Needled to Death

Needled to Death

Maggie Sefton

This Large Print edition is published by Wheeler Publishing, Waterville, Maine USA and by BBC Audiobooks Ltd, Bath, England.

Published in 2006 in the U.S. by arrangement with The Berkley Publishing Group, a division of Penguin Group (USA) Inc.

Published in 2006 in the U.K. by arrangement with The Berkley Publishing Group, a division of Penguin Group (USA) Inc.

U.S. Softcover 1-59722-189-9 (Cozy Mystery)
U.K. Hardcover 1-4056-3731-5 (Chivers Large Print)
U.K. Softcover 1-4056-3732-3 (Camden Large Print)

A Knitting Mystery

The text of this Large Print edition is unabridged.
Other aspects of the book may vary from the original edition.

Set in 16 pt. Plantin by Ramona Watson.

Printed in the United States on permanent paper.

British Library Cataloguing-in-Publication Data available

Library of Congress Cataloging-in-Publication Data

Sefton, Maggie.
Needled to death / by Maggie Sefton.
p. cm. — (Wheeler Publishing large print cozy mystery)
ISBN 1-59722-189-9 (lg. print : sc : alk. paper)
1. Knitting — Fiction. 2. Knitters (Persons) — Fiction. 3. Colorado — Fiction. 4. Large type books. I. Title. II. Wheeler large print cozy mystery.
PS3619.E37N44 2006
813′.6—dc22 2005034005

Acknowledgments

My thanks to all the helpful alpaca breeders and ranchers in the Northern Colorado area who were kind enough to allow me a peek into their fascinating business. Most especially, I want to thank Marjean Bender of Kitchell Kriations Alpacas in Fort Collins, CO, who welcomed me to several alpaca shearings — as well as into her home. Over many cups of coffee and tea, she never ran out of patience with my endless questions about the alpaca ranching and the beautiful animals with the to-die-for soft wool.

One

Kelly Flynn grabbed her empty coffee mug as she opened the glass patio door leading to her cottage's small backyard. "Go for it, Carl. Another sunny day. Squirrels are waiting." She gave her rottweiler a parting pat as he raced outside, clearly eager to face the furry tormentors that kept him running.

Spying the deep rose circlet of yarn that rested on the dining room table, Kelly snatched her knitting bag with her latest project. The silk-and-cotton, raspberry sherbet yarn had tempted her for months in the knitting shop across from her home.

Kelly paused near her desk, nestled in a sunny corner of the cozy white stucco and red-tiled roof cottage. It was her cottage now. When Aunt Helen was killed, Kelly inherited everything, and her life turned upside down.

Glancing at her corporate client's folder beside the computer keyboard, she checked the clock. The analysis of the client's financial statements was going smoother than she'd anticipated. Some accounting issues were easier to solve than others. There was ample time for a knitting break.

The caffeine lobe deep in her brain sent out another insistent signal — coffee, now. Kelly headed for the front door. She could almost taste Eduardo's potent brew. The knitting shop had an attached café with the best regular coffee Kelly had ever tasted. Eduardo, the genial cook, always laughed when she asked about his secret for the coffee that kept her coming back for more.

July's intense heat radiated in the Colorado air even though it was only mid-morning. Afternoon would be brutal and in the high nineties, Kelly decided as she glanced at the shimmer coming off the adjacent golfing greens. That reminder caused her to turn and check on her dog's whereabouts.

Carl had developed an unfortunate habit these last three months she'd stayed in Fort Connor. Golf balls. They were an irresistible temptation to which Carl frequently succumbed. Kelly had tried several tactics to discourage him from climbing the fence and racing onto the greens to steal balls. Memories of angry golfer encounters were still fresh in Kelly's mind.

She spotted Carl standing, paws up on

the chain-link fence. "Don't even think about it, Carl," she warned in her best attempt-to-control-dog voice. Carl looked over his shoulder in pleading mode. "Nope. You've gotten us in enough trouble already. Go play with your legal stash over there." Kelly pointed to a cluster of golf balls near several decorative pots filled with colorful shade plants.

Carl rolled his soft brown eyes in an obvious last effort to convince, then lay down in the grass and stared longingly at the greens.

"I know it's more fun to chase down stray balls, but you just can't. I don't want to have to bail you out of doggie jail," Kelly warned as she headed across the driveway toward Aunt Helen's former farmhouse, now turned knitting shop.

Passing by the oaken front door with its carved sign that read HOUSE OF LAMBSPUN, Kelly followed the flower-bordered pathway around the sprawling stucco and red-tile roof building to the café entrance. The enticing aroma of coffee greeted her as soon as she opened the door. She glanced around at the tables filled with customers lingering over late breakfast and brunch until she spotted a familiar face. One of her knitting friends, Jennifer, worked mornings at the café and afternoons as a real estate agent.

Kelly aimed straight for her. "Cof-fee, cof-fee," she demanded in a deep, raspy voice, mug in outstretched hand.

"Look, it's the return of the Coffee Zombie," Jennifer joked to the café owner. "Hide, Pete. She hasn't had her caffeine yet."

Pete's round face spread with a wide grin as he poured orange juice into a glass pitcher. "It'll only be a minute, Kelly. Eduardo's got some brewing. We had a business breakfast group in here this morning, and they drained the last drop."

Kelly's heart almost stopped. "Pete, don't even joke about something like that," she warned.

"It'll only be a moment. You can make it," Jennifer teased. "C'mon, have a doughnut." She gestured to the tempting pastries displayed in a nearby glass case.

Kelly tried to ignore them, but one lemon-glazed creation called her name. "Okay, but sugar's not gonna do it. I need coffee. I can only last so long on that supermarket brand I have at home. I've already spent most of the morning combing through one corporate account, and I've got several more waiting."

"Boy, you're surlier than usual this

morning," Jennifer observed, handing her the napkin-covered doughnut. "Numbers not adding up? Clients getting unruly? I can help with that." She winked.

"Actually, everything's going smoothly. I just want to work ahead so I can take the whole day off tomorrow," Kelly said before she sank her teeth into the sugar.

"You guys have a game tomorrow?"

"Games all day. It's the Fantastic Fourth at the Fort tournament. Teams are coming from all over the state."

"I'd better tell Eduardo to put some more shoelaces in the coffee, then. You'll need it," Jennifer said with a laugh as she took Kelly's mug and headed for the kitchen.

Kelly brushed sugar flakes from her T-shirt and checked the barrette holding back her chin-length, dark brown hair. One of the best things about telecommuting to her office in Washington, D.C., was she could dress the way she liked. And in Colorado in the summertime, that meant a T-shirt and shorts.

Tomorrow would bring back a ton of memories, she was certain. She remembered playing in that same softball tournament years ago when she grew up here in Fort Connor. Lots of memories. In fact, that's all she had left from the past. The people were all gone — her dad, her aunt Helen, everyone.

"You're saved," Jennifer announced, coming toward her, mug in hand. "Coffee's ready, and you're all set. Go forth and knit." She handed the mug to Kelly. "I'll be over on break."

"Thanks," Kelly said and headed for the doorway that led into the knitting shop.

As always, her senses went on overload the moment she entered the shop. Room after room of the renovated farmhouse was filled with yarns of every hue and texture — frothy mohairs in ice cream colors, nubbly wools and luscious alpacas, seductively soft silk spun with cotton or wool or all alone. Kelly couldn't get through a room without stroking a fat skein or squeezing some enticing fiber. She'd become a "fiber fondler," as the shop's knitting regulars called themselves.

Rounding the corner into what was once the farmhouse living room, Kelly went straight to the long library table that now dominated the room. "Hey, there," she greeted two of her friends who sat around the table knitting.

"How's the sweater going?" Lisa asked,

glancing up from the lacy ribbon vest she was creating.

"Well, okay, I guess. I'm still doing the ribbing along the edge," Kelly replied as she settled into a chair.

"Getting used to the circular needles?" Megan asked, pausing over the vivid purple froth that lay piled in her lap. Was that one of the new boa eyelash yarns that were so enticing?

"Yeah, gradually. It still looks strange, but I hope to finish the ribbing soon so I can start knitting the sweater. I mean, it doesn't feel like a sweater yet, just this circle of yarn." She held up the circle of rosy red yarn. The two slender wooden needles were connected end to end by a ribbon of thin plastic. Kelly scrutinized the rows of ribbing that covered the entire circumference and frowned. "You sure this is gonna work?"

Lisa grinned and brushed a lock of blond hair from her forehead. "Ohhh, it'll work all right. Trust us."

"Wait'll you see those rows of stockinette stitch appear, then you'll be convinced," Megan added with her usual bright smile. With her fair, fair skin and almost black hair, Megan always looked delicate to Kelly — except, of course, when she was on the softball field. Underneath the porcelain, Megan was tough as nails.

"Okaaaay," Kelly said, still skeptical. "If you say so. I still don't understand how I'll get stockinette if all I do is the knit stitch. I mean, when I did my first easy sweater with the chunky yarn, I had to do it the regular way — one row of knitting, one row of purling. How do you get stockinette without doing that?"

"It just happens," Megan reassured.

Kelly pondered that and drank deeply from her mug, savoring the coffee's familiar harsh assault on her taste buds. "That's no answer. There has to be a reason why it works."

"Trust in the process," Lisa said with her enigmatic smile.

"That's what Jennifer always says, but that's hard for me," Kelly admitted, picking up the circular needles. "I mean, I spend most of my days examining the process with all my accounts. It's hard to switch off."

Mimi, the owner of the shop, leaned around the doorway. "It's magic," she said with a smile. "I couldn't help overhearing you, Kelly. Don't worry. It'll be fine."

"What'll be fine?" Jennifer queried as she approached the table, knitting bag over her arm.

"Oh, Kelly's worrying about knitting in the round," Mimi explained and went back to straightening the surrounding shelves of books and magazines.

"That's Kelly's standard operating procedure," Jennifer said, pulling a luscious, multicolored fringed yarn from her bag. "Whenever she starts a new project, she always worries that it won't turn out."

"Hey, not always," Kelly protested, compelled to defend herself even though she knew her friends were right.

"Yeah, you do."

"Always."

"I rest my case." Jennifer grinned. "You'll be fine. Just trust —"

"In the process, I know, I know." Kelly drank from her mug as she reached out one hand to fondle the glistening and vibrantly colored fibers that Jennifer was knitting into one of those new trendy scarves. Yummy soft. "I'm going to have to make one of those scarves. They are simply irresistible."

"Get a little further along on your sweater, first, before you leave it," Megan advised. "I know what it's like to be tempted away from a bigger project."

Kelly nodded and went back to creating the ribbing that would be the bottom of her new sweater. At first, it seemed strange to knit two stitches, then purl two stitches, but after a few rows, she actually saw the ribbed effect appear. Another few rows and she'd have created the inch required to form the sweater's edge.

Lisa broached another subject, one that had been niggling in the back of Kelly's mind. "How long do you think your boss will let you work away from the office? Did he give any clue when you went back to D.C. last month?"

"I don't know. He was doing his cool, aloof routine when I spoke with him. He does that whenever he wants to keep someone off balance." She frowned at the memory of sitting in her corporate CPA firm's offices, pleading her request for an extension of family leave.

With the death of both her aunt and her long-lost cousin, Martha, Kelly was suddenly the heir and beneficiary of a good deal of property. It would take several months to sort through both estates, even with trusted family lawyer Lawrence Chambers overseeing the process. Kelly didn't have a clue when she'd be able to return to Washington — or if she even wanted to.

"Well, you know how we all feel," Megan

spoke up. "We want you to stay here with us."

Kelly felt her heart give a little squeeze. Deep inside, that's what she wanted, too.

"Any chance of that happening?" Jennifer probed. "You're managing those huge mortgage payments on the cottage, right? And you've got a renter for your town house back in Virginia. How's that working?"

"Oh, Chuck is great. He absolutely loves the place," Kelly replied. *All the more reason to let him have it,* the little voice inside whispered. If it were only that simple, Kelly thought. "But it's a delicate balance. The only way I can manage the cottage mortgage payments is with my CPA salary." She shook her head. "I can't quit my job."

"Well, we'll simply have to find a way for you to earn money here," Jennifer declared.

"Boy, that's not as easy as it sounds," Kelly said. "Consulting on my own simply wouldn't cut it. I've done some checking, with Megan's help."

"Something will come up. I can feel it," Jennifer said.

The front door's jingling bell sounded. More customers. Over the past three months that she'd been a regular, Kelly had noticed the ebb and flow of customers. Mid-morning to lunchtime was often hectic, with classes and customer questions. Then a brief pause often occurred before the afternoon press of customers and more classes began. Of course, weekends had no pause at all. It was nonstop shopping and classes the entire day. Kelly marveled at how Mimi managed to handle the constant flow of questions and instruction and helping customers find "just the right yarn" while staying so warm and reassuring. It must be her passion. It flowed over into everything she did and all she'd created. Kelly glanced to the billowy mohairs that draped against the walls and the stacked bins that bulged with summer-bright yarns. Mimi had truly created a wonderland here. No wonder knitters flocked to the shop.

"Well, hello, everybody," a woman's voice spoke from the doorway. "Looks like half the Tuesday group is here."

Kelly turned in her chair and recognized Vickie Claymore, another of the Tuesday group regulars. "Hey, Vickie. What brings you out of that beautiful canyon and into town?"

"Nothing much. Errands, that's all," Vickie said as she joined them at the table.

"When are you bringing some of your weavings?" Lisa asked. "I've got a friend who's been dying to buy one ever since she saw mine."

"That's great! Thanks, Lisa," Vickie said, her suntanned face breaking into a grin. "I hope to have some more ready by next week." She brushed her dark brown hair off her shoulder.

Vickie was one of the few fifty-plus women Kelly knew who could still wear her long hair hanging behind her back in a ponytail. Even mixed with gray, it still looked good on her. Kelly admired Vickie not only for her lively personality, but also for her artistic creativity and her shrewd business sense. Vickie was a successful alpaca breeder and rancher as well as a talented spinner and weaver. Instead of knitting on Tuesdays, Vickie would spin, sometimes on the drop spindle. Other times, she'd borrow a wheel from Mimi.

"Boy, if I lived in that gorgeous canyon, I wouldn't want to leave," Megan said.

"You would if you wanted to buy groceries and eat," Vickie said with a laugh. "Plus, it's good to get a break from the ranch. Makes me appreciate it more." She poured herself a cup of tea from the always-present teapot at the center of the table.

"Are all your baby alpacas born? Any more deliveries?" Kelly asked, remembering Vickie's concern for her herd.

"Yep," she replied, brushing dust from her jeans. Ninety degrees or not, boots and jeans were necessary around the ranch. "All the cria are safely delivered — thank goodness and natural alpaca mother instinct."

Lisa looked up from the ribbon vest. "Cria?"

Vickie nodded. "That's the name for baby alpacas. We've got twenty new ones."

"Wow. Is that a lot to care for?" Megan asked.

"Actually, the mothers do most of that. I just have to make sure the moms are well-fed and cared for." She grinned, and her eyes lit up. "Just like with humans, moms do most of the work."

"Doesn't your cousin, Jayleen, help out?" Mimi asked as she rearranged a bin of eyelash yarns. "You have nearly forty animals."

"Thirty-eight with the babies, and, yes, Jayleen comes every day."

"Oops, I almost forgot! I need to ask you a favor, Vickie," Mimi said, abruptly turning from the bins. "There's a group of out-of-town knitters from the Midwest who're visiting Fort Connor. They're a touring group. Apparently they take yearly trips to different areas of the country."

"Wow, touring knitters. Now that's something new," Jennifer observed.

"Actually, there're several knitting groups that tour, I've heard," Mimi added. "This group is coming to see the shop after July fourth, and they asked if I knew of any alpaca ranches they could visit. I know this is short notice, Vickie, but would they be able to tour your ranch Friday afternoon?"

Vickie leaned back in the chair and sipped her tea. "Friday. Yes, I think that would be all right. What time would they come?"

"They're planning to have lunch at Pete's, so we can drive them into the canyon afterward. Probably about two o'clock. Does that work?"

"That'll work," Vickie agreed, smiling. "I take it they've never seen an alpaca before, right?"

"Probably not."

"Okay, I'll give them the grand tour." Vickie drained her teacup before she stood up.

"Vickie, you're a doll," Mimi said, her face losing its worried expression. "Thank you so much. Now all I need are some volunteers to take them to the ranch." She surveyed the table. "Any of you girls want to take a drive into the canyon Friday? We'll need shepherds for this flock."

Kelly started to speak up, but Jennifer beat her to it. "I'll be glad to escort them, Mimi," she said. "I've been wanting to drive past some property in the canyon anyway."

Picturing herself driving through the shady, deep green canyon northwest of Fort Connor, Kelly chimed in, "Count me in, too, Mimi. I could use an afternoon in Bellvue Canyon."

Mimi beamed. "Thank you so much, girls. I'll take care of all the arrangements."

"I'll see you two on Friday, then," Vickie said as she headed toward the doorway. "If your flock behaves, I'll show them my looms. I'm weaving a new piece now with some of my herd fleeces. It's really striking, if I do say so myself."

"I'll bet it is," Kelly said. "I remember that beautiful rug you showed us last month. The patterns were gorgeous."

"You can see it when you come. It's on my floor now. Take care, folks." Vickie gave a wave as she left.

"Boy, Kelly, I didn't think you'd be up for supervising knitters after the last time," Megan teased.

Kelly remembered helping Megan last spring when they escorted a group of senior knitters to the regional Colorado wool festival. "Ohhhh, yeah," she grinned, recalling one mischievous knitter's antics. "Well, let's hope we don't have any 'Lizzies' in this flock."

Mimi threw up her hands in remembered horror as she scurried back to her office while Kelly and her friends laughed out loud.

Kelly sat down on one of her teammates' blankets that dotted the ridge above the city reservoir. She'd forgotten to bring a blanket of her own. Heck, it was all she could do to get to the field this morning.

After a long night spent poring over her client accounts, Kelly had overslept, awaking to the sound of an angry golfer's shout outside. "Damn dog! I knew he stole my ball," the man yelled.

Bolted awake, Kelly was about to go to Carl's rescue when she saw the time. It was past eight o'clock, and her softball team's first game was at nine. She vaulted out of the bed and into the shower, setting a new speed record even for her. She raced through the kitchen, poured a double ration into Carl's doggie dish, and shoved it under his nose. The golf ball scolding would have to wait. Carl, clearly ecstatic at the unexpected bowl of plenty, dug in.

Grabbing her first baseman's glove and her dad's USS *Kitty Hawk* baseball cap, Kelly raced out the door and into her car, hoping she had all her clothes on. There was no way she'd let her teammates down by not showing up on time. Thanks to uncommon good fortune with traffic lights and an unexpected parking spot, Kelly raced onto the field where her team gathered. Two minutes to spare.

"Boy, girl, you like to live on the edge, don't you?" Lisa joked.

"No, she just likes to give us all heart attacks," Megan said over her shoulder as they took the field. "I'm backup first base, and I'm lousy at it. So don't do that again."

Kelly swore alarm-clock vigilance and took her base, grateful for green lights.

Relaxing now under the blue velvet night sky, Kelly let out a sigh. So many stars. She was always surprised when she returned to Colorado and noticed the night sky. Not only was she a mile closer to the heavens, but there were more stars to see. Big-city light pollution kept her from stargazing back in the D.C. metro area. Occasionally, she'd driven out into the Virginia countryside to find a beautiful Blue Ridge mountain knoll just so she could see the heavens more clearly.

But it wasn't the same. The sky looked different here. And this ridge was right on the edge of town. She gazed up and tried to spot her favorite constellations, the ones her dad had taught her to see back in her childhood. She visually outlined the Big Dipper, then found the North Star and was looking for the Little Dipper when a familiar low voice sounded beside her.

"Want one? It's your favorite," Steve Townsend said as he sank to the blanket beside her.

"Thanks," Kelly said, accepting the bottle. "You read my mind."

Steve seemed to be doing a lot of that lately, Kelly noticed. Whether it was running interference for Carl with the angry golfers or taking time from his busy construction business to appear at her door with coffee when she needed a break from corporate accounts, Steve showed up. He was a nice guy. A really nice guy who had turned into a good friend — even if he was the star player for a rival team.

Kelly tipped the bottle with the colorful

label and drank. Her hometown had developed into a center for special microbrewed boutique beers. The amber ale's cold, crisp tang fit perfectly with the summer night. The intense heat of the day had subsided now, and the air was gradually cooling, especially up on the ridge — one of the many benefits of mountain living.

"How's your knee?" Steve asked as he leaned back on his arm, stretching out his long legs, which were even longer than Kelly's.

Kelly checked her newly-scraped right knee. The sting of injury had lessened so much that Kelly had forgotten about it.

Her knees were always skinned when she was growing up. Softball, basketball, soccer — all took a toll. She was used to bandages. But living in the corporate world these last several years had taken her far away from simple pleasures like sliding into base, knees be damned. Suits and stress were the uniforms and routine of the day with no time allowed for standing outside in the sunshine. The clock inside Kelly's head ruled her schedule in six-minute intervals — billable hours. These last three months had given Kelly a taste of a different kind of life, delicious and tempting like a forbidden dessert. If only she could find a way to stay here and not starve.

"Oh, it's fine. I completely forgot about it. Actually, it feels kind of good to have skinned knees again."

Steve grinned. "How's that?"

Kelly let out a sigh and leaned back on her hands, staring out over the brightly lit city spread out in a carpet below. The fireworks display in City Park would be starting soon. "It reminds me of when I was growing up here and all the other places my dad and I lived. I was always playing ball and getting hurt. It's amazing I have any knees left." She laughed softly in the gathering darkness. The blue velvet sky had turned to black. "I didn't know how much I missed it until I came back and met Lisa and Megan and started playing again."

"Wasn't there a team in D.C. where you could play?"

"Oh, sure. Lots. But it was always a question of time. Never enough time. I worked late a lot at the office. Until my dad got cancer, that is. Then I made sure I visited him every night." Kelly felt an old familiar tug of remembrance as she pictured her father.

"That must have been tough."

"It was."

The aroma of hot dogs and hamburgers drifted by. "Last chance for hot dogs and burgers," Lisa called to the scattered players relaxing along the ridge. She wound a path through the blankets and chairs, a platter in each hand piled with cookout leftovers.

"Hey, I'll take another burger," a guy said as he slipped up behind Lisa and made off with his prize. "Who's got the beer?"

"Beside the grill, over there," someone else called out.

"I've got some chardonnay, if anyone wants it," Wendy, the team's catcher, said, waving from a nearby blanket.

"Boy, hot dogs and chardonnay," Steve joked. "That just doesn't work."

"Hey, I can't help it," Wendy explained with a laugh as she grabbed a glass from the guy beside her. "I don't like beer."

"And you call yourself a catcher."

Kelly let the sound of relaxed laughter float over her like the evening breezes that came over the mountains. It felt good here. Really good. Deep inside, she felt the warmth that always came whenever she considered staying in Colorado.

"Well, for what it's worth, you sure look a lot more relaxed and happy than when you first came into town back in April," Steve said.

"Yeah," Kelly admitted with a sigh. "That's because I am."

"Relaxed or happy?"

"Both."

Steve didn't reply. After a few minutes of comfortable silence, which Kelly spent tracing star patterns, he spoke up. "Well, maybe that means you should stay."

"If it were only that easy."

"You know, Kelly, there's a huge amount of business going on in this town. There're all sorts of ways to consult —"

A collective "Ahhhh!" spread along the ridge as the fireworks display blazed into the sky.

"Whoa," Kelly said. "I'd forgotten how pretty it is from up high. Even prettier than being right beneath. That's where I usually was back in D.C. My dad and I would go find a spot near the Washington Monument."

"Sounds like fun."

"Yeah, it was. If you don't mind being crammed in with several thousand people. We could barely move."

"More than at City Park?" Steve teased.

Kelly sent him a look. "Ohhhh, yeah. Way more." She watched a spectacular flare of reds, blues, purples, and greens shoot through the black mountain sky. "It's nicer here," she said softly. "It's good to be back."

"Well, for the record, I'd be glad if you could stay, too." He gestured to Kelly's teammates, oohing and aahing at the colorful displays. "Even if you guys did beat us this afternoon."

Kelly grinned. "I'll take that as a compliment."

"Do that."

Two

Kelly eased the huge SUV around the curving canyon road more slowly than usual. These monster vehicles had a different feel to them, not at all like her sporty, super-responsive road car. She glanced into the rearview mirror. Jennifer was right behind her in Mimi's blue minivan, loaded like the SUV with touring knitters.

"How much farther is it? I thought you said it was 'just up the road,' " the knitter in the front seat asked for the third time in twenty minutes.

Kelly took a breath and searched for patience. This woman was something else. She'd done nothing but complain ever since she'd gotten into the automobile. It was too hot. The air-conditioning was too cold. She was tired. She was thirsty. Weren't there some alpacas they could visit in town? She didn't like curving roads.

Noticing the other women's rapt attention to the beautiful scenery outside the windows, Kelly tried to distract the woman, or at least her impatience. "This canyon is much greener and more deeply wooded than some of our others. That's because it's a north-facing canyon, and it holds the snow longer. That means there's more water available."

Fussy knitter piped up, pushing her glasses to the ridge of her nose. "Yes, and more snow to shovel, too, I'll bet."

"Absolutely," Kelly said with a laugh. "In fact, some of the upper roads don't get plowed by the county. The homeowners have to pay to have it done."

"Now, I wouldn't like that at all," Fussy declared, setting her mouth. Kelly noticed hard lines already etched in her face. Too much frowning, she figured.

"Well, the people who don't like it usually move back into the city after a couple of years, I'm told," Kelly observed. "You have to love being in the mountains to live comfortably here."

"Ohhhh, I'd love it," a woman's voice spoke up from the middle seat.

"Me, too," agreed another.

"Is that the place, over there?" Fussy asked, pointing to a farmhouse nestled between trees. Cows grazed in the pastures.

"No, but we're getting close," Kelly answered. "Just around this curve." She spotted Vickie's sprawling farmhouse in the distance and slowed as they approached the driveway.

"Well, finally!" Fussy declared.

Kelly kept her smile to herself as they bumped along the rutted driveway, listening to the stream of complaints coming from the next seat. The other women were laughing and chattering excitedly as they approached the farmhouse.

"Oh, look! Alpacas!" a woman proclaimed, pointing to the corral and pastures adjacent to the weather-beaten red barn.

"How do you know they're alpacas?" Fussy asked. "They look the same as llamas."

"Well, you're right. They are very much alike. But I've been to Vickie's ranch before. Otherwise, it's hard for most people to tell."

"What's the difference?" a woman asked.

"About a hundred pounds. Alpacas are smaller than llamas," Kelly replied as she pulled the SUV into a graveled area near the barn and parked beside Vickie's beat-up gray pickup truck. Exiting the auto, she motioned to a parking spot for Jennifer, who was coming up the driveway behind them.

"Okay, ladies," Kelly addressed the

women who were unfolding themselves from the vehicle. “Let’s get everybody together, then we can start our tour. Meanwhile, smell that mountain air.” She took a deep breath. Out of the close confines of the car at last.

Jennifer parked the van, then hopped out and helped her charges alight, laughing and talking the whole time. Kelly wished she could be as entertaining as Jennifer, but she seemed to be missing that gene. Maybe she could foist Fussy off on her for the ride back into town.

“Wow, this is one beautiful place,” Jennifer observed as she approached Kelly. “I haven’t been here before, have you?”

“Yes. One time I came with Mimi when she was doing some weaving with Vickie. They were developing a workshop together.” She glanced toward the farmhouse across the drive, wondering why Vickie hadn’t come out to greet them. It certainly wasn’t for lack of noise.

The gaggle of knitters had gathered around the fence, pointing and exclaiming at the alpacas scattered about the pastures. For their part, the alpacas simply gazed back with huge brown eyes and continued to graze peacefully. Kelly noticed one or two headed toward the fence, clearly as curious about the visitors as the visitors were about them.

Of course, their approach delighted the knitters no end, and cameras appeared from purses. Digital and film, the cameras snapped away as the women leaned over the fence. Thank goodness it was sunny, Kelly figured, or the flashes would have spooked the gentle beasts for sure. It did halt their approach, however, much to the ladies' disappointment.

"Will they let you pat them?" one woman asked.

"Some will. But we'll let Vickie be in charge of that," Kelly replied, wondering again why Vickie hadn't come out to greet them.

Checking her watch, she saw it was after two o'clock, so they were right on time. Maybe Vickie was in her sunny workroom in the back of the house, absorbed in her latest weaving project.

"She may have forgotten that we're coming," Jennifer offered, stretching, arms overhead. "Does she have a workroom or something?"

"Yeah, in the back. She may be working and waiting for us to ring the doorbell. I'll go check. You keep track of them," Kelly suggested and started across the gravel driveway.

She headed toward the front porch with its rough-cut pine beam posts and overhang that created an inviting, shady spot for the rocking chairs that were angled to enjoy the mountain view. A wide wooden deck also extended around the corner of the log home and along the side, creating a large, sunny patio.

As Kelly's foot touched the front step, she heard an altogether too familiar voice right behind her.

"Why isn't she out here to greet us?" Fussy demanded, catching up with Kelly. "Isn't that her truck in the driveway?"

"She's probably in her workroom in the back and couldn't hear us. Why don't you wait with the others while I go get her, okay?" Kelly suggested as she crossed the porch, hoping Fussy would take the hint.

She didn't. "I've already seen the animals. I want to see those weavings the shop owner was talking about."

Kelly reached for the doorbell, then stopped when she noticed the door was ajar. She rang the bell anyway and waited. And waited. Fussy wasn't good at waiting, she noticed, so Kelly rang again and waited some more while Fussy fidgeted.

"Well, where is she?" Fussy demanded. "Don't tell me we came all the way out here for nothing."

"Oh, she probably didn't hear it, that's all," Kelly reassured. She pushed open the heavy door, and they stepped into the entryway. "I'll go check her workroom. Why don't you stay here and admire the décor, okay?" This time Kelly let her voice assume a formal tone, and she gave Fussy an I-mean-business look for good measure. Fussy stayed put.

"Vickie? Hello?" Kelly called. "Jennifer and I are here with the tour group. Where are you?"

No answer. Kelly stood for another moment, letting her gaze sweep over the spacious log home. One whole side of the living room was floor-to-ceiling windows, affording a gorgeous view of the canyon and the mountain ranges in the distance. Vaulted ceilings and skylights allowed light to flood the room, highlighting the furnishings, some rustic, some modern.

Vickie had eclectic tastes as well as an excellent eye for art. Patterns and fabric and color were everywhere. A still life in the style of the old masters was separated from a colorful abstract by one of Vickie's striking weavings. Everywhere Kelly looked she saw art — painted, sculpted, woven, or carved. It was a visual feast.

Wishing she could simply stand and drink it in for several minutes like she did on her last visit, Kelly headed through the living room toward the back of the house. Once the touring group was enthralled in Vickie's demonstrations, she and Jennifer could enjoy their surroundings. Glancing over her shoulder, she noticed Fussy was edging out of the entryway.

"Wait right there," Kelly said, gesturing to the woman. "I'll be back in a minute."

When she skirted around the rust-colored leather sofa, however, Kelly came to an abrupt halt. Vickie lay on the floor, her dark hair spread out on the handwoven rug in stark contrast to her pale face. A pool of blood, blackish red, swirled across the intricate pattern woven into the gray and white wool.

Kelly's breath caught in her throat. What had happened? Why all this blood? Was Vickie still alive? Suddenly, she spotted an ugly red gash across Vickie's neck. Kelly swallowed down her revulsion. Vickie's throat had been cut.

She knelt beside her friend and gingerly placed her fingers on Vickie's wrist, hoping to feel a pulse. There was none. Vickie was dead. She'd bled to death. And hours ago, too, from the look of the blood. It was dried already in places where it had soaked into the fabric. The icy lump in Kelly's throat sank to her stomach. Was this a suicide? Or was it murder? Who would kill Vickie?

"Oh, my God!" cried Fussy, right behind Kelly's shoulder. "Would you look at that! There's blood everywhere!"

That did it. Kelly snapped into command mode. She jumped up and wheeled on Fussy, pointing straight at her. "*You!* Out! This minute. Go get Jennifer and tell her to bring her cell phone right away!"

"Well, I never —" Fussy huffed.

Kelly dropped her voice two octaves into the I'm-warning-you-Carl range. "Do it. *Now.* This is a crime scene, and the police need to be called. Go!"

Mention of the police clearly got Fussy's attention, because all color drained from her pinched face. She turned and ran from the house. Kelly took a deep breath and forced herself to look at her dead friend once more. How was this possible? Vickie was always so full of life and energy. Who would kill her? It had to be murder. Vickie had so many plans for the future. Kelly remembered her friend excitedly describing how her baby alpacas were already sold to other breeders. As soon as they were weaned from their mothers, she'd be "playing stork," as Vickie laughingly referred to her delivery trips. No. Vickie hadn't killed herself. Kelly was convinced.

She slowly walked around the great room, trying to absorb every detail she could in case she was asked later. She disturbed nothing but noted everything. There was no sign of a knife anywhere. Did the killer sneak up on Vickie? There was no way Vickie would stand still and let a crazed person slit her throat. So, what happened? Kelly wondered.

As she circled behind the sofa, Kelly spied a bronze bust lying on the floor beneath an end table. She remembered that piece because Vickie nearly knocked it over when she was hauling a huge weaving into the room to show them on their last visit. The Mozart bust. Kelly glanced to the cherry wood bookcase where she'd remembered it last. The space was empty.

Jennifer burst through the front door and raced into the room. "Kelly! Is it true? Did someone kill — ?" She skidded to a stop when she saw Vickie. "Oh, my God," she breathed, hand to her throat. She went almost as white as Vickie.

"Jen! Jennifer, give me your cell," Kelly ordered in a sharp voice to snap her out of it.

Color started to rise in Jennifer's cheeks, and she shook her head as if to clear it. "Here." She offered the phone. "I'm not sure we'll have a signal, though. I lose it a lot in the mountains."

Kelly snapped open the cover, and, sure enough, there was no signal. One of the downsides of mountain living. "Damn," she said. "I didn't want to use the land-line."

"Why?" Jennifer asked, turning away from the gruesome sight.

"There may be fingerprints. I don't want to smudge any before the police get here." She searched her pockets. "Do you have a tissue or something I can use?"

"Yeah, here." Jennifer dug in her back pocket and handed one over.

Kelly approached the kitchen, searching for a phone. Spying one on the wall, she carefully draped the tissue over the receiver and used her T-shirt to cover her dialing finger while she punched 9-1-1. She sincerely hoped she hadn't accidentally wiped off any other fingerprints in the process.

When the police operator came on the line, she calmly reported what she had found, where they were, and identified herself. The operator informed her that an investigative unit would be on the scene right away. Kelly gave the woman the description of Vickie's farmhouse as well as how far up the canyon it was located before she hung up.

Turning back to Jennifer, she saw her hovering at the edge of the sofa casting furtive peeks at Vickie. Death held an undeniable fascination for most people. Kelly remembered how her father looked when he died, but he was barely recognizable having wasted away with lung cancer. It wasn't the same. Vickie had been in the prime of her mature life, full of anticipation for the future and joyful, loving her work and her art. Kelly glanced at her dead friend. It wasn't the same. It wasn't the same at all.

"Do you really think someone killed her?" Jennifer asked softly, as if someone was listening.

"It has to be murder," Kelly declared, even more emphatically now. "Vickie wouldn't kill herself. But even if she planned to, she would have done it another way. If she'd wanted to bleed to death, she'd have done it in the bathroom or in the tub or something. Not on top of her gorgeous rug." Kelly shook her head.

Jennifer shuddered. "What a gruesome thought. I mean, I've been down sometimes, but never enough to do that." She grimaced again. "Who in the world would kill Vickie?"

"I don't know. I can't imagine —"

Suddenly, voices. Voices everywhere as the flock of touring knitters swarmed into the house and scattered about the great room, tittering and squealing and shivering in turns as they pointed and peeked.

Kelly and Jennifer stood rooted in the kitchen, both clearly appalled at the sight. Vickie had been their friend, Kelly fumed within. Her death was not a stop on the tour schedule.

Fussy fluttered to the head of the flock and pointed to the victim. "There she is!" she proudly proclaimed. "I found her just like that!"

"That does it!" Kelly exploded as she strode over to the women. They were just like a bunch of magpies. She purposely stood between the flock and her fallen friend, then pointed to the door.

"Get out now!" she ordered. "Vickie was our friend and you have no right to invade her privacy like this. *Out!*"

"That's right, ladies," Jennifer spoke up. "This is a crime scene. You could get in trouble with the police for disturbing it. Now leave." She shooed them away.

Jennifer's stretching of the truth worked. The flock squawked and scattered out the door. Fussy, however, held her ground. She puffed out her chest in full huff. "What about you two? You have no right to be here, then."

Kelly was beyond the point of politeness. Manners be damned. She pointed right between Fussy's eyes. "You. Not another word. I mean it, or you'll walk back to Fort Connor." If Kelly's voice sank any lower, it would be in the river at the bottom of the canyon.

Fussy blanched, then turned and stalked out of the house, feathers dropping in her wake.

"Whoa, you go, girl," Jennifer teased. "I'd hate to see you really mad."

Kelly released a huge breath. "It's not a pretty sight, trust me."

Just then, the sound of a wailing siren pierced the air, farther away, then coming closer. The police. Thank God, Kelly sighed in relief.

"C'mon, let's get out of here," Jennifer prodded and motioned to Kelly.

Kelly took one last look at her murdered friend and followed Jennifer out the door.

Three

Kelly paced beside the pasture fence while she watched police detectives spread across Vickie's property — interviewing visiting knitters, searching the barn, and hurrying in and out of the sprawling log home. Since Bellvue Canyon was in the county, not the city of Fort Connor, this case belonged to the county police. It was their jurisdiction, and Kelly was relieved to see the number of squad cars lining the driveway.

The more cops, the sooner they'll find whoever did this, Kelly told herself as she paced. The horror had worn off, and the sense of outrage that someone could snuff out a life as vital and worthwhile as Vickie's took hold of Kelly now. Who could have done this awful thing?

Uniformed policemen were scattered from pasture to front porch, each with a pair of overwrought visitors. The women chattered, and the officers dutifully wrote everything down. Maybe one of them had seen something Kelly hadn't.

Another policeman strode by with a man

carrying a large video camera setup, and they both entered the house. Kelly imagined them photographing every inch of the great room. Who knew where clues might be hidden? She only hoped the flock of magpies hadn't disturbed anything.

She glanced toward the pasture and observed the alpacas scattered about, grazing and studying all the human activity. Kelly searched for any sign of agitation but wasn't exactly sure what to look for. Her knowledge base about alpacas was pretty shallow. Vickie had been the one to educate most of them in the Tuesday evening group when she'd regale them with stories about the gentle beasts with the to-die-for soft wool.

Fleece, she corrected herself. Kelly had learned that much, at least. Just like sheep, alpacas were sheared of their heavy coats in late spring or early summer. Once the wool was cleaned of debris, it was carded, then spun into yarn. She'd seen an alpaca shearing only last month, when Vickie had invited the knitting group to her ranch.

Kelly'd been amazed how thick and heavy the fleece was, and how relieved the animals seemed to be when it was gone. Summer heat had already descended by early June. Kelly couldn't imagine wearing her winter coat outside in those temperatures. No wonder the animals were glad to be rid of it, noticing how they carefully sniffed and inspected each other as they returned to the common pen. Kelly still remembered the loud buzz of the huge razor and the methodical, efficient, almost rhythmic way the female shearer moved around each animal.

Jennifer's voice sounded behind her. "Well, I told them everything I saw, and I was finished in two minutes. Your favorite has been enthralling that guy for at least ten." She snickered and indicated Fussy across the driveway, still holding forth, gesturing animatedly to an attentive officer.

Kelly turned away with a shudder. "I can't look. Remember, you're taking her home."

"I know, I know. You can have one of mine."

"A quiet one, please."

Jennifer laughed softly. "Boy, an afternoon with you without caffeine can sure turn ugly."

"Don't even go there," Kelly warned.

"Too bad they won't let us use the kitchen. I'll bet Vickie has some coffee. Whoa, here comes another cop, heading for you, I'll bet," Jennifer observed. "I'll make myself scarce and see if I can hunt up a cola or something."

"Please," Kelly begged, watching a middle-aged, suit-clad policeman approach.

"Ms. Flynn, I'm Lieutenant Peterson, the detective in charge. Can you go over some things with me, please?" the man asked, his notepad already open and poised.

"Surely, detective, uh, Lieutenant Peterson. How can I help?"

He paged through the notepad. "You said you noticed a bronze statue or bust lying on the floor near the victim, is that correct?"

"Yes sir," Kelly replied. "I noticed it because I'd seen the bronze before on an earlier visit. It usually sat on the cherry wood bookcase against the wall."

He scribbled away dutifully, then looked Kelly straight in the eye. "Ms. Flynn, can you think of anyone who might have wanted Vickie Claymore dead?"

Kelly met his gaze. "No sir, I cannot. I never heard her say a bad word about anyone." Something in the back of Kelly's memory sent a niggling thought forward. Oh yes she did. There was one person Vickie had spoken of harshly.

The detective's gaze narrowed. "Are you sure?"

"Well," Kelly hesitated, not sure how much she should say. "She did say some strong things about her husband. Or, soon-to-be ex-husband, Bob Claymore."

"They were divorcing?" he asked as he wrote.

"Yes, they were, but it wasn't final yet."

"Was he still living here, do you know, or elsewhere?"

"Vickie said he was living in town. In Fort Connor. He's . . . uh . . . he's a professor at the university. That's all I know about him." That wasn't entirely truthful, but Kelly was already feeling uncomfortable talking about her friend's personal business.

"Was it amicable? The divorce, I mean?" The detective fixed her with his tell-the-truth look, which Kelly felt all the way down to her toes.

"Not exactly," she admitted. "I recall Vickie complaining to some of us at the knitting shop about Bob and, uh, the situation." Complaining put it mildly, Kelly recalled. Vickie had been in a white-hot fury when she discovered Bob was having an affair with a fellow weaver — a woman named Eva Bartok.

"Complaining about what?" he continued to grill, scribbling in the notebook.

Oh, brother, Kelly sighed within. Better tell him. "Vickie found out he was having an affair with a friend of hers. And . . . and she was pretty irate, to say the least."

"She was angry?"

"Oh, yeah. Furious is more like it. She filed for divorce the following week."

"Do you know the other woman's name?" he continued.

"Yes, Vickie said it was Eva Bartok. I don't know the woman personally and have never met her, so I'm afraid I can't help you there," Kelly answered, hoping the detective would let her go. He was like a pit bull.

"Was Ms. Stroud present when Ms. Claymore spoke of her husband and the divorce?"

Darn. Now Jennifer would be grilled, too. "Well, yes, she was, detective. You see, we're both part of the same knitting group that Vickie belonged to. We meet every Tuesday night at the shop in town — House of Lambspun."

The detective glanced around the grounds. Most of the visitors had finished their interviews, Kelly noticed, and she was grateful that Jennifer had corralled them together near the barn. All except Fussy, that is. She was still holding forth.

Kelly closed her eyes. What was that woman saying?

"Are all these women in your knitting group?" he asked.

"Heck, no." Kelly caught herself before emitting her first response. "The rest of these folks are visiting from out of town and wanted to see a working alpaca ranch." She shook her head. "I guess they saw more than they wanted on this trip."

"Probably so, Ms. Flynn," he agreed and lowered his notebook. Kelly almost sighed in relief. "Thank you for your cooperation. You've been most helpful."

"I hope so, detective. I want whoever did this awful thing to Vickie to be caught and put in *jail,*" Kelly declared.

"We'll do our best, Ms. Flynn, I promise," he assured her. "Can you think of anyone else that we should interview?"

Kelly paused for a moment but couldn't resist. "See that woman over there, gesturing?" She pointed toward Fussy. "I had the dubious pleasure of riding into the canyon with her. I'm sure she'll tell you exactly how to run your investigation, detective." She gave him a wry smile.

"I'll bear that in mind, Ms. Flynn. Thank you again," the detective replied, a twinkle in his eye.

Kelly watched him cross the driveway and head straight for Jennifer. She knew she should supervise the visitors while Jennifer was being grilled, but Kelly simply didn't think she could stand by calmly while they bombarded her with questions. Not now.

The sound of a truck engine approaching caught her attention, and Kelly watched as a mud-splattered navy blue pickup pulled to a jerking halt near one of the police cruisers. A slender woman with sandy blond hair pulled back with a scarf jumped out of the truck and raced over to the closest police officer who was not engaged in interviewing.

Curious who the woman was, Kelly started walking toward them. As she drew closer, she noticed the woman appeared distraught and grasped at the officer's arm. Approaching close enough to overhear, Kelly paused.

"Officer, you've got to tell me what happened," the woman pleaded. "I'm Vickie's cousin. I'm the closest relative she has here. We work together every day. Please, please, tell me if Vickie's all right!"

The younger policeman hesitated for a moment before he answered. "No, ma'am, she isn't. I'm afraid she's dead."

The woman's mouth dropped open, and she gasped, "No . . . that can't be . . . how . . . ?"

"Let me get the detective in charge, Lieutenant Peterson. He'll want to speak with you. He'll explain everything. Stay right here, ma'am, okay?" the officer advised as he left.

The woman clasped both arms around herself and took a deep breath. Her head bent forward, and her shoulders began to shake. Kelly assumed she was crying and purposely glanced away for a few moments, not wanting to intrude on the woman's grief.

Kelly figured she must be Vickie's cousin who helped out at the ranch. Glancing back, Kelly saw the woman wipe her eyes with the back of her hand as she stared at the house. Kelly slowly approached, wanting to offer her condolences. "Excuse me, I don't mean to intrude, but I couldn't help overhearing your saying you were a relative of Vickie's."

The woman looked up, her eyes red, her face mottled from crying. "Yes, yes, I am. I'm her cousin, Jayleen," she said. "Can you tell me what happened here?"

Kelly shook her head. "I'm afraid not. We just arrived this afternoon with a group of knitters who're visiting from out of town." She gestured, indicating the crowded driveway and yard. "My friend and I offered to show them around a working alpaca ranch. Vickie was kind enough to volunteer." Kelly's voice softened. "When we walked in, we found her lying on the floor. I'm afraid she was already dead."

"My God . . . ," Jayleen whispered, closing her eyes.

"I just wanted to tell you how sorry I am about Vickie." Kelly extended her hand. "I'm Kelly Flynn, one of Vickie's friends from the knitting shop. She used to come and visit with us every Tuesday night. She'd weave while we knit."

"Jayleen Swinson," the woman said, giving Kelly a firm handshake. "I remember her talking about that group."

"We all grew very fond of Vickie. She was so vibrant and full of life. . . ." Kelly gestured as she lost the words.

"Excuse me, ladies," Lieutenant Peterson's voice interrupted as he strode up. "You said you're a relative of the deceased, Vickie Claymore?" He directed the question at Jayleen.

Kelly took that as her hint to leave, and she quickly walked toward the fence. She leaned over and pretended to watch the alpacas while she strained to catch parts of the conversation. Maybe cousin Jayleen had some idea who could kill Vickie. Why she was deliberately eavesdropping, Kelly wasn't sure. Something inside her was curious.

Peterson's questions were often lost, since his back was turned to Kelly, but Jayleen's responses carried clearly on the slight mountain breeze.

"I'm here every day, Lieutenant Peterson. I work with Vickie and help with her business. I would know if she had any enemies. We grew up together in Colorado Springs, Lieutenant. We're very, very close. We do not keep secrets from each other. At least, we didn't. . . ." Jayleen's voice faded.

Kelly heard a low mumble she took to be Peterson's question, which brought an irate response from Jayleen.

"Absolutely not! Vickie would never commit suicide. Never. She had too much going for her. Her . . . her business was successful, she had plans, she . . ."

The rest was lost as the breeze shifted. So far, everything Kelly heard confirmed what she believed. Vickie didn't have enemies, and she wouldn't kill herself.

Another low mumble was followed by an

angry explosion from Jayleen. "You bet she was divorcing Bob! Do you know what that —" She went on to describe in detail all of Bob Claymore's sins and transgressions, punctuated by colorful expletives.

Kelly smiled and imagined Lieutenant Peterson scribbling furiously in his little notebook. It was certainly an entertaining narrative, she had to admit. Even the alpacas had gathered closer to the fence, as if to listen. She held out her hand, palm up, and one came over to sniff.

"Sorry, no food," she apologized to the gentle creature as she reached to pat its graceful, long neck. Newly shorn, the animal felt nubbly and soft at the same time. Kelly noticed the tawny brown and white pattern covered the skin in the same pattern it appeared on the heavy coat when sheared.

Jayleen's responses continued to float over to Kelly as she patted the animals adventurous enough to approach. Meanwhile, she heard a litany of divorce demands and counterdemands. Vickie's business was more successful than Kelly knew, and apparently, her husband, Bob, wanted half of it.

"Can you imagine?" Jayleen demanded. "Bob Claymore didn't build that business!

Vickie did, and it took her fifteen years. He has no right! That . . ."

More expletives drifted by, and Kelly noticed the alpacas seemed to pay attention. It made sense, she decided. After all, Jayleen helped Vickie on the ranch every day, so the alpacas knew her, were comfortable with her. If Jayleen was upset, the animals would probably notice. Carl always sensed her moods, Kelly reminded herself and wondered if alpacas did the same thing.

"Her estate? I don't know. I'm sure she'd be leaving it all to her daughter in Arizona."

This change of subject caught Kelly's attention. The divorce wasn't final, so legally, Vickie and Bob Claymore were still married at the time of her death, which meant . . .

"What!" Jayleen exclaimed. "You can't be serious. No way he gets half! That can't be right. They were divorcing!"

This time the string of curses must have startled not only the alpacas but Lieutenant Peterson as well, because Kelly heard him speak.

"Calm down, Ms. Swinson. I know you're upset, but —"

"Hey, look what I dug up from someone's backpack," Jennifer declared as she appeared at the fence beside Kelly. She dangled a can of soda. "It's not cold, but it's caffeine."

Kelly's caffeine lobe started vibrating. All attempts to eavesdrop were forgotten. Priorities beckoned, and right now she needed caffeine. Hot, cold, or lukewarm. "Wow, thanks, Jen," she said as she accepted the soda. Popping the top, Kelly took a huge gulp.

Jennifer grinned. "Maybe we'd better round up these ladies and head down the canyon. What do you think? It's nearly five o'clock now."

Kelly's stomach growled, reminding her of the time. She glanced toward the cluster of knitters, who were actually staying in one place this time. Police power, Kelly figured. She also noticed Fussy was among them, having obviously finished relating her story. Or, maybe the officer's ear had dropped off.

"Yeah, you're right. Last thing we want is to be stuck in a car filled with starving women. They could get surly. We'd better feed 'em."

"It's not them I'm worrying about — it's you," Jennifer teased. "I've seen you hungry, and it's scary."

"I wonder if the detective will let us leave," Kelly asked aloud. Watching Lieutenant Peterson close his notepad as he spoke with Jayleen, Kelly took that as a sign and approached them. "Excuse me, detective," she ventured. "Is it all right if my friend and I gather up these visitors and take them back to Fort Connor? We need to get them fed and to their hotel."

"Ah, yes, Ms. Flynn, that's fine," Lieutenant Peterson answered, his suntanned face cracking a smile. "They've had a busy day. Better take them home. If we need any more information, we'll be in touch with you."

"Thanks, Lieutenant Peterson, and I'll be glad to help any way I can," Kelly said.

"As will I . . . sir . . . uh . . . Lieutenant," Jayleen spoke up. "Do you want me to call Vickie's daughter, Debbie, in Arizona?"

"That's okay, Ms. Swinson. We'll be contacting the family. Is the daughter the only living relative other than yourself?" Peterson asked, opening his notebook once more. "Do you know her address and phone number?"

"Yes, she's the only other family Vickie has." Jayleen shoved her hands in the back pockets of her jeans. "I don't know the phone number off the top of my head, but

I can get it for you real quick. Everything's right inside Vickie's office. I keep her books, so I'm in there every day. It'll only take me a sec."

She pointed toward the log home, which now had yellow police tape wrapped around the entire front porch and doorways. It looked to Kelly like a bizarre present, gift-wrapped in its mountain setting. Completely out of place.

"I'm sorry, but we can't allow anyone inside the house now. Our investigators have to complete their work. We're treating this as a crime scene. Do you have a record of the daughter's address and phone elsewhere? Does anyone else know her?"

"I may have her number at home in my office, somewhere. I'd have to look," Jayleen said. "My desk is a mess, but I should be able to find it — after I put the animals in the barn, that is. We can't leave them out overnight. I'll be able to do that, won't I? I mean, I'm here every morning helping Vickie around the ranch. It's one of my jobs."

Peterson pondered for a second. "I think the barn's been checked, so that should be all right. But you'll only have access to the barn and pastures. Don't touch anything else. The house will be locked up."

Jayleen's eyes got huge. "No sir. I wouldn't. Honest. Just the animals. That's all."

Kelly spoke up, "You know, if you can't find that number, Jayleen, I can ask Mimi Shafer, the owner of the knitting shop. Maybe she knows the daughter. Mimi and Vickie are, uh, were friends."

Lieutenant Peterson scribbled, then reached into his coat pocket. "Thank you, Ms. Flynn. Here's my card. Please tell Ms. Shafer to call if she has any information. Oh, and you can take your group and go now." He gestured toward the flock, clustered by the barn. "Good luck going home."

Taking that as her cue to go, Kelly sent him a warm smile. "Thanks, Lieutenant. We may need it."

Waving to Jennifer, she beckoned for the group to join her, then headed toward the SUV. With any luck, they could be out of the canyon and in Fort Connor by six o'clock. Kelly sincerely hoped the promise of a quick stop at a fast-food restaurant would be enough to keep the visitors docile on the trip back.

Carl nosed and sniffed the thick bushes lining the backyard fence, investigating every inch of the perimeter of his small kingdom. Kelly leaned back and sipped her coffee. She loved this time of the evening. The last light of summer sunset illuminated the treetops while the evening breeze seduced the leaves, whispering its night song.

Kelly relaxed into the shape-hugging chair. No matter how busy and stressful her workday turned out, it all disappeared during these hours. She gazed at the outline of the mountains, shadowed by impending twilight. The mountains nourished her. The breeze nourished her. Being outside nourished her. Heck, just being back in Colorado nourished her.

She took another sip of coffee, grateful for the umpteenth time that she was out of the close confines of the SUV and away from all those chattering women. The promise of food had worked, and the ladies kept their questions to a minimum, obviously content to entertain themselves on the return drive. Even so, Kelly had the beginnings of a headache, which started when she and Jennifer deposited their charges at the hotel and headed home themselves. Jennifer offered to call Mimi and tell her the sad news, and Kelly gratefully agreed. She didn't think she could answer another question.

Now, relaxed outside in the gathering dusk, Kelly felt all the accumulated tension from the disturbing day disappear. Only questions remained, darting in and out of her mind, as she watched night slowly capture the sky.

Who could have killed Vickie? Her husband, Bob? Remembering the angry accusations Jayleen had hurled this afternoon, Kelly had to admit he might have a motive. Apparently, Vickie wasn't about to divide up her successful alpaca business with him in a divorce settlement. But if she died before a settlement was reached and the divorce wasn't final, then Bob Claymore was still legally her husband. As such, he was entitled to a portion of her estate.

Kelly pondered the thought. Money could definitely be a motive for murder. People had killed each other over money since the beginning of time. But Bob Claymore was also the most obvious suspect. All of their friends knew he and Vickie were involved in a bitter divorce. Bob Claymore had the most to lose from the divorce and the most to gain from Vickie's death.

The last time Kelly had gotten close to a murder investigation, the obvious suspect turned out to be innocent. When her aunt Helen was killed, the police quickly arrested a suspect they believed responsible. But Kelly sensed the real killer was still out there and went on to prove it.

She took a deep, satisfying drink of coffee. A bird hidden in the treetop above warbled an evening song. Kelly listened to the lilting cadence, releasing all thoughts of motives and murder, and simply let herself drink in the delicious summer night.

Four

Megan looked up from the other side of the shop's long library table as Kelly dumped her knitting bag and sat down. "Kelly, how are you? I'm so sorry you were the one to find Vickie. That must have been awful!" she exclaimed, her naturally pale skin almost white with concern.

"It was," Kelly admitted as she set a mug of Eduardo's delectable nectar on the table. "I hope I never have to walk in on something that horrible again."

"Jennifer told us all about it this morning. Lisa was here for a while between therapy patients," Megan went on, picking up her needles again. The scarf of purple eyelash yarn was almost finished. "I had to go back for a conference call with my Boise client, but I promised Mimi I'd return after lunch. I was hoping you'd show up."

"How's Mimi taking it? Vickie seemed to be a very close friend."

"Oh, she was. Mimi said they'd known each other for over twenty years. Ever since Vickie moved here with her first husband.

In fact, Mimi was the one who taught her how to weave."

Kelly sipped the flavorful brew. "They go back a long way, then. This must be hitting Mimi pretty hard."

The sound of Mimi's voice coming around the corner caught their attention. Mimi appeared, arms filled with pattern books, talking to Rosa, one of the shop assistants.

"I thought that lace pattern was in the latest issue of this knitting magazine. Maybe I'm wrong," Mimi said as she dumped the books on the far end of the table. Glancing up, she gave Kelly a wan smile before she went back to Rosa. "See if you can find it, would you, please? It's got the scalloped edges and roses."

Mimi walked toward their end of the table, straightening magazines and yarn bins along the way. Finally, she sank into a chair. She looked tired to Kelly. Grief was wearing on her. She'd lost a good friend with Helen's death a few months ago, and now another dear friend was gone.

"How're you doing, Mimi?" Kelly asked.

"I'm okay," she said quietly, staring into her lap. No knitting needles, Kelly noticed, to keep Mimi's restless hands occupied. "Still stunned, I guess. I mean, it's all so senseless. Who would kill Vickie Claymore? She was a warm, generous, caring person — a gifted craftsman and a successful businesswoman." Mimi wrapped her arms around herself and shook her head sadly. "I don't understand."

Kelly debated how to bring up the subject that had been playing through her mind last night, ever since hearing Jayleen's accusations. She'd have to work up to it. "Mimi, you know Vickie's cousin, Jayleen, don't you?"

"Yes, I've met her a few times over the years. I don't actually know her real well, but Vickie was always saying how much work she did around the ranch."

"She arrived at the ranch yesterday while the police were there," Kelly went on. "She was really upset, understandably."

"I imagine so," Mimi added. "Vickie has been like a big sister to her. Helped Jayleen straighten her life out after her last divorce. I think she even helped Jayleen get a job as a bookkeeper, too, if I recall."

Kelly sipped her coffee. "Well, that explains her forceful and rather colorful defense of Vickie's interests — in the divorce, I mean."

Mimi managed a small smile. "Yes,

Jayleen can be colorful, all right. She's got quite a tongue on her."

"Ohhhh, yeah. She was describing all of Bob Claymore's transgressions to the police detective. And she was as furious as Vickie that Bob wanted half of the business. But then she really exploded when the detective told her he'd wind up with half the business now that Vickie's dead." Kelly gave a wry smile, remembering Jayleen's wrath. "The detective had to calm her down."

"Well, he's right. The divorce wasn't final, so Bob Claymore is still legally her husband," Mimi observed.

"That doesn't seem fair," Megan said, glancing up from her scarf.

"What isn't fair?" Lisa's voice spoke up as she appeared at the table and settled into a chair.

"Finished with therapy already?" Megan looked up in surprise.

"Yeah, two rescheduled, and I had some errands to run anyway," Lisa explained as she pulled the multicolored ribbon vest from her bag. "I take it you guys are talking about Vickie. That was horrible, just horrible." Lisa scowled. "What lowlife would sneak in and kill Vickie?"

"Maybe the killer didn't sneak in," Kelly suggested.

"You think she knew the killer?" Megan asked, her blue eyes growing as huge as demitasse saucers.

Kelly nodded. "I think it's a strong possibility. There's no way Vickie would let some deranged intruder cut her throat."

Lisa nodded. "You're right. Vickie would probably punch him out. And not just an intruder, either. Face it, Vickie wouldn't let anyone attack her. She was tough."

"What do you think happened?" Mimi asked, peering anxiously at Kelly.

Kelly glanced over both shoulders, checking for nearby customers, then said in a quiet voice, "I think she was killed by someone she knew. Someone she allowed into her home. Yesterday, I saw a bronze bust lying on the floor near Vickie. I think someone knocked Vickie unconscious, then killed her."

Mimi blanched, then shuddered. "Oh, that's so gruesome."

"Wouldn't she have regained consciousness before she died?" Megan whispered.

Lisa shook her head vehemently. "Not if her throat was cut right through the jugular vein. She'd bleed out quickly. Even if she awoke from the head trauma, she'd pass out from blood loss."

Both Mimi and Megan shuddered visibly this time. "How diabolically cruel," Mimi whispered.

"Yes, and only someone who knew Vickie would have been able to do it," Kelly added. "And that brings us back to Bob Claymore."

"Vickie's husband?" Lisa asked, clearly surprised. "I don't think so. I've worked with him on a community housing project. He's this laid-back literature professor. No way."

"Anyone can kill, Lisa," Megan said darkly, her fingers nimbly working the purple yarn.

"Boy, that sounds scary. Let me see if I can guess what you guys are talking about," Jennifer announced as she dumped her knitting bag on the table and pulled up a chair beside Kelly.

"Well, I'm not talking about this anymore," Mimi said forcefully as she rose. "I just can't. I still remember when we all came to Fort Connor and the university years ago. We were all happy. We raised our children, we went to parties, we built our businesses . . ." Mimi's voice trembled as she gazed outside. "And we didn't go around killing each other." She turned and rushed from the room.

"Poor Mimi," Megan ventured. "This is so hard on her."

"She was in tears on the phone last night when I called," Jennifer added. "I felt so bad."

"I sure hope the killer made lots of mistakes for the police to find, so they can catch him quickly," Kelly said.

"Do you really think her husband could have done it?" Megan probed.

Kelly released a sigh. "I don't know. But he sure sounds like suspect number one, judging by everything we've heard. He was the one with the most to gain from her death."

"Was that who Vickie's cousin was going off about yesterday?" Jennifer asked, taking the multicolored fringed yarn and needles from her bag. "Brother, I haven't heard that much swearing since my freshman year at an all-girls' college."

Lisa's knitting fell to her lap. Megan's jaw dropped. Kelly stared at Jennifer, incredulous. "You went to a girls' college?"

"Yeah. I promised my parents I'd try it for a year. Damn near killed me."

Kelly joined the laughter that rippled around the table as she reached into her knitting bag and withdrew her new sweater project. She examined the newest rows of stockinette stitching that she'd finished that morning while downloading files. Her friends were right. Knitting in the round produced stockinette. Kelly didn't care if it was magic or not. She was proud of herself. It looked good. The raspberry silk-and-cotton stitches were nice and even. She held up the rosy red circlet of yarn and noticed the twist that had appeared in the circle this morning.

How'd that happen? she wondered. It hadn't been there yesterday.

"Hey, look how much I've finished," Kelly announced, proudly holding up the circlet. "I had a ton of client files to download from my office this morning, so I got a lot done."

Lisa glanced up. "Looks like it's really coming along —" She stopped, peering at the circle. "Uh-oh."

That was enough to capture Megan's attention. She eyed the twisted circlet and asked, "What happened? It looked fine yesterday."

"Oooops," Jennifer observed and went back to her silky yarn.

Kelly sat perplexed, still holding the rosy red circle. She'd expected to hear a heartening string of "good job" and "looks good." Not this.

"What's with the 'oops' and the 'uh-oh'?" she demanded. "What's wrong?"

"How'd it get twisted?" Lisa asked.

Kelly shrugged. "I don't know. I must have shoved it into my knitting bag before I left for the canyon yesterday. It was twisted like this when I took it out this morning."

"Did you notice the twist?" Megan asked.

"Yeah," Kelly admitted. She didn't like the way this conversation was going.

"But you kept knitting," Lisa added, her needles working the ribbons in her lap.

"Yeah, I figured it would straighten out somehow."

"Like magic?"

"We gotta stop using the M-word with her. She's an accountant."

"Don't worry, Kelly, we've all done it," Megan reassured with an encouraging smile. "It happens easily when knitting in the round."

"*What* happened?" Kelly exclaimed, exasperated now. "What'd I do wrong?"

Jennifer turned to her and smiled. "Congratulations. You've created a Möbius strip. Start frogging."

Kelly stared at her. What? Möbius strip?

Frogs? What did that have to do with yarn? "Möbius strip?" she asked, totally clueless as to what Jennifer was talking about. "You mean those twisty things that hang from the ceiling?"

"Yep. That's what the sweater turns into when the circle gets twisted."

"But won't the twist come out?" She placed the circle on the table and started working the yarn with her fingers around and around the circle.

"Let me know if it disappears," Jennifer said. "We'll call the knitting magazines. You'll make the front cover."

Kelly scowled at the uncooperative circle of yarn. Whenever she straightened the twist on one side, it corkscrewed on the other. Around and around, over and over. "Darnit," she fussed. "Now what?"

"Start frogging."

"Enough of this!" Kelly protested, disappointment mixing with annoyance now. "What do frogs have to do with anything?"

Megan giggled. "It's an expression we use for unraveling."

"You remember the sound frogs make. *Rip-pit! Rip-pit!*" Lisa joked.

Kelly stared at the circlet in disbelief. "Rip it out? All of it? But I've done so much, I —"

"Well, you can hang it from the ceiling as a decoration or rip it out and start over. Your choice," Jennifer added.

"I don't believe this." Kelly shook her head, still dumbfounded at her mistake. How could she do something like that? She thought she was doing so well. The stockinette looked so good. And all along, she was doing it wrong.

"Now, don't go beating up on yourself," Lisa advised. "We've all done it, Kelly. Knitting in the round is tricky until you get the knack of it. It's a common mistake."

"Yeah, yeah, yeah," Kelly grumbled.

"Uh-oh. Knitting angst is about to descend. I can feel it," Jennifer teased.

"You're right, it is," Kelly complained. "I thought I was doing so well. My stockinette really looked good."

"And it does look great," Lisa reassured. "Just think of this as extra practice."

Kelly released a dramatic sigh and listened to her friends chuckle. "Okay, what do I do to start unraveling, or frogging, or whatever it is?"

Jennifer reached over. "Here, let me get you started. First, we have to gently pull the yarn off the needles and plastic circle, like this." She started slowly working the slender wooden needles and attached plastic cord from the top row of stitches. "There, all out." She tossed the needle contraption on the table and handed the forlorn sweater attempt back to Kelly. "Now, just pull gently and it'll all start to unravel."

"Okaaaay," Kelly said dubiously, giving the yarn a tug. It cooperated, and the entire first row of stitches unraveled before her eyes.

"Here, wind the yarn around this," Lisa said, reaching into her bag and offering an empty paper towel roll. "You don't want to get knots in the yarn."

"Why not?" Kelly complained, indulging in a little self-pity. "I've managed to bungle everything else about this sweater."

"Oh, boy. The angst is getting deeper. She's about to go under. Look out," Jennifer teased.

"All right, all right," Kelly started to laugh, joining her friends. It was impossible to stay in a bad mood when she was around them.

The shop's doorbell jingled, followed by a familiar duet of voices. One high and girlish, the other low and deeply resonant, told Kelly the Von Steuben sisters had arrived. Both were elderly retired school teachers and two of the most accomplished knitters Kelly had seen yet.

"Hello, hello," Lizzie Von Steuben trilled as she fluttered into the main room, a vision of white and pink. "How wonderful to see all four of you this afternoon. What a treat!" She daintily set down her lacy knitting bag as she joined the others.

"Good afternoon, ladies," boomed Hilda Von Steuben as she strode through the room and settled at the end of the table.

The better to conduct class, Kelly thought and smiled to herself. Both spinster sisters were accomplished interrogators, Kelly had learned. Only their styles differed. Lizzie would flit and flutter around the subject, circling ever closer, while Hilda steamrollered right to the point.

"Hilda, Lizzie, good to see you," Megan greeted.

Kelly joined in the ensuing small talk, waiting for Hilda to start questioning. She could tell Lizzie was about to explode with curiosity.

"Kelly, I'm profoundly sorry you were the one to make the dreadful discovery yesterday," Hilda intoned.

"Ohhhh, yessss," Lizzie rushed in. "Such a horrible thing to see. Are you all right, dear?"

"I'm doing fine, thank you, ladies," Kelly replied and launched into a condensed version of yesterday's events in the canyon. Lizzie and Hilda both sat rapt, not saying a word. While she talked, Kelly watched Lisa check her watch and slip away from the table, as did Jennifer. Kelly wound the sad tale to a close.

Lizzie bent her head over the misty gray shawl she was crocheting and didn't say a word, clearly affected by the death of one of their own. Hilda seemed content to concentrate on the peach wool that appeared to be forming into a baby blanket. Kelly glanced at her watch, timing this welcome break from analyzing accounts.

"Has Vickie's daughter been notified yet?" Hilda asked after a moment.

That comment caught Kelly's attention and reminded her she told the detective she'd ask Mimi to search for the daughter's number. "Thanks, Hilda, that reminds me of something." She started to push back her chair when Mimi appeared around the corner, daytimer in hand. "Mimi, I just remembered. Do you know Vickie's daughter's name and phone number? I think she lives in Arizona."

Mimi stopped where she was, clearly startled. "What? You mean Debbie hasn't been notified yet? Good heavens!"

Kelly dug in her knitting bag and withdrew Lt. Peterson's card. Handing it over to Mimi, she said, "I told the detective in charge, Lieutenant Peterson, that you would call with the number. Just in case Jayleen couldn't find it at her home. No one was allowed in Vickie's office where all the phone logs would be, naturally."

Mimi took the card and headed toward the front of the shop. "I'll call right away."

"This will come as a terrible shock to the girl, I am sure," Hilda continued in a resonant contralto. "She's such a delicate little creature. I sincerely hope she's able to bear up under this tragedy."

"Oh, my, yes," Lizzie murmured, making soft little *tsk*ing sounds as more flower designs appeared in the smoky gray shawl.

The shawl looked scrumptious to Kelly, and she couldn't resist reaching over and squeezing the soft yarn. Lusciously soft. So soft it must be . . . "Alpaca?" she guessed.

Lizzie beamed, her round cheeks tinged pink. "Why, yes, it is. Good for you, Kelly. You're learning your fibers."

Kelly suppressed her smile and watched Megan do the same at the verbal pat on the head. "What sort of health problems does the daughter have?" she asked after a second.

"Debbie is afflicted with the most serious

form of asthma. Truly life-threatening. That's why she lives in the drier climate in Arizona. She needs to be away from the irritants that could trigger an attack. She's been hospitalized countless times since she was a child, according to Vickie."

"That's awful," Megan exclaimed.

"And her mother was always such a picture of health," Lizzie commiserated, shaking her head. "I always thought it unfortunate that a woman as robust and strong as Vickie Claymore would have such a frail and fragile child as this Debbie appears to be."

"You've never met her?" Kelly asked, continuing her unraveling. It was actually a strangely soothing activity, she noticed, but not one she'd like to indulge in frequently. Kelly liked results, and the quicker she got results, the better.

"No, we haven't seen her since she was a young girl living with her family here in town," Lizzie answered. "Her asthma was serious but not as bad as it is now."

"It was the ranch that did it," Hilda decreed. "When Vickie divorced her first husband, she used the property settlement to buy an old ranch house up in Bellvue Canyon. She'd dreamed of raising and breeding alpacas. Unfortunately, it was that dream that spurred Debbie's disease to the next level."

Hilda's fingers worked the peach yarn, producing a spreading fan design in the blanket. The Von Steuben sisters' artistry always amazed Kelly. "What do you mean?" she continued to probe. "Was she allergic to the alpacas?"

"Oh, no," Lizzie spoke up. "It wasn't the alpacas."

"It was the ranch setting itself, apparently," Hilda picked up the thread. "The hay and dust in the stalls and pastures, the grasses the animals grazed, the surrounding trees and bushes. All of it triggered a dangerous attack when she was ready to go to college. Poor girl. She had a scholarship to Stanford, too."

"What happened?" Megan prodded, clearly as enthralled with this story as Kelly. "Did she drop out of college?"

"Unfortunately, yes," Hilda continued. "She was in and out of hospitals for over a year. That's when she had to move to Arizona to recuperate. She enrolled in the state school when she was stronger." She glanced up at Mimi, who was quietly rearranging yarn in the corner. "Exactly what did Debbie study, do you remember, Mimi?"

"Yes, it was biology. She's a researcher now, looking for a cure for these dreadful respiratory diseases." Mimi's voice had an edge to it.

"You sound like you spent a lot of time with Vickie," Megan addressed Hilda. "I'm sure this is hard for you."

Hilda set her needles down and was uncharacteristically pensive for a moment as she stared out the window. "Yes, it is. I'd grown quite fond of Vickie over the years. I taught her some of the advanced knitting techniques, and she tried to teach me to weave. I wasn't a very good student, I'm afraid."

"She was fond of you, too, Hilda," Mimi said in a small voice. "She said so many times. You reminded her of her mother."

That seemed to rouse Hilda, and she returned to the peach wool. "Poor misguided girl. An old fussbudget like me."

"Did you call the detective, Mimi?" Kelly asked, noticing her edge around the table.

"Yes, and he said he's already contacted Debbie. She told him she'd be coming to Fort Connor as quickly as she could." Mimi paused near the fireplace, decorated with hanging summer tops, and gazed out the window. "I feel sorry for Debbie. She was so close to her mother."

"I'm surprised she's able to come back here at all if her asthma is that serious," Megan commented as she rose to leave.

"Vickie said there're newer medicines now that allow Debbie to travel more. I believe she actually stayed with Vickie at the ranch last year for over a week."

Kelly checked her watch. Corporate accounts beckoned. "I'm afraid I have to get back to work, ladies. Maybe I'll see you tomorrow," she said as she carefully placed the circular needles and ball of unraveled yarn back into her bag and rose to leave.

"You'll see me tonight," Megan reminded her on the way to the door. "Practice, remember? Seven o'clock."

"Ohhhh, yeah," Kelly said, hitting her forehead. "Brother, I thought I put it on my calendar." Throwing a wave over her shoulder, she headed for the door. "See you, folks. Gotta run." She'd really have to push now to finish that client file before practice.

As she raced down the flagstone steps leading from the shop, Kelly heard her cell phone's insistent ring. Darn. She didn't need any interruptions right now. "Kelly Flynn here," she snapped into the receiver.

"Whoa, hello to you, too," Steve's voice

sounded in her ear. She could hear the amusement.

"Sorry, Steve. I'm just hurrying back to my office to finish up some files before dinner. Totally spaced about tonight's practice. What's up?" she asked as she maneuvered the cottage door open and dumped her things on the sofa.

"We've got an invitation to dinner tomorrow night. From Curt Stackhouse and his wife, Ruth. I saw Curt at a builders' meeting this morning, and he reminded me we said we'd come over for dinner some night."

"We who?" Kelly played dumb, deliberately stalling. She'd been hoping Curt had forgotten his offer.

"You and me who." She could almost see Steve's smile.

"You and me, huh?"

This time she heard the chuckle. "Yeah, unless you want to bring Carl, too. We could let him run loose in the field. Or he can play with the sheep."

Kelly laughed, remembering the last time she'd been to Curt Stackhouse's ranch. Carl spent the entire time galumphing through the tall field grass, chasing scents and scampering creatures. "Curt would not be amused," she said, settling at the computer. "Neither would the sheep."

"Okay, so it's back to us. You and me. For dinner. At Curt's. Think you can handle it?"

"Okay, okay," Kelly gave in with an exaggerated sigh. "What time are we talking about tomorrow night?"

"Seven o'clock. Does that work?"

"Yeah. Okay. Seven." She hesitated. "I'll meet you there."

Steve laughed out loud this time. "You want us to drive separate cars? Won't that look a little strange? What are we gonna do, meet in front of Curt's barn?"

He was right. It would look stupid. Rats. She hated it when he was right. She was being borderline ridiculous, but she couldn't help it. "Okay, I'll meet you at the Crossroads coffee shop. I've got some errands to run on that side of town anyway."

"You just don't want anyone at the shop seeing me pick you up, that's all."

Steve hit dead center on that one. Darnit, Kelly smarted. "No, that's not it —"

"Yeah, it is," he teased. "Listen, I've got a better idea. Why don't you pick me up? I'll be at my new site in Wellesley. Corner of Newport and Hampton streets. Six thirty, tomorrow. See you." And he clicked off before Kelly could say another word.

Five

"Thanks, Pete," Kelly said as she lifted her coffee mug and edged around the café tables, heading for the hallway that led to the shop. She'd been working at the computer ever since her morning run on the river trail. She deserved a fiber break, as she referred to her daily visits to knit and talk with friends.

Sometimes the workaholic inside her tried to make Kelly feel guilty for leaving her home office. Fortunately, it didn't last very long. She needed those breaks. She worked all alone now, not in the midst of an office filled with colleagues. Kelly missed the camaraderie. She didn't realize how much until she'd started telecommuting to her firm three months ago. Besides, she reminded herself, she got twice as much work done without all the interruptions for meetings that used to mark her daytimer. Now, she could actually leave her work without worry and was thankful she'd made so many good friends in the short time she'd been here.

Rounding the corner to the front room, Kelly stopped short. Once again, elves had come in and worked their magic overnight. Frothy new yarns were everywhere, spilling across the round maple table in the center of the room and tumbling from wooden crates that lined the walls. Steamer trunks that held scrunchy wools only months ago now brimmed with fat balls of new fibers that begged to be touched.

Kelly couldn't resist and set her knitting bag and mug on the floor, then sank her arms elbow deep into the chest of brilliant and bold boa yarns. Soft, soft, with little fibers that stuck out like eyelashes, and in every color imaginable. She squeezed strawberry scarlet and lime green, pineapple yellow and tangerine orange. Jelly bean colors. She'd been let loose in the candy shop and was playing in the candy bins. There was a big difference, though. These "candies" weren't fattening.

Moving to the bins along the wall, Kelly stroked longer-lashed yarns, some spiky in combination colors and others so silky soft they seduced her very fingers. Burnished copper and lemony yellow tempted next. She fingered a particularly seductive skein the color of good claret, then one of antique gold, another of moss green. Yummy,

Kelly thought, picturing the gorgeous autumn scarves she could make from those colors.

That was it. She had to have one. Jennifer was knitting a similar long-fringed scarf, and Megan had finished the purple eyelash scarf and was working on a pink one now. Kelly wanted one, too. Now that she'd gotten her knitting-in-the-round back on track, she could take a break, couldn't she? Besides, everyone said these scarves knitted up quickly.

Now, which color to choose, she pondered, wandering back to the chest of boa eyelash yarns. Something other than red this time, noting that her very first chunky wool sweater was cherry red, and her latest project was a luscious raspberry silk and cotton. She wanted something different. Decisions, decisions.

Kelly was still immersed in color when she heard her name called. She turned to see Rosa in the doorway and another woman Kelly didn't recognize.

"Kelly, this lady wanted to talk to you," Rosa explained, then dropped her voice. "She's a friend of Vickie's and wanted to know what happened."

Scarves and jelly bean colors had to wait. Kelly scrambled from the floor. The woman stepped over to her, hand outstretched.

"Kelly, I'm Geri Norbert. Vickie was my closest friend. I live up in the canyon about two miles from her ranch. And I . . . I just wanted to ask some questions, if you don't mind."

Kelly shook her hand. It was warm and callused. "Sure, I'll be glad to answer whatever I can, Ms. Norbert."

The woman's suntanned face creased with a grin. Kelly guessed her to be midfifties like Vickie. Her long, dark hair mixed with gray hung down her back in a fat braid. "Please call me Geri. Everyone does," she said.

Glancing over her shoulder at the knitting class taking place around the library table, Kelly gestured toward the café. "Why don't we have a cup of coffee at Pete's and talk, okay?" She reached to snag her knitting bag and mug before she headed back to the restaurant.

"Looks like you've already got yours," Geri said, following after Kelly.

"Yeah, I get a fill-up every morning. Helps me make it through all that computer work," Kelly replied as she aimed for a table in the back alcove. Noticing Jennifer wasn't working the morning shift,

Kelly signaled another waitress, then added, "I can personally recommend their cinnamon rolls. They're wicked."

Geri pulled up a chair as Kelly sat down. "I shouldn't. My sweet tooth is too easily awakened. Better let it sleep."

"I'm not sure mine ever goes to sleep," Kelly joked as Geri ordered coffee. She purposely waited until the steaming cup arrived before she started relating the events of that day. Geri sat without saying a word, solemnly watching Kelly with wide gray eyes until the sad story was finished.

Kelly took a long drink of coffee and waited for Geri to speak. Remembering those events took a toll, she noticed. Each time she told the story, the emotions of fear and horror and anger returned to pull at her again. She shivered, despite the hot coffee.

"I still can't believe it," Geri said, stirring her coffee without looking up. "I'm sitting here listening to you, and it still doesn't seem real. I'm . . . I'm stunned. I still expect to see Vickie's truck pull up in my driveway." She swiped at her eyes in a brusque way, as if the tears had startled her.

"I know it must be hard," Kelly said quietly. "Especially if you and Vickie saw each other a lot."

"All the time. We helped each other out with the animals. I have twelve alpacas. I've also got a few sheep." Geri stared out into the café. "Vickie was going to get some lambs from me this spring and start a small flock of her own."

Kelly heard a slight tremor in Geri's voice and purposely stayed quiet while Geri stirred her coffee. It must be stone cold by now, Kelly observed. Geri had barely had a sip and yet stirred enough to dissolve a pound of sugar.

Geri cleared her throat. "Vickie's daughter, Debbie, called me last night. She was in tears. We both were by the time she hung up. She'll be coming in today. I told her I'd pick her up at the airport."

"That's wonderful, Geri," Kelly said, impressed at how quickly she'd stepped into a difficult situation and made herself useful. "I assumed her cousin, Jayleen, would handle things like that. After all, they're family."

"Jayleen's got too much on her plate right now. She's trying to take care of Vickie's animals and her own and handle all the bookkeeping she does." Geri shrugged. "I offered to help with Vickie's alpacas, but Jayleen told me she could handle it."

Intrigued, Kelly followed up. "How many clients does she have? I'm a corporate accountant, so I know how consuming the work can be. And I don't have alpacas waiting to be fed, either."

Geri leaned back in her chair, and Kelly sensed she was relaxing a bit. "Well, I guess she's got about twenty alpaca breeder clients by now, plus any other stray clients she may have picked up. Enough to keep her busy." She swirled the cold coffee. "Vickie recommended Jayleen to other alpaca ranchers every chance she got."

"Did you use her services?"

"I do as much as I can myself, then I give it to Jayleen to put all the numbers together. That way, she charges me less. I've got a much smaller operation than a lot of the ranchers. Plus, I don't have a 'cash reserve,' either."

"Okay, you've got to explain that," Kelly said. "Now you've got me curious."

Geri grinned, highlighting the weathered lines around her eyes. Nice eyes, Kelly noticed. "That means I don't have a separate source of income coming in to run my ranch and pay the bills. A lot of people go into alpaca breeding when they retire from their regular jobs. That way there's steady money coming in. Me, I sink or swim based on how well my animals do."

"How many did you say you have?"

"I've got eleven females that are bred every year and one young herd sire that I use as stud. You've seen Vickie's prize-winner, Raja? Well, my Raleigh is Raja's son and has the same coloring. He's a gorgeous smoky gray like Raja. I'm expecting Raleigh to throw the same colors and females that Raja does."

Kelly held up her hands. "Wait a minute. What's this about throwing colors and females?"

"It's a term breeders use that means a stud whose particular color interacts with the females in such a way as to produce some beautifully colored offspring. Also, if he can produce more females than males, you make more money. The stud business is always a gamble, especially with a young male. Your income fluctuates, depending on the cria." Geri ran her finger around the rim of the cup. "But, I think my luck is about to change."

"What does luck have to do with it?" Kelly asked.

She looked up with a grin. "More than you think."

"Cria are the babies, right?"

"Right. And the female cria are your

bread and butter, because they can produce a baby a year. That's why you can sell the females for more money. Lots more."

"Ballpark?" Kelly probed, her inner accountant thoroughly engaged now.

"Thousands or tens of thousands, depending on the bloodlines."

Kelly pondered. Brother, this alpaca business was much more complicated than she'd ever imagined. "Boy, I never knew it was so involved. I guess I assumed you just let them breed, then sold the babies."

Geri laughed. "Well, I guess that's what we are doing, but it's a helluva lot of work. We can't leave it up to the animals. The females are kept separated from the males until their babies are sold and they're ready to be bred again. That's why we don't need more than one herd sire until he's about to retire. Most of the time, we send our females out to be bred to other males."

"Around here or out of state?"

"Both. Those gals are on the road a lot."

"Do they come into season right after they wean the babies?"

"Actually, alpacas only ovulate when they mate," Geri continued. A musical jangle sounded then, and Geri slipped a cell phone from her back pocket as she rose from the table and stepped into a hallway.

Kelly did the same. Her inner clock was ticking away. Work was waiting, and she only had the afternoon left. Tonight was already scheduled. Dinner with the Stackhouses and Steve.

Geri snapped her phone shut. "Sorry, had to take that call." She extended her hand again and gave Kelly a warm smile. "I want to thank you so much for taking the time with me, Kelly. It's helped a lot."

"You're welcome, Geri. I enjoyed talking with you, too. And the alpaca lesson," Kelly said with a grin. She liked Geri. Maybe because Geri reminded her of Vickie Claymore — sharp, down-to-earth, with a good sense of humor.

"I wouldn't be surprised if Debbie comes to see you as well once she settles in," Geri added, heading toward the door.

Kelly followed after. "Please tell Debbie how sorry we all are for her loss. Our loss, too. If there's anything I can do to help, please let me know."

"Thanks, Kelly. I'll be sure to tell her," Geri said with a wave as she opened the door to a faded green pickup truck.

Kelly hurried across the gravel driveway to her cottage, dumped her knitting bag on the sofa, and headed for the sunny corner of the dining room that doubled as her office. She'd barely glanced at the client file when her cell phone gave its insistent ring.

"Darnit! Why does it always ring when I'm super busy?" she complained to the empty room as she flipped the phone open. "Hello, Steve, if this is you reminding me about tonight, don't bother. I haven't forgotten. Corner of Newport and Hampton in Wellesley, right?"

"Well, not really, Kelly," an elderly gentleman's voice answered. "I'm still here in Fort Connor. Where are you?"

Oooops, Kelly thought, suddenly embarrassed. "Ohhhh, Mr. Chambers, I'm so sorry. I thought you were a friend who was giving me a hard time."

Lawrence Chambers chuckled. "I'm glad you've met so many good friends here, Kelly. Helen would be pleased. And, as your *friendly* legal adviser, I have some good news. We've moved through the first legal hurdle in Wyoming in regard to your cousin Martha's property."

Kelly set her mug on the desk and leaned back into her chair, ready to absorb one of Lawrence Chambers's legal updates on her inheritance rights to Martha Schuster's Wyoming ranch. The fluttery sensation that always settled in her stomach whenever Chambers brought up the subject returned.

What on earth was she going to do with a ranch? With cattle, yet. Five hundred head, Chambers had estimated. It had been years since she was around livestock. She'd been a city girl for so long, the only thing she remembered was to watch where she stepped in a pasture. She'd be totally out of her element and totally useless. And Kelly hated feeling useless.

"Okay," Kelly said. "We've passed through the first phase. How many hurdles do we have left?"

"Well, we've still got several left to go. After all, the property is literally passing through Ralph Schuster's estate to his wife, Martha, then through her estate to your aunt Helen, then through Helen's estate to you." He laughed softly again. "It's certainly one of the most convoluted inheritances I've ever seen, to be truthful. But don't you worry, Kelly. All is going well and proceeding in perfect order. These things just take time, that's all."

The fluttery sensation lessened somewhat. "That's all right, Mr. Chambers. Take all the time you need. I'm not ready to even think about owning a ranch anyway," she admitted.

"Well, you might want to start thinking about it, Kelly," he suggested. "Why don't you go up there and take a look at the property? The ranch manager I hired says it's really nice."

"Ohhhh, I wouldn't want to interrupt him," Kelly demurred, not too crazy about the idea.

This time Chambers laughed out loud. "You won't be interrupting him, Kelly, I assure you. Besides, I hired him, and since I'm acting on your behalf as your attorney, technically, you're his boss."

Kelly understood that concept, but somehow she couldn't picture herself bossing cowboys around. Accountants, yes. Cowboys, no. "I dunno, Mr. Chambers. I'll think about it."

"You know, Kelly, you could always take some friends along when you go up there. Your knitting friends would particularly enjoy it, I think."

Kelly's antennae started to buzz. She'd heard the smile in Chambers's voice. "Why is that?"

"Ohhhh, didn't I tell you? There's approximately one hundred sheep on the ranch in addition to the cattle. So you'll be inheriting lots of wool along with the land. You take care, Kelly. Bye now."

"Sheep? I have sheep? What — ?" Kelly exclaimed before she realized Chambers had already hung up. She could have sworn she heard him laugh.

Six

Kelly swirled the melting vanilla ice cream into a deep purple puddle of fresh blueberries, melt-in-your-mouth pie crust, and luscious blueberry sauce oozing into the cream. Homemade blueberry pie and ice cream. Yummmm. Kelly thought she'd slipped back in time to her childhood when Ruth Stackhouse placed the enormous, lattice-top dessert in the center of the table. Aunt Helen's blueberry pie was the best she'd ever tasted until tonight. Kelly had to admit, Ruth and Aunt Helen were tied for the honor.

She lifted another delectable spoonful to her mouth and savored it while the gentle hum of conversation surrounded her. Kelly was enjoying herself immensely. Curt and Ruth Stackhouse were wonderful hosts, warm and genial, and clearly loved entertaining guests. She had felt comfortable in their beautifully-appointed ranch home from the moment she entered.

Kelly stirred her coffee, which was surprisingly rich and strong, while she watched Ruth tease Curt about his refusal to wear a business suit. Curt responded in kind, and Kelly got the feeling that they'd been lovingly teasing each other for years. Something about watching Curt and Ruth together like this felt good inside. She didn't know why. It just felt good.

She leaned back in her chair and smiled, watching them enjoy each other, still teasing and joking together after nearly fifty years of marriage. Kelly toyed with the last piece of pie in her purple puddle.

She could tell both Curt and Ruth thought of Steve and her as a couple. It was understandable, she supposed. After all, Steve had been with her the first time they met, when Kelly was trying to unravel the cause of her aunt Helen's death three months ago. It was understandable, but it was wrong. Steve was just a friend. A softball friend. A provider of a steady supply of used golf balls for Carl. A good friend. But, still, just a friend. This "couple" thing was a place Kelly couldn't go. She'd been part of a couple once, years ago, and it ended painfully. Old memories still hurt. But she'd learned an important lesson: relationships were risky. And they often ended in loss.

After that, Kelly threw herself into her

budding corporate career, taking time only for her dad and an occasional softball game — until her dad was diagnosed with cancer. Then, everything changed. Kelly's life narrowed its focus even more and revolved exclusively around her job, her dad, and hospitals. No time for softball, and certainly no social life. She even stopped seeing the few friends she'd made. After her dad died three years ago, Kelly felt numb for months — until her uncle Jim's heart attack. And the whole heartbreaking cycle of loss started all over again. By now, Kelly was an expert on loss.

Finishing the last spoonful of pie, Kelly closed her eyes in enjoyment. "Mmmm, Ruth, this is delicious," she said after swallowing the morsel.

"Why, thank you, Kelly," Ruth said, her lined face crinkling into a broad smile. "I love to cook for folks who enjoy eating."

"Well, you cooked for the right people, ma'am," Steve said. "That was a delicious dinner. And dessert. I hate to be disloyal to my own mom, but that's gotta be the best pie I've ever tasted, Ruth."

"Oh, go on," she shooed at him, a blush coloring her cheek.

"No exaggeration, Ruth," Kelly agreed. "I thought my aunt Helen's blueberry pie was the best, but yours beats all."

"See, I told you, Ruthie," Curt said, wagging his head. "You should enter your recipe in the county fair."

"Now, don't you start about that fair again." Ruth patted Curt on the arm as she rose from the table. "You know I don't like crowds." Grabbing the coffeepot, she offered it around. "Who'd like more coffee?"

Steve was right there, cup extended, and Kelly was next in line. She'd already downed the contents of her first cup and was ready for more.

"There's plenty more pie, Kelly," Curt teased. "I've been watching you keep an eye on it."

Kelly laughed as she settled back into the upholstered chair and relaxed. "I may need it, Curt. Especially after the news I've had today."

"Does your boss want you back in Washington?" Steve asked, his smile disappearing.

"No no, not that. I had a call from Lawrence Chambers. He's the lawyer who's trying to straighten out all this inheritance stuff. You know . . . Helen's estate and then Martha's. It seems I'm the only remaining heir to both." She shook her head. "Today he told me I've got sheep. Last time we talked, he told me I had cows. I swear, I'm afraid to talk to the man."

"Wait a minute, wait a minute," Steve said, holding up a hand. "That little place in Landport isn't big enough for livestock, is it?"

Kelly stared at Steve blankly.

"You told me you were inheriting Martha's property, right? Didn't she live in Landport?"

"No no," Kelly said, realizing the mix-up. She had deliberately left out some significant details when she'd told her friends about Cousin Martha's property. "She was renting that place. But she and her husband owned land up in Wyoming. That's where the sheep are. And the cows." She took another sip of Ruth's rich coffee and brushed invisible pie flakes off the tablecloth.

Steve leaned back in his chair and crossed his arms, a hint of a smile showing. "Okaaaay, so how many sheep do you have?"

Kelly swished the coffee in her cup, acutely aware that the others were focused on her intently. Both Curt and Ruth were leaning forward on the table, watching.

"About a hundred," she said, straightening her napkin.

Steve grinned. "And the cattle?"

Kelly glanced out into the kitchen, trying her best to look nonchalant. "Ohhhh, about five hundred. I think that's what Chambers said."

Steve turned to Curt, and they both started to laugh. Kelly heaved a dramatic sigh and tried to ignore them.

"Goodness, Kelly, that's a lot of livestock to take care of," Ruth commented.

"Oh, Mr. Chambers took care of that," Kelly said with a dismissing wave. "He's hired a ranch manager to handle everything."

"A ranch manager, huh?" Curt observed with a grin. "Tell me, Kelly, how much land are we talking about here?"

Nonchalant and offhand hadn't worked. And trying to ignore both Steve and Curt at the same time would take more energy than she had at the moment. So Kelly resorted to complete honesty. She looked Curt straight in the eye. "A little over three hundred acres, I'm told. And damned if I know what I'm going to do with it."

Curt just laughed in reply. Steve raised his coffee cup to her, a wicked gleam in his eyes. "Congratulations, Kelly. You're a rancher, and you didn't even know it."

"That's not funny."

"Yeah, it is," he said, then burst out laughing.

"Don't start," she warned, trying to look severe, but that only made Steve laugh harder. He could be so annoying at times.

"That's a nice spread, Kelly. Have you gone to see it yet?" Curt asked.

She shook her head. "No. Chambers said I need to go take a look, but I don't really want to."

"Why?" Ruth asked.

Now that she'd gone the honesty route, she might as well go all the way. "Because the manager would probably ask me all sorts of questions, and I wouldn't know what he was talking about. I know nothing about running a ranch. The mere thought of all that land and livestock belonging to me is, well, it's scary. What am I supposed to do with it all? Martha mentioned she wanted the ranch to be turned into a nature preserve. How in the world am I supposed to do that? Do I sell all the cows? What about the house? And the equipment?" She gave an exasperated gesture.

Steve leaned over. "Hey, you're not alone, Kelly. We can help you. Both Curt and I can check out the land and the livestock. We can help you with all that. You don't have to do it by yourself."

"Damn right, Kelly," Curt said. "I'll be happy to help you. I do this all the time. And I know the people and places in Wyoming to contact for whatever we need."

Kelly felt the fluttery sensation in her stomach melt away, just like Ruth's delicious pie. She wouldn't have to do it alone. She'd have help. Suddenly the image of Martha's ranch didn't seem so foreboding.

"So, when would you like to go?" Steve asked.

"You mean up there?" Kelly pointed toward the kitchen.

Steve chuckled. "Yeah, up there, except Wyoming's north, so it's thataway." He pointed over his shoulder. "Where is it, exactly?"

"Wellll, I don't know exactly," Kelly hesitated. "All Martha said was it was west of Cheyenne."

To his credit, Steve did not burst out laughing at her comment, but Kelly could tell Curt was trying to hide his amusement and not doing a very good job.

"That leaves some pretty big territory, Kelly. We're gonna need some directions," Steve teased. "Or else we'll just head north till the wind starts to blow, then turn left."

Both Curt and Ruth laughed out loud at that, but Kelly bristled. She'd never liked being teased. What was it about her that made people tease her? Why was she so eminently teaseable? And, of course, whenever Steve succumbed to the urge, it annoyed Kelly all the more.

"I'm sure Chambers will give us all the directions we need," she said in her best attempt to appear haughty, which only succeeded in amusing Curt even more.

"Lord, Kelly, you've been out of the West too long," he said with a chuckle. "It's a good thing we've got you back. Don't you worry. We'll get you acclimated pretty damn quick. First, we'll get you something to wear that's better suited to tromping around pastures."

"We've got several pairs of extra boots you're welcome to use," Ruth suggested. "Boots and jeans will do a lot better."

Kelly was about to thank her, but Curt was clearly in a planning mode and already on a roll.

"Okay, then, what's your schedule like next week, Kelly? I'm booked all this week. Steve, how about you?"

"I'm afraid it'll have to be late next week or the week afterward for me, folks," Steve replied. "I don't want to leave the new site until the framers are in there. I've been putting out fires every day on this one.

Can't risk being that far away yet."

"I know what you mean, son," Curt said, nodding in agreement. "Always a crisis or someone's screwing up. Well, the week after will work for me, too. How about you, Kelly."

Kelly ran through her mental daytimer. Since they were planning almost two weeks out, she'd have plenty of time to work ahead on her accounts. "No problem. I'll be able to work around it. But if you two are super busy, we can postpone the trip."

"Oh, no," Curt admonished, shaking his head. "You need to go up there and see what you'll be inheriting. We need to make plans. Besides," he added, "I'm really anxious to see this spread you've been teasing us with. You've got my nose for land itching. Now I've gotta go out and sniff." He grinned.

"Me, too," Steve agreed. "I'm curious. I want to check out the cattle. See what you've got. Who knows? Maybe Martha had some good bloodlines going."

Kelly shrugged. "Martha had been away from the ranch for over four years when she was killed. Helen took her in and kept her hidden in Landport after Martha ran away from her abusive husband. When they learned that he died in a car accident last year, Helen asked Lawrence Chambers to take care of Martha's inheritance."

The table fell quiet now, all laughter forgotten. "That's dreadful," Ruth said, her pale, thin face pinching with a frown.

"Was there a divorce? Are there any children?" Curt probed.

"None living. Their only son died in an auto accident and is buried on the property, Martha said. And her husband never filed for divorce, so they were still married."

"Sounds like a pretty complicated inheritance," Steve said after a moment. "All the more reason for you to go up and take stock of what's there, Kelly. You're the heir to all of it."

"Don't remind me," she said, grimacing. "I'm not sure I'm ready for all that extra responsibility. I mean, I'm still trying to figure out how to keep making those huge mortgage payments on the cottage."

Steve reached over and placed his hand on her shoulder. "Let's see what we can do to help you with that. This ranch could actually help you solve those problems."

"You bet, Kelly," Curt concurred. "Let's go up there and see if we can get some cash flow started. I imagine you could use that."

Cash flow? Now they were talking about

something Kelly understood quite well. "Really? You think that's possible?"

Curt sent her a savvy smile. "Ohhhh, yeah. Think about it, Kelly-girl. You've got five hundred head of cattle. And sheep. You'll make something off their sale to start. Then, we'll go from there."

"And Kelly, if you've got sheep, then there're bound to be some fleeces to sell," Ruth added with the enthusiasm of the spinner and miller that she was. "What you and your friends don't want for yourselves, we can sell online. Spinners and weavers will snap them up if they're good quality. I'll be glad to help you with that. And what we don't sell as fleece, I'll mill and spin for you, and I guarantee you'll sell that. Mimi will probably buy them all to custom dye and sell in her shop."

Kelly stared at Ruth in surprise. Selling wool fleeces online to spinners and weavers. What a combination of Old World craft and New World high tech. "Wow, Ruth. That sounds great. You'd help me with that?"

"Of course, dear." Ruth gave her a motherly pat. "I'll be more than happy to help. I do this all the time."

Kelly felt the fluttery sensation take flight. At last. Muscles that had been tensed without her even knowing relaxed. This ranch business could work out. She didn't have to understand it all by herself. She had people to help her with each part of it. Like consultants. Now that made sense. And it made her feel a lot better. So much so, Kelly could feel the blueberry pie beckoning to her across the table.

She eyed the tempting dessert, blueberries and sauce oozing into the plate. The vanilla ice cream had softened during their discussion. Perfect. She could taste it already.

Curt chuckled. "I see you eyeing that pie again."

"You're right," Kelly admitted. "Thanks to you folks, I feel a lot better. And I hear that pie calling me."

"Ruth, go ahead and carve the girl a slice. And pile on the ice cream, too," Curt suggested.

"While you're at it, Ruth, leave a slice for me," Steve jumped in, plate in hand. "Can't let it go to waste."

"Don't mention 'waist,' " Kelly joked. "I may not have one after this slice. I'll have to run an extra mile tomorrow."

"Oh, for heaven's sake," Ruth fussed, placing a huge slice on Kelly's plate. "You're slender as can be." She plopped a large dollop of melted ice cream on top of the pie.

"Not after tonight," Kelly laughed and accepted the bowl that was filled to overflowing.

She'd barely gotten her spoon into the purple nectar when Steve spoke up. "Tell me, Kelly. Has Chambers mentioned anything about oil and gas deposits?"

"Yes, he said he was going to make some phone calls, but I haven't heard anything more," she said, then blissfully closed her eyes and savored the blueberry delight. When she opened her eyes again, she saw Steve and Curt grinning at each other, then her. "What? What's so funny?"

"Kelly, girl, if you're lucky, you may never have cash-flow problems again," Curt decreed as he leaned back in his chair.

Kelly pondered that for about two seconds, then succumbed to the sinfully rich summertime dessert.

"Good boy," Kelly said, rubbing Carl's shiny black head as she settled into her favorite patio chair. "Did you behave yourself while I was gone tonight?"

Carl placed his chin on her bare leg, all brown-eyed doggie innocence. Kelly laughed softly and continued patting her dog, letting the familiar night sounds close in around her. She'd just relaxed completely into the comfortable chair when her cell phone jangled, shattering the night sounds and probably scaring away the soft-voiced evening songbirds.

"Kelly here," she said into the phone, unable to disguise her reluctance to talk.

"Hey, Kelly, Burt here," a familiar deep voice sounded, catching her by surprise. "I can tell you're tired. Why don't I call back tomorrow?"

"No no, Burt, it's okay," Kelly replied, straightening in her chair. Retired police investigator Burt Parker never called unless he had something important to say. His calm advice and presence during Kelly's investigation into her aunt's death had been a godsend. "What's up?"

"Well, I thought you might be interested in what I've learned from my contacts back on the force — about Vickie Claymore's death, I mean. I know how hard that must have been for you to walk in on something like that, Kelly."

"Yeah, it was. How on earth did you handle that stuff, Burt? Did you ever get used to it?"

"Never."

Kelly could picture big old Burt, hovering like a protective bear, standing near the crime scene. "What did you find out? Did you guys find any fingerprints to trace?"

"Nope. None other than Vickie's. Everything was wiped clean. Doorknobs, tabletops, the phone, and most importantly, that bronze bust on the floor. I heard you saw it lying not far from the victim."

"Well, now, that's interesting, wouldn't you say?"

"Oh, yeah. It definitely looks to be a murder. And the killer had time to clean up afterward, too."

"Sounds like he wasn't afraid of being caught," Kelly added. "Which means it probably was someone she knew, right?"

Burt chuckled. "Go on."

Emboldened, Kelly pressed further. "Another reason I think it was someone Vickie knew is because she'd never turn her back on some crazed intruder so they could hit her on the head and kill her."

"Smart girl," Burt replied. "And you're right about her being knocked unconscious. The investigation shows she was hit on the head with that Mozart figure, then her throat was cut so she'd bleed to death before regaining consciousness. The weapon looks to be a small knife, like a pocketknife."

"Dammit! Who would be so cruel? The cops better find out who did it."

"Well, I'm certain they're doing their best, Kelly. Now, the other reason I'm calling is so we can have this conversation in private and not in the shop with listening ears. I want to know if there's anything else you noticed that was amiss? You've got a keen eye for detail, Kelly. What did you see?"

Kelly closed her eyes and pictured herself walking through Vickie Claymore's living room that awful day. "I saw Vickie lying on her beautiful handwoven rug. I checked her pulse when I saw the deep gash on her neck and all the blood. I also noticed the pool of blood had dried mostly and soaked into the fabric, which I figured meant she'd been killed hours earlier, right?"

"She was killed between nine p.m. and eleven p.m. the night before," Burt answered.

"All the more reason to believe it was someone Vickie knew. Who else would be visiting her that late at night?" Kelly probed. "I mean, we've eliminated the crazed intruder."

"Well, you've eliminated him. The police can't afford to eliminate anyone. So, tell me, did anything else strike you while you were there?"

Kelly searched her memory. "Nothing else was out of place other than the Mozart bust. Everything looked to be in the same place that I remembered seeing it two months ago."

Burt paused, and Kelly pictured him writing everything down in a little notebook similar to Lt. Peterson's. That brought a question to mind.

"Burt, I remember the county police were handling this case since Bellvue Canyon is in their territory, not the city's. You've got contacts with them, too?"

"Sure I do, Kelly. We've worked together on lots of things. Particularly something like a murder. Anything else you remember?"

"No, but I've got a question of my own."

"Shoot."

"Any suspects jumping out at your friends?"

"Well, it's a little early. No one is jumping out yet."

"Just fishing. I couldn't help but overhear Jayleen Swinson's tirade about Bob Claymore while I was standing around outside. And I remember Vickie talking about the divorce, too. It was bitter, Burt. Both of them seemed to be dug in and fighting each other. Sounded awful to me."

"Yeah," Burt sighed. "I've watched several friends go through that. Sounds like hell on earth. Listen, Kelly, I'll let you go. Take care of yourself, and I'll see you folks over at the shop when I next come in. Probably later this week."

Remembering something, Kelly tossed out a teaser. Burt was an excellent spinner and spun several of Mimi's fleeces for her. "When you're there, I'll tell you how I'm about to become the owner of several fleeces. At least, I think I am."

"Well, you've got me interested already, Kelly," Burt said with a laugh. "See you."

Kelly snapped her cell phone shut and went back to patting Carl while visions of woolly lambs carrying bags of fleeces danced through her head.

Seven

"Looks like you're making progress on the sweater," Megan observed, glancing up from the bubble-gum pink eyelash yarn in her lap.

Kelly held up the second version of her sweater in the round. "Yep, still straight, no twists, and I've got at least two inches of stockinette, too," she said proudly.

"Hey, look at that," Jennifer commented as she sat down to join them. "Good job." She leaned over and peered at the raspberry circle. "Stitches look good, too. See? It was worth all that frogging."

"Yeah, yeah," Kelly mumbled. "I just hope I never have to do that again."

"You won't. But there'll be other times you'll choose to unravel and start over," Megan added, fingers working at warp speed. "It's all a part of trying something new. If you don't like it, you frog it out, then try it again. Or something else."

Kelly looked up to see Connie, another of the shop's assistants, standing in the doorway. "Kelly, there's a woman out front to see you," she said, pointing toward the front room. "She said her name's Debbie Hurst, and she's Vickie's daughter."

Kelly dropped the knitted circlet and pushed away from the table. "Thanks, Connie. I'll go into the café. See you guys later," she said as she followed Connie to the front of the shop.

Standing beside the counter was a slightly-built young woman with short brown hair and a striking resemblance to her mother. The sight of those familiar features caused a tug at Kelly's heart. She approached the young woman, her hand extended.

"Debbie, I'm Kelly Flynn. Your mother was a dear friend of ours. We're all deeply sorry for your loss. It was our loss, too."

Debbie looked up at Kelly with clear green eyes and shook her hand. It felt cool to Kelly, even in the midst of summer. "Thank you, Kelly. That's very kind of you to say." Glancing around to Connie, she added, "You're very kind. My mom talked about all of you a lot. You were very important to her."

"Geri Norbert told me she was picking you up at the airport yesterday. Are you staying here in town?"

"I stayed at the ranch last night," Debbie

replied. "There's so much I have to do, so many details with her death and all, I barely know where to start."

Kelly had more questions but didn't want to stay in the midst of the shop. Plus, something told her Debbie might want to sit down. "Why don't we go into the café and sit down with some tea or coffee, okay?" she suggested.

"Oh, that sounds wonderful. I could use some tea," Debbie said with a smile.

Kelly guessed her hunch was right and led the way, choosing a quiet table in the back alcove. She pulled out Debbie's chair, then sat down herself and signaled the waitress. After she ordered, she looked at Debbie with concern.

"How are you feeling, Debbie? Mimi said you had to be careful coming back to the ranch environment."

Debbie nodded and leaned back into her chair, giving Kelly a chance to notice how thin she really was. Not much meat on those bones, Kelly thought, feeling positively pudgy beside Debbie, especially after all that blueberry pie last night.

"I'm doing okay," Debbie said after a deep breath. "There's a new medicine I'm on now which gives me more freedom than ever. Last year I actually stayed up there with Mom for over a week." She smiled, clearly proud of her accomplishment.

"Wonderful," Kelly enthused. "That will help a lot when you have to be up at the ranch. But you may want to stay in town at night while you're here. That way, you won't overtax your system." Kelly knew she sounded pushy, but there was something about Debbie that reached out — a fragility, vulnerability. Whatever it was, Kelly couldn't help responding.

"You know, Kelly, I was thinking the same thing. That way I'll only be around the grasses and other stuff when I absolutely have to."

Kelly leaned out of the way while the waitress set tea and coffee before them. She waited until Debbie had loaded her cup with sugar and cream before she broached the subject that had brought Debbie to the shop. "I have a feeling you want me to tell you about that day at the ranch. Am I right?"

Debbie set her cup in the saucer, then fixed a clear emerald gaze on Kelly. "Please. And don't leave anything out, no matter how awful it is."

Kelly took a deep breath and did as she was told, even though her insides still twisted with the telling of this terrible tale.

She fervently hoped this was the last time she'd have to relate this story. Lowering her voice so no one else would hear, Kelly covered everything she and the others saw, said, and did that summer day.

While Kelly spoke, Debbie traced invisible patterns on the wooden tabletop, her face growing paler by the minute. Watching this, Kelly began to worry. Debbie'd looked pale and fragile when she entered the shop. Now, she looked like she might pass out. Kelly deliberately skipped her description of the detectives and their investigation and wound the tale to a close.

Debbie sipped her tea in silence, which Kelly didn't care to break. She'd talked enough. She also needed the quiet to dispel the ugly thoughts and feelings that the story always brought with it. Like a toxic residue, it clung to her whenever she touched it.

"Do you think the police are doing a good job of investigating this . . . this murder?" Debbie asked quietly.

"They certainly appear to be. I mean, they had scores of policemen up there as soon as I called, and they interviewed everyone thoroughly. Even those visiting knitters."

Debbie closed her eyes and took a shaky

breath. “I still can’t believe she’s gone,” she whispered. “Mom was so . . . so alive and . . . and healthy, and so . . . so joyous. She can’t be gone.” Her lower lip trembled, and Kelly spotted a tear sliding down Debbie’s pale cheek.

Kelly felt her own heart ache. Debbie’s grief so closely matched her own when she’d lost her dad and then Aunt Helen. A yawning emptiness had opened inside and threatened to swallow her whole. She reached out and placed her hand over Debbie’s.

“I know what you mean,” she said gently. “I lost my dad three years ago and my aunt Helen in April. She was like a mother to me. You can’t believe they’re gone at first. It hurts so much.”

Her words turned the trickle into a flow, and Debbie placed her face in her hands and wept, her thin shoulders rising and falling beneath the blue cotton fabric of her dress. Kelly gave a reassuring wave to the concerned waitress and motioned for her to bring more tea, then reached over and placed her hand on Debbie’s shoulder.

“That’s okay, Debbie. No one’s here. Just us. Go ahead and cry,” she reassured.

Debbie’s tears slowly subsided into wet snuffles. Grabbing the extra napkins the waitress had kindly supplied, she wiped her face and blew her nose. "I'm sorry," she said in a ragged voice. "I thought I had cried myself out."

That sounded familiar. "You know, my tears kept coming too. All it took was for someone to say something kind, and" — Kelly gestured — "a deluge would start to flow."

"Thanks for saying that," Debbie said, wiping away. "And thanks for this." She lifted the extra cup of tea and drank it down.

Changing the subject, Kelly ventured, "Do you need any help arranging the funeral or anything? We'd be glad to help. Especially Mimi. She and Vickie were close friends."

"Thank you, Kelly, but Geri's already handling it for me. Thank goodness. I wouldn't know who to call or anything." She took another deep breath and sank back into her chair. "What I really need help with is sorting through all the records. I mean, there's so much there. I have to find insurance policies and contact them and notify her friends in Denver, and then I have to sort through all the business records." She gestured helplessly. "The lawyer says all the accounts have to be in order before he can start examining the estate. I'm a biologist. I don't know anything about financial records. My mom was good at it, but I'm lost." She shuddered in visible disgust.

Kelly recognized that shudder. She saw it a lot when she used to keep small business accounts, years ago. Numbers can confuse people. One of the things she remembered enjoying was helping people understand what was happening. Now she knew how she could help Debbie.

"Listen, Debbie, I'm a CPA, and I'd be happy to help sort through those records for you. Once I do, I'll be able to create whatever financial statements you'll need for the lawyers."

Debbie's green eyes turned puppy-dog grateful. "Ohhhh, Kelly, are you serious?" she breathed. "I mean . . . I would be so grateful if you could. And I'd pay you, of course."

Kelly waved the offer away. "No, that's okay. I'd do it for your mom."

Debbie sat up straight and lifted her chin. "My mom always paid her bills. I cannot accept your help unless you let me pay you. After all, anyone else I'd call in the community would charge a lot, and I'll bet most of them don't have your credentials."

Kelly opened her mouth, but she didn't have anything to say. Debbie had stated her terms clearly. It was up to Kelly to accept or decline.

"Okay. I accept your offer, but I'm clueless what to charge. So, I'll have to check into that."

"Good. Could you start tomorrow? That office is filled with stuff, and I don't know where to begin."

Kelly had to laugh at Debbie's eagerness. "Well, probably. It would be the afternoon before I could finish with my own office work. I'm telecommuting to my job back in D.C."

"That would be great," Debbie enthused, her relief obvious. "I promise I'll try to make some order of the papers on her desk. At least separate the bills from vendors and suppliers and all that. And I'll check the bank statements to see if they're accurate."

"Geri told me that Jayleen Swinson took care of your mom's accounts, so there should be a file somewhere of income statements at least," Kelly suggested. "I'll bet your mom also had a computer file."

"I'm sure she does. Mom was very thorough about her business."

Another thought intruded, and Kelly

added, “Have you spoken with Jayleen? She’d know where everything is. Maybe she should do this for you. After all, she’s been keeping the books. I don’t want to step on anyone’s toes here.”

Debbie looked out into the café. “She left a message on my cell phone this morning, but I haven’t talked with her yet. But, you know, I just don’t think she’s qualified to do this level of financial work. She’s a bookkeeper. You’re a CPA. I’d feel a lot better with you looking at Mom’s accounts.”

“Okay, then I’ll be happy to help.”

“You don’t know how much I appreciate that, Kelly,” Debbie said, her expression hardening. “The sooner I can get those records to the lawyer, the sooner I find out what that weasel is up to.”

Kelly didn’t have to ask who the “weasel” was. She had a pretty good idea Debbie was referring to Vickie’s almost-but-not-quite-divorced husband, Bob Claymore.

Debbie eyed Kelly. “I take it you know all about the divorce proceedings? Mom said she told everyone.”

“Aaah, yes. Vickie was quite forthcoming.”

A smile flirted with Debbie’s mouth before she bit it off. “Mom was furious. And so was I. The very idea that that weasel would try to steal half my mom's business. Dammit! It took her years to build it up. And he never contributed a thing! He was too busy screwing around at the university! Bastard. I never did like him."

Kelly had to lean away from the heat of fury that radiated from Debbie now. "It's certainly unfortunate the divorce was still unsettled when Vickie was killed."

Debbie snorted. "Unfortunate, yes. The timing is more than unfortunate for my mother. But not for him. It's all too convenient for Bob Claymore. A few more weeks and he would be out in the cold. Instead, he's salivating over my mother's business. Bastard."

Kelly watched the storm clouds contort Debbie's delicate features into an ugly mask. Her hatred of Bob Claymore was palpable. It was also evident that Debbie had already found the chief suspect in her mother's death.

"Listen, Debbie, do you have a cell phone?" Kelly ventured, hoping to change the subject. "I can call you when I'm on the way into the canyon tomorrow."

"Ohhhh, yes, of course," Debbie said and reached into her purse, withdrawing a business card. "But you'd better use the landline. You know how the canyon eats cell phone signals. Just come when you can. I'll be there, sorting papers."

"Will do. By the way, do you need a ride somewhere?"

"No, thanks, I've rented a car. I'm fine." She leaned on the table as she stood up, steadied herself, then caught her breath.

Kelly scrambled to her feet, reaching out. "Are you okay? You look like you're having trouble breathing."

Debbie waved away her concern as she headed for the doorway. "No, it's . . . it's just the altitude. It takes a while to acclimate."

Kelly wondered how much the intense emotion she'd just witnessed played a role in Debbie's sudden wooziness. "If you want to rest a little more, you're welcome to sit at our library table. We've always got a pot of tea there, too," she offered.

"Thanks, Kelly. I'll be fine. And thanks again for helping me with all this. I can't tell you how much it means to me."

Kelly was about to reply, but Debbie swiftly hurried out the door, as if she felt tears encroaching once more and wanted to leave quickly.

Feeling strangely unsettled, Kelly headed toward the main room. She needed some quiet time to think. There was so much going on inside Debbie — so many storms and different emotions. She seemed so vulnerable, and yet, Kelly sensed strong — almost violent — emotions erupting inside.

Megan was still across the table knitting as Kelly settled into a chair and picked up her circular sweater.

"Hey, how'd the visit go with Vickie's daughter?" Megan asked.

Kelly paused for a moment and simply knitted. "I think it was good for her. She got to cry some more. I sensed a lot of relief, too."

"Poor thing. I feel so sorry for her. I can't imagine losing my mom like that, can you?"

Her question caused an old wound to twinge way down deep. "Well, it was kind of like that for me when Aunt Helen was killed. She was the closest thing to a mother I ever knew. So, it was like losing my mom."

Megan peered over at Kelly. "You've never talked about your real mom, Kelly. Did she die when you were real young or something?"

"Nope. She walked out on my dad and me when I was just a baby," Kelly said, repeating the line she'd practiced since she was a child. Even so, it never lost its sting. "That's why my dad and I were so close."

"Oh . . . ," Megan said softly and ducked her head. "I'm sorry."

"Don't be. It's okay. My dad and I did great. We were a team." Deliberately changing the subject, she said, "Guess what? Debbie wants to hire me to help figure out Vickie's business accounts and draw up financial statements to take to the lawyers. I offered to do it for free, but she refused."

"Wow, good job," Megan said, her smile returning. "See how easy it is to find consulting? Sometimes it lands in your lap."

Kelly looked up from the neat rows of raspberry stockinette. Consulting? She hadn't really thought of it that way. "Well, I'm not sure you could call it consulting, but —"

"What else would it be?" Megan declared. "You're doing specialized work at her direction for payment. Sounds like consulting to me."

Kelly let that last thought play around in her head as the rows of stockinette slowly increased.

Eight

Kelly stared out the large window in Vickie's home office, which looked directly out onto the pastures and corrals. Several groups of alpacas were scattered about, grazing in separate pastures, their long, graceful necks bending to the ground as they searched for tasty grasses. She leaned back in her chair and took a drink from her ever-present coffee mug as she paged through the file folder of income statements.

Vickie's business was definitely profitable. Expenses and revenues both fluctuated month by month but were directly correlated with the business cycle of owning alpacas — breeding, shearing, babies, showing, breeding, over and over. Now that she had the accounts in front of her, Kelly could envision what Geri had tried to explain — the variability of income from stud fees and sales of alpaca offspring. What kept Vickie from "living on the edge" like Geri was that Vickie had a fair amount of cash reserves put away, either the result of thrifty saving or high demand for her alpaca services over the years.

Kelly picked up the folder containing the balance sheets for the business and paged back a few years, watching how carefully Vickie had built up her savings. Smart, very smart, Kelly thought, admiring Vickie's financial discipline. That was usually the Achilles heel of most small businesses, she'd witnessed. Whether they tried to make a go without sufficient capital to begin with or they simply neglected to pay their required taxes, most small companies went belly up within five years. Kelly was always happy to find the ones that went on to succeed.

Noticing that the last balance sheet in the folder was dated three months ago, Kelly jotted a note on the pad beside her elbow. So far, so good. She was beginning to get a picture of what was there, what was missing, and what she needed to do.

"Aaaah! There it is," Debbie spoke up from across the office. She leaned over the papers spread out on a side table.

Kelly had set up a place for Debbie to sit and sort through documents while she used the desk and computer. "I thought you already found the insurance policy. What're you looking for now?"

"I was looking for the sheet with the funeral arrangements. I knew she had it here somewhere." Debbie looked over at Kelly and smiled. "Mom told me she had a file with everything in it. I thought she meant one folder. She meant the whole cabinet."

"Oh, boy," Kelly smiled ruefully. "What else do you need? I can stop this and help you get the policies."

"No, it's okay. I've already called the insurance person and gotten that started. Now, I can tell Geri —"

"Tell Geri what?" Geri asked, poking her head around the doorway. "I saw two cars parked outside, so I thought I'd drop by and see who was here. It's about time that yellow police tape was removed. I see you beat me to it."

"Hey, Geri, good to see you," Kelly greeted.

"Ohhhh, yes, Geri, come in, come in," Debbie beckoned. "We're trying to put all these papers in order, and thanks to Kelly, I think we can do it."

Geri pulled out a straight-back chair and straddled it backward. "Have you found those instructions yet?"

Debbie handed over the sheet. "Yes, here they are. It only took me two hours of searching." She shook her head.

Geri smiled. "No hurry. I'll handle everything. If I need your signature, I'll bring the papers to you."

"Geri, I don't know what I'd do without you," Debbie said, her gratitude obvious. "You've been a lifesaver ever since I arrived."

"It's the least I can do, Debbie. Your mom was my best friend. Is there anything else you need? Any help with the animals?"

"No, Jayleen must have been here early in the morning, because they were already out in the pastures. We keep playing phone tag. She left me another message saying she was taking care of them."

A loud slam of the front door sounded, and a voice called out, "Helloooo! Who's here?"

Kelly recognized Jayleen's voice, having listened to it at top volume when she vented her anger to the police detective.

"We're here in the office, Jayleen," Geri called out.

The sound of boots stomping across wooden floors got louder until Jayleen appeared in the doorway. Kelly noticed she looked surprised to see all of them there. "Hey, guys, what's up?" she asked, strolling into the office.

A slight look of displeasure seemed to

pass over Debbie's face, then was gone, Kelly noticed. "We're trying to get all these papers in order, Jayleen. Insurance policies, bank accounts, things like that," Kelly explained in her best offhand manner.

"Hey, I can help with that," Jayleen offered. "I do the accounts. I know where everything is —"

Debbie held up her slender hand. "That's okay, Jayleen. We've got it covered. The lawyer needs financial reports, and Kelly's going to take care of everything since she's a CPA and knows how to do all that."

"Oh . . . oh, sure, I understand," Jayleen said, appearing slightly crestfallen. "Well, if there's anything I can do to help, you know, please let me know."

Feeling really uncomfortable now, Kelly jumped in. "I've got the file with all the income statements and balance sheets. You've done a great job, Jayleen. That makes it much easier when I do the financial reports."

Jayleen found a crooked smile. "Thanks. It's just good software, that's all."

Kelly grinned. "Don't give me that. I know the business. Software doesn't do it. You do. And you've done a good job."

"Thanks, Kelly."

Kelly nodded, then remembered something. "By the way, Jayleen, I noticed the last balance sheet was dated three months ago, yet the income statements are right up to date. Have you run an updated version yet?"

Jayleen shook her head. "Nope. I was waiting on the quarterly reports from Vickie's investment account. They should be in by now, but I wasn't able to get into the office to run them."

"No problem. I'll do it," Kelly offered.

"All the other statements are in the files." Jayleen jerked her thumb toward the cabinet.

"Thank you, Jayleen. You've been very helpful," Debbie said, the sound of dismissal in her tone all too evident.

Kelly flinched inwardly, feeling really embarrassed for Jayleen.

Jayleen responded by staring at her boots for a second before she turned toward the door. "You know, I noticed Raja wasn't acting like himself. I mean, he usually comes over whenever I come to the fence and whistle. The gals came, but Raja just stood out in the pasture and looked at me."

"He must be missing mom," Debbie said sadly.

"Maybe he picks up signals like our pets do," Kelly suggested. "My dog, Carl, always picks up on my moods, so maybe alpacas do, too."

"Maybe so," Jayleen said. "Well, it looks like you folks have everything in control here, so I'll just get along. You still want me to take care of the animals, don't you? I mean, they're used to me. I've been doing it for years now."

Debbie nodded, a flicker of gratitude appearing for a moment. "Yes, that'll be great, Jayleen. I simply cannot be carrying feed and letting them in and out. I'm afraid all that dust is already taking a toll." She took a deep breath.

Geri rose from her chair. "You okay?"

Debbie gave a little wave. "Yes, but I think I'd better go back into town soon."

Kelly noticed Debbie's pallor. "You know, I was about to head back into town, too. I can review these folders at home tonight. Why don't we both leave now? That way, I can follow after you."

"Oh, would you, Kelly? I'd be ever so grateful," Debbie said. "Let me get my things together."

Kelly did the same, gathering the files she needed to review and shoving everything into her briefcase.

"Well, see you later, folks," Jayleen said as she left.

Geri paused at the door. "Listen, Debbie, if you need anything at all, let me know. Meanwhile, I'll get on these arrangements. Talk to you tomorrow."

Kelly waved good-bye to both women, logged off the computer, and pushed back her chair to leave. She felt unsettled suddenly and didn't know why. There was a lot more bubbling under the surface of Vickie's family than she'd ever imagined.

Carl was at the fence yelping a greeting as Kelly headed toward the cottage's front door. "I'll feed you in a minute, Carl. Hold on —"

She broke off when she noticed a white paper attached to her outer screen door. Kelly snatched the typewritten note from the screen and read as she let herself into the house.

"What the . . . ," she said when she came to the second paragraph. "Carl!"

Dumping her things on the dining room table, Kelly yanked open the patio door to the yard. Carl was already jumping about, long pink tongue dangling, clearly anticipating dinner.

Kelly brandished the note and glared at

her dog. "Carl, you've been stealing golf balls again, and I told you not to."

Carl's happy-dog expression disappeared, and his "Who, me?" face materialized.

"Don't give me that look," Kelly accused. "This is a warning from the greenskeeper. He says if you steal balls one more time, we'll have to go to court, and there will be a big fine."

Carl cocked his head and stared, obviously curious as to what had perturbed his owner. Kelly let out an exasperated sigh and glanced around the yard. Sure enough, there were several more golf balls than usual.

"Okay, that's it, big guy. You may not care if you get a police record, but I do. I do not want to pay to bail you out of doggie jail."

Kelly proceeded to walk around the yard, snatching up every newer-looking ball she found. Steve had brought Carl old used-up balls, so it wasn't hard to tell the difference. Carl, of course, was right behind her, protesting ownership every step of the way. Once, he almost got to a ball before Kelly, but she snatched it first.

"Don't even think about it, Carl," she warned, with her sternest naughty-dog-scolding voice. "You can keep the old ones, not these."

Kelly then swung her legs over the fence, strode to the edge of the course, and threw all the balls as far as she could. Being a really good ball player, Kelly could throw pretty far. She returned to the yard to find Carl lying on the ground, head between his outstretched paws, sulking.

"Pout all you want," Kelly said. "You're coming inside with me after dinner. Furthermore, you'll have to stay inside while I work on the computer, and I promise it won't be any fun at all."

She wasn't sure, but Kelly thought she saw Carl screw up his face in displeasure.

Nine

Mimi was draping a turquoise sleeveless sweater over the antique dry sink in the knitting shop's center room when Kelly entered.

"Why, hello, Kelly. I haven't seen you over here early in the morning for a while," she said with a bright smile. "Has your work load lightened up a bit?"

"Actually, it's increased, Mimi," Kelly replied as she set her knitting bag on the library table. "I've agreed to help Debbie Hurst with her mother's business accounts and prepare financial statements for the lawyers. So I guess you'd say I'm consulting, in addition to my regular office work, of course."

Mimi positively beamed. "That's wonderful, Kelly! I knew you'd find some consulting sooner or later."

Noticing several bright eyelash yarn scarves dangling from a nearby cabinet door, Kelly fingered electric limeade and tangerine crush, envisioning one of her own. The last time she'd thought about making one of these scarves, she'd been interrupted. Maybe now was a good time.

"Go ahead and indulge yourself, Kelly," Mimi tempted. "I can tell you want to make one. Do it. It knits up so fast, you'll have it done in no time."

Kelly shook her head with a rueful smile. "I've heard that before. You folks always say that, because it doesn't take you guys any time at all. But me . . . ha!" She laughed. "Every time I start a new project, I find a way to screw it up."

"Not every time," Mimi protested, giving Kelly a maternal pat on the arm. "What about your chunky wool scarf? Your very first project. You didn't screw that up, did you?"

Kelly had to admit she hadn't. Hmmmm, she pondered. This would be a scarf. Maybe that's a good sign. Maybe she could knit this up as easily as she knit the woolen scarf. The bold colors beckoned to Kelly again. Touch, touch. She couldn't resist.

"Okay, okay, I'll give it a try," she said, sinking her hands into the chest filled with jelly bean colors. "Can you help me get started?"

"Absolutely. You pick a color while I get some size fifteen needles." Mimi headed for the front of the shop.

Kelly played in the overflowing chest, squeezing one yarn after another, even though they were equally soft. Which to choose? A brilliant turquoise blue and green combination, peacock bright, teased her, and Kelly held it up. Why not? She usually didn't choose those colors, but it was fun trying something different. Walking to a side room to check the mirror, she held the fuzzy ball of yarn under her chin. Not bad, she decided.

"Ohhhh, I love it," Mimi concurred enthusiastically, peeking around the corner, needles in hand. "It'll look great on you."

"I agree," Lisa said, leaning around Mimi. "I was coming in and saw you picking yarns. It's about time you made one of those scarves. You've been dying to try it."

Buoyed by the wave of enthusiasm from her friends, Kelly floated back toward the main room, convinced the scarf was hers to do. "Okay, here goes," she said, settling into a chair beside the long table. "Thanks for getting the needles, Mimi. Now, how many do I cast on?"

"For that kind of yarn and scarf, ten would be fine," Mimi replied. "That'll give you a scarf about this wide." She held her fingers approximately three inches across.

"They're supposed to be long and narrow."

Kelly nodded as she poked into the soft ball to find a dangling end, and, finding it, she pulled enough to start knitting. "Okay, first I measure about three times the width to cast on, right?" she said, pulling the yarn between her fingers.

"Good for you. You're remembering," Lisa said, settling at the table. She withdrew a colorful ribbon shawl from her bag.

"I'm sure you won't need any reminders how to cast on, Kelly," Mimi said with a laugh as she headed toward her back office. "Not after starting your new sweater twice."

"Don't remind me," Kelly said with a groan, recalling all the casting on required for her sweater in the round. "That took forever, and I had to do it twice." She wrapped the peacock yarn around her thumb and forefinger and began the intriguing movements required to cast stitches onto the needle.

"Just think how good you are now, though," Lisa reminded.

"Yeah, yeah." Kelly counted the stitches appearing on her needle. Six more to go. This new yarn definitely felt different. Each strand was soft but also skinny, with little fronds or "eyelashes" of fibers sticking out at intervals.

"Hey, I didn't see old Carl barking around in the yard when I drove up. He usually bounds over and says hello when I come."

"Carl is staying inside the house all day. He's been a naughty dog."

"Uh-oh. Let me guess. Golf balls?"

"Yep. I found a note on my front door yesterday, warning me that he'd be arrested and thrown in the slammer if he stole again."

"C'mon, what'd it really say?"

"That there would be an official nuisance warning issued against Carl if he touched any more balls. And I'd have to go to court and pay a hefty fine."

"Ooooh, ugly."

"Definitely. I do not want to appear before some cranky judge and plead doggie mischief."

"Poor Carl. Stuck inside all day."

"Poor Carl, nothing. He brought this all on himself," Kelly declared righteously. "I told him not to chase any more balls."

"C'mon, he's a dog. He can't stop chasing balls any more than he can stop trying to catch the squirrels."

"I know," Kelly conceded, remembering a downcast Carl lying on the floor staring out the glass patio door, watching squirrels race across the fence unimpeded.

Without Carl on patrol, the squirrels would have a high old time — digging in the flower pots, stealing apples from Aunt Helen's apple tree. Kelly envisioned scores of insolent squirrels dancing about on the patio, deliberately teasing Carl behind the glass. The squirrels in her backyard were a sassy bunch. She'd even witnessed a squirrel steal one of Carl's bones while he was stretched in the sun sound asleep. She found it in her gutter two weeks later.

"You could always buy a long chain. That way he could still be outside," Lisa suggested, her nimble fingers twisting ribbons around her needles.

"Hey, good idea," Kelly said, perking up at the thought. "Do we still have the big outdoors store north of town?"

"Yep. They probably have fifty-foot chains you could use. That way, Carl could still enjoy the yard but not get over the fence. And even if he did, he wouldn't get very far."

Kelly smoothed out the three rows of stitches she'd created with the new yarn. The larger needles gave the fluffy yarn its loose, open effect. It was pretty already. Peacock blue and green cried, "Wear me! Wear me!"

"I'll buy a chain today. I just hope Carl doesn't choke himself the first time he tries to chase a squirrel," she said, pushing her needle beneath a slender fiber. Sometimes the fibers were hard to pick up with the bigger needles, she noticed, and it took several tries to slide beneath each stitch.

"How's the consulting going?" Lisa asked. "Megan told me you're helping Debbie. That's great."

Kelly smiled. The knitting shop's grapevine was alive and well. News traveled faster here than in most offices she'd experienced. "She needed help with all the accounts. I haven't a clue what to charge, though."

"Megan will help you with that."

"Well, well, look how much you've done, Kelly," Mimi said as she drew up a spinning wheel at the end of the table. "I thought I'd join you gals while I finish up this fleece."

Kelly loved to watch Mimi spin, or Burt spin, or anyone else for that matter. She found the sound of the wheel soothing as it hummed its song. Mimi pulled the roving apart in her lap and started the wheel turning, her fingers working the fibers into strands, feeding the wheel. Yarn wound around the bobbin, fatter and fatter.

"This is the last of Vickie's fleeces," Mimi said in a sad voice. "I'm going to mix this one with mohair and dye it shamrock green. That was Vickie's favorite color."

The jangle of Kelly's cell phone intruded. She slipped it from her purse and spoke softly, not wanting to shatter the quiet moment entirely. "This is Kelly."

"Kelly, I just wanted to tell you that I won't be going up into the canyon today," Debbie's voice came through. "I've lain awake nearly the whole night. I couldn't sleep, I was so angry. I'm going to the police today. Geri's taking me."

"The police?" Kelly replied, startled. "Why? What's the matter?"

"I took out the will from the file cabinet again, and you know how upset it made me when I first read it."

Kelly remembered all too well. Yesterday in Vickie's office, Kelly had worried Debbie's fury would trigger an asthma attack. "Yes, I remember." She noticed Mimi's wheel had stopped turning as she and Lisa listened intently.

"Well, I'm taking the will to the police detective today. I'm going to show it to this Lieutenant Peterson. It's so clear, a blind man could see it! Bob Claymore gets half of all my mother's property now that she's dead. Not just the house and the bank accounts but half of the business she spent years building. But she was divorcing him! He shouldn't get a thing. She was cutting him out!"

Kelly heard Debbie draw a ragged breath. "Debbie, are you all right? Please, don't get so upset. You have to be care—"

Debbie cut her off. "Dammit, Kelly, I don't care what happens to me. He's got to pay for what he did to Mom. I *know* he killed her! And the will helps prove it. Listen, I've got to go. We'll talk later. Bye."

Kelly bid her good-bye and flipped off her phone. Debbie's anger was so raw it was hard to listen without some of it rubbing off. "That was Debbie. She's taking the will to the police detective who interviewed us in the canyon to tell him her suspicions about Bob Claymore."

"Mimi, what's your feeling about Bob?" Lisa asked. "I worked with him on a community housing committee last year, and he seemed almost mousy to me."

Mimi's wheel picked up speed again. "Well, I don't know if I'd call him 'mousy.' But I also can't picture him hating Vickie enough to kill her."

"Maybe it wasn't hate, Mimi. Maybe it

was simply greed. And maybe he'd fallen in love with that other woman," Kelly suggested. She noticed Rosa was nodding in agreement as she straightened the bookshelves behind Mimi.

"You mean Eva Bartok?" Mimi shook her head. "Bob would be crazy to choose Eva over Vickie. Eva's so . . . so . . ."

"Hateful," Rosa supplied. She brought a pile of magazines to the table and started sorting. "Eva tried teaching a weaving class at the community center once, and I swear, half the students left after two lessons. I was one of them."

"Oh, yes, I remember. I don't think Eva was ever asked to teach anywhere more than once," Mimi said with a rueful smile. "She's such a gifted artist, a truly exceptional weaver, but she lacks, I don't know, warmth, uh, people skills, whatever."

"You're being too nice, Mimi," Rosa said with uncharacteristic vehemence. "Eva was just plain mean. She was always making cutting remarks to students in her classes. I know some people who stopped weaving altogether because she'd said something cruel."

"Ooooh, really ugly. And sad," Lisa decreed.

"And she's also got a nasty temper, too. I

heard she deliberately kept a weaver out of a competition because she was mad at her. Probably jealous. She was always bragging about her awards." Rosa's face betrayed signs of past slights.

"Bad karma," Lisa said sagely.

Rosa looked up from the magazines, and Kelly could tell she was debating whether to say something else. "You know, I accidentally walked in on Eva and Vickie having a big argument at the weaving conference last month. They were in the ladies room, and ohhhh, boy, they sounded about ready to claw each other's eyes out."

"The Denver conference?" Mimi asked. "You're right, Rosa, I remember seeing both of them."

"Oh, they were there all right," Rosa nodded vigorously, her brown eyes wide with remembering. "They tried to shut up when I came into the restroom, but not before Vickie called Eva a . . . well, it was pretty ugly."

"I shudder to think what Eva said in reply," Mimi commented.

Rosa glanced toward the windows. "Actually, Eva didn't say anything. Vickie slammed out the door before she could. I just remember the expression on Eva's face." Rosa closed her eyes and shivered.

"It was ugly. Really, really ugly. Worse than any name."

Kelly could almost feel the animosity coming off that scene Rosa described. She didn't know Eva Bartok, but she noticed the strong feelings she aroused in people who had crossed her path. Eva sounded like a woman who did not like being crossed. Did she harbor a grudge against Vickie? Had that grudge festered and brought forth enough hate to cause her to kill?

"How did Vickie and Eva get along before Bob's affair?" Kelly probed. "They were both weavers, so they must have interacted. Fort Connor isn't that big a place. Did they get along?"

Mimi seemed to ponder while her wheel spun. "Now that you mention it, I always got the feeling they didn't really care for each other. There was never anything said or anything overt, just something I felt." She gave a little shrug. "Whenever I was in the same room with them, it was like, well, like you could almost see the fur rise on their necks."

"Meow," Lisa said with a grin.

Kelly joined the soft laughter. "Well, that's interesting. Maybe Eva harbored animosity toward Vickie that spilled over after that confrontation in Denver."

"Look out, she's sleuthing again," Lisa teased.

"Ohhhh, Kelly, please, no," Mimi said. "I can't stand to think about it."

Kelly shifted her needle to start the next row of stitches. This scarf was easy. Just the knit stitch, exactly like her chunky wool scarf. She smoothed out the three inches she'd completed.

What the — ? she thought, noticing the bulging curve along one side of the scarf. The bottom two inches of the scarf were nice and even, approximately three inches wide. But that was followed by another two inches of scarf that grew wider and wider with each additional row.

How'd that happen, she wondered? She counted the stitches in the even bottom rows. Ten stitches across. Then she counted the stitches in the row she'd just completed — while she was conjuring images of Eva Bartok as villain. Eighteen stitches.

"Eighteen?" Kelly complained out loud. "How'd I get eighteen? I cast on ten. What happened?"

Lisa glanced over and smiled. "Uh-oh. That can happen with those eyelash yarns."

"Please, not another 'uh-oh.' " Kelly slapped her hand to her forehead. "Why me? I'm doomed. Every time —"

"Angst alert. Dive, dive," Jennifer said as she dropped her knitting bag on the table.

"It's not funny. I've done it again. I've screwed something up. I tell you, I'm cursed," Kelly moaned.

"Quick, administer caffeine," Jennifer ordered. "Where's her mug?" Spying Kelly's mug, she shoved it near Kelly's nose. "Don't talk, just breathe deeply and take a drink. Better yet, drink deeply, then breathe."

Kelly deliberately suppressed the laughter inside, even though it bubbled around the table. "Coffee won't cure it," she said, but took a long, deep drink anyway. Then another. It might not cure it, but the caffeine rush sure helped.

"Cure what?" Mimi asked.

"Knitting incompetence," Kelly replied, sulking now. "Oh, it's so *easy!*" she mimicked, then gave a Bronx cheer. "Riiiight."

"Here, let me help you." Jennifer reached out for the misshapen scarf. "We can unravel these last few rows and get you back to where you went astray."

"Yeah, yeah, yeah."

"She's going down."

Kelly scowled at Lisa, who just laughed. "I know you get tired of hearing this, Kelly, but that happens to everyone. Those yarns are slippery little things."

"Then why do you all say 'it's so easy'?" Kelly demanded, pique at fever pitch. "It's . . . it's unfair advertising."

Everyone laughed at that. "Oh, Kelly, you are a delight," Mimi declared.

"Here we go," Jennifer said, showing her the much-shorter scarf again. "I unraveled the uneven rows, then threaded the needle through the loops, and you're ready to go." She handed it over. "My advice, count after every row to make sure you've still got ten. If eleven appear, then just knit two together to get back on track. Much easier to catch mistakes early."

"Thanks," Kelly grumbled, looking at the rows. "Okay, count after every row. Count after every row."

"And let's not discuss murder suspects anymore, okay? I'm sure that's where she got off," Mimi suggested.

At the sound of the doorbell jangling, Rosa looked up, and her expression changed. Kelly wasn't sure, but Rosa's face paled. "Mimi, uh, we have a visitor," Rosa said, pointing behind them.

Kelly turned to see a uniformed police officer approach from the front room — a county policeman, she noticed, when he drew close enough to see his shoulder patch.

"Excuse me, ladies," the officer began. "Is Mimi Shafer here? The shop owner?"

Now it was Mimi's turn to go pale, Kelly observed. "Y-yes, officer. I'm Mimi Shafer. What can I do for you?" She started to push away from the silent wheel.

"No need to get up, ma'am," he said and hastily approached. "I'm simply here to ask you if you could identify an item our investigators found at Vickie Claymore's home. We were informed you and the victim were close friends, correct?"

"Yes, sir, we were," Mimi said in a small voice.

The officer, who appeared to Kelly to be in his mid-thirties, withdrew a small plastic bag from his pocket. He held it out to Mimi. "We found this bracelet in the room where Ms. Claymore was murdered. We don't know if it belonged to her or to someone else. We've already asked Ms. Swinson if she recognized it, and she did not. We're hoping you might help us out."

Mimi took the package and scrutinized it. Kelly watched her expression carefully and saw the light of recognition go on in her eyes. "Yes, officer, I do recognize the bracelet."

The officer appeared relieved and withdrew a small notepad from his shirt pocket. "Excellent, Ms. Shafer. So you recognize it as belonging to Ms. Claymore?"

Mimi took a deep breath. "No, officer. It belongs to someone else. It's Eva Bartok's diamond tennis bracelet. I can tell because she had this little silver lamb especially made for it." Mimi fingered the tiny charm dangling at the end of the bracelet. "She wore it regularly. Eva claimed it was her good-luck charm."

Ten

Kelly ran up the steps to the century-old white frame church on a shady Old Town corner. She'd tried to keep track of the time but had gotten lost in a client's morass of numbers. The next time she glanced at her watch, another hour had magically evaporated. Suddenly, it was twenty minutes before Vickie Claymore's funeral, and Kelly hadn't changed clothes. She was still in shorts and a T-shirt.

Racing through her bedroom, she'd grabbed a sleeveless black dress, wiggled into it, and snagged some dressier shoes. Balancing on one foot, she struggled to finish dressing and caught site of Carl-in-Chains in the backyard.

Kelly had felt so guilty, leading Carl outside to race around, only to snap a fifty-foot chain to his collar. She'd bought a metal stake for the yard as well. Carl was pretty strong, and when he got excited, could exert a lot of rottie pulling power. A nearby water pipe looked too flimsy to Kelly. Besides, she didn't want to return to a flooded yard if the squirrels started tormenting Carl.

Pushing open the church's front door, Kelly stepped inside. Immediately, the hot, dry air of the old building enveloped her. Oh, boy. No air-conditioning, and it was ninety-five degrees already. Noticing the wooden pews were nearly full, Kelly searched for the familiar faces of her friends. She spied them near the front in a pew that looked tightly packed.

Kelly glanced about for a place to sit and heard a familiar soft voice speak up beside her. "Kelly, you can sit here. There's enough room." Kelly turned to see Rosa scoot over on the pew, leaving space.

"Thank you so much, Rosa," Kelly whispered as she gratefully settled into the spot. "I was working on the computer and lost track of time. Story of my life."

Rosa smiled. "Don't worry. I was late, too. I offered to stay at the shop until one of our student helpers could come."

Looking around at the full church, Kelly said, "This is quite a turnout and a tribute to Vickie that so many people have come."

"Yes, it is. Vickie was a good person, and she touched a lot of lives."

Kelly detected a slight rise in the subdued murmur of voices and noticed a slender and very stylish blonde about Vickie's age walk down the aisle.

"That's Eva Bartok," Rosa leaned over and whispered as the woman found a seat midfront.

Kelly had only caught a fleeting glimpse of her features, but she appeared very attractive. "Vickie's age?" she asked.

Rosa gestured. "Give or take a few years, I think."

Peering toward the front pews, Kelly scanned the heads. "Which one is Bob Claymore? I've never met him."

Rosa craned her neck, staring toward the front. "He's in the first pew, left-hand side. Starting to go bald on top."

Kelly spotted him. She also noticed there was no one else sitting beside him on that pew. Bob Claymore sat totally alone. Across the aisle on the other front pew, Debbie Hurst was surrounded by Geri on one side and Mimi on the other. Jayleen Swinson sat at the far end of the row, her curly blond hair held back with a black ribbon.

"You know, I don't know anything about him, but I almost feel sorry for Bob Claymore," Kelly whispered as a black-robed minister approached the lectern. "No one will go near him."

Rosa nodded in agreement, and Kelly let her gaze finally settle on the long casket at the front of the church. She'd deliberately not focused on it before now. The sight of a casket made her uncomfortable, reminding her of all the loss in her life. Her father, Uncle Jim, Aunt Helen, Cousin Martha.

The minister's voice rose with practiced ease, his words floating out into the sultry summer air. Kelly prepared to zone out for the rest of the service. She'd heard all those words before. There were no words written that could truly console those left behind when cherished loved ones were stolen away.

"My gosh, I thought I was going to melt in there," Rosa exclaimed as she and Kelly finally broke free of the stifling church. "Fresh air, at last." She fanned herself.

Kelly shaded her eyes. The air might be fresh outside, but it was still hot, even in the shade. Softball practice would be brutal tonight. The sun would still be blazing at seven o'clock. She glanced around for Lisa or Megan but didn't see them. What she did see was Bob Claymore approaching Debbie Hurst, who was standing beside a black limousine and still flanked by Mimi and Geri.

"Look at that," she discreetly motioned to Rosa. "I wonder what Debbie will say."

Rosa shook her head, her long black braid slipping behind her back. "I don't want to know. She might take his head off."

Kelly watched Debbie's expression freeze despite the July heat. She drew closer to Geri, while Mimi looked dreadfully uncomfortable. Bob Claymore gestured as he spoke and appeared agitated. Then, a mask of disgust claimed Debbie's features, and she turned without a word and entered the limo, slamming the door behind her. Geri scurried around to the other side while Mimi took a moment to say a few words to Bob. His dejection obvious, he stared at the ground until the limousine drove away.

Kelly pulled her car to a stop in front of the cottage and jumped out, slamming the door. She had to get out of this dress before she died. After hours of a stifling, hot church service and a graveside burial in the blazing noontime sun, Kelly swore the fabric had been heat-sealed to her body. Racing inside her house, she peeled off her clothes and jumped into the shower. Afterward, she returned to her summer attire of choice — shorts and a T-shirt.

Grabbing a cold soda from the fridge, Kelly checked on Carl through the window. He was lying in the sun in the exact same position he'd been before she left. Kelly took a long drink, letting the cold soda chill her inside. She peered at Carl again. Was he all right? Had he been sleeping all that time in the hot sun? Why didn't he go under the tree in the shade?

Suddenly, the vision of Carl running to chase a squirrel and snapping his neck in the process appeared before her eyes. Horrified at the possibility, Kelly flung back the patio glass door and ran outside. "Carl!" she yelled. "Are you all right?"

Carl raised his head just enough to look over his shoulder at her, then flopped back down.

"Ohmygosh," Kelly cried, convinced that Carl had injured himself while she was gone. He'd been lying in pain for all these hours, baking, roasting in the hot summer sun, waiting for his neglectful owner to return and take him to the vet. Kelly sank to her knees next to her dog and ran her hands over his back and legs. "Carl, are you all right? What's the matter? Did you hurt yourself?"

Staring balefully at her, Carl lifted his head enough to lick her hand, then let it flop back to the ground. Tears sprang to Kelly's eyes. "Oh no! You really did hurt yourself. We've got to get you to the vet."

At that, Carl lifted his head again. But this time he appeared to be tracking a squirrel's mad dash along the fence super-highway. The squirrel paused long enough to fuss at Carl in that chattering squirrely squeak. Clearly annoyed at the exchange, Carl suddenly scrambled to his feet and began to bark. Then, he took off for the fence, only to be yanked back rudely at the end of the chain. That did not stop the barking, however.

Kelly pulled herself from the ground. That old faker, she thought, smiling at her dog. He was trying to make her feel guilty. Watching Carl desperately try to reach the squirrel, barking ferociously, Kelly did feel guilty. The squirrel seemed to pause at intervals, as if he were teasing Carl to come and get him, knowing full well Carl could not. Finally, the squirrel leaped to a nearby cottonwood, gave Carl a rodent version of a Bronx cheer, then scampered into the leafy branches above.

"I'm sorry, big guy," Kelly apologized as she patted Carl's head. "I don't know what else to do."

Instead of enjoying the pat, however,

Carl immediately started barking again, staring toward the driveway beside the cottage. Kelly turned to see a man tentatively approach the fence, then draw back at Carl's ferocious barking. Something about the man looked familiar.

"Can I help you?" Kelly said as she approached the fence.

The man hesitated and looked over her shoulder. "Is he okay?" he asked, clearly concerned. "I don't want to make him mad."

"No no, it's all right," Kelly reassured. "Did you wish to speak to me?"

"Yes, yes I did," he answered, looking her full in the face.

Kelly remembered where she had seen him — that morning at the funeral. "You're Bob Claymore?" she inquired, offering her hand across the fence. "I'm Kelly Flynn. I believe I saw you at Vickie's funeral this morning."

Claymore almost looked grateful as he shook her hand. "Thank you. I was hoping you might do me a favor, Ms. Flynn. Mimi Shafer told me you were assisting Debbie with Vickie's business accounts, I believe."

"Yes, that's correct," she replied, adopting a businesslike tone. She had no idea where this conversation was going. "What sort of favor are you talking about, Mr. Claymore."

"I simply wanted you to ask Debbie if she would please meet with me, if only for a few minutes. She's refused to talk with me since her mother died. I can understand her anger and grief, but . . . but now she's making wild accusations to the police."

Claymore's face took on the desperate look Kelly had seen that morning when he'd obviously tried to plead his case to Debbie. "I'll certainly mention it to her, Mr. Claymore, but I'm not sure my saying anything will make a difference."

Claymore's whole body seemed to sag with that. He ran his hand through his thinning gray hair. "I've asked everyone, Ms. Flynn. Mimi Shafer, Geri Norbert, Jayleen. I . . . I don't know anyone else who might get through to her. I know how much she loved her mother, but to think that I could kill Vickie, why, it's . . . it's unthinkable. I loved Vickie. I couldn't hurt her." He stared off toward the golf course. "And now she's gone to the police with all these awful accusations. It's . . . it's unbelievable! They came to my office at the university, for God's sake. And they interviewed me there. I was so ashamed. I couldn't even look at my colleagues afterward. What must they think of me? Do they believe me to be capable of murder?"

Kelly watched the anguish play across his face and decided that Bob Claymore would have to be an excellent actor to feign all that emotion. Her earlier feelings surfaced, and she softened her tone. "Mr. Claymore, I promise I will try to convince Debbie to see you. All this animosity isn't good for either of you. And it certainly doesn't serve Vickie's memory."

Claymore glanced back to Kelly, gratitude evident in his eyes. "Thank you, Ms. Flynn. I . . . I appreciate that more than you know."

"She may bring others along with her. I'm sure you'd understand if she did."

Claymore nodded. "Of course. She's free to bring anyone she wants. I just want to have an opportunity to clear myself in her eyes."

"I understand, Mr. Claymore. I'll do what I can."

Carl started barking again, and Claymore gave Kelly a wan smile as he backed away. "Thank you," he repeated as he walked away.

Kelly watched him all the way to his car, wishing she didn't feel so unsettled.

* * *

"See you tonight at practice," Megan called over her shoulder as she sped through the knitting shop door.

"Don't forget your sunscreen," Kelly teased with a wave as she headed toward the main room.

Burt sat in his favorite sunny corner, spinning a smoky gray fleece. Kelly settled into a nearby chair and pulled the peacock blue and green scarf from her bag.

"How are you, Burt?" she said, picking up the scarf where she left off. It was really looking good now, and she was almost finished. The pudgy ball of boa eyelash yarn had dwindled to the size of a walnut. "You heard about the visit we had from the police, didn't you?"

Burt smiled, feet moving back and forth, setting the wheel's rhythm. "Yes, Mimi told me about the bracelet and the visit."

"I imagine Eva Bartok was questioned. I mean, after all, she's the woman who'd been screwing around with Vickie's husband."

"She was questioned yesterday as a matter of fact," Burt replied.

Kelly waited, anxious to hear what had transpired, or whatever Burt could reveal. "Well, what came out of it?" she demanded after Burt sat silent for over a minute.

Burt glanced toward the adjoining rooms. They were alone at the library table. "She has an alibi," he said in a hushed voice. "She was with a book discussion group at the university the night Vickie was killed."

The hum of the wheel filled the room as Kelly sat quietly knitting while Burt spun. Try as she might, she simply could not come up with a suspect other than Bob Claymore. Problem was, now that she'd met him, seen the anguish in his eyes, and heard the despair in his voice, Kelly felt sorry for him. And that made it harder for her to picture him as a killer.

Was all of that a ruse? Kelly wondered. All of that anguish and despair looked real. Was it possible Bob Claymore really was the killer?

She paused to count stitches again. That was the only way she'd been able to control the yarn's tendency to multiply. Whenever she found an extra stitch, Kelly would simply knit two stitches together.

"Burt, is he the only suspect the police have so far?" she probed again.

Burt gave her a smile. "Well, let's just say he's the best suspect the detectives have at the moment."

"Because of the divorce and the terms of the will, I'll bet."

"Well, that, and the fact that he doesn't have an alibi. He says he was home reading. All alone."

Kelly sighed out loud. "Oh, brother. That doesn't look good."

"Now that they've questioned Eva Bartok, he may get another visit from the detectives."

"Why's that?" Kelly asked, noticing two customers chatting in the adjoining room.

Burt leaned closer. "Eva claims she lost the bracelet two weeks ago, right after she'd spent the weekend with Bob Claymore."

Kelly stared at Burt. "Sounds like Eva thinks Claymore is trying to frame her. What do you think?"

Burt shrugged. "It depends on whether you believe her story. The detectives said she only mentioned Claymore after they told her where they'd found the bracelet. Apparently she got pretty mad after that."

"And Eva has an alibi, right? So it can't be her," Kelly mused in a low voice. "So, she couldn't have dropped the bracelet at the scene. And that leads us right back to Claymore. Assuming, of course, that he's the one who stole it."

"Or that it was stolen at all," Burt reminded her with a smile. "Who knows, maybe it dropped off her arm when she was visiting Vickie one day."

Kelly shook her head. "From what I've heard, Vickie and Eva were not on visiting terms. In fact, I heard they had a really bad argument at the Denver weaving conference the week before Vickie died."

Burt sat back. "We'd picked up lots of gossip about the bad blood between those two women, but our network missed that. Where'd you hear it, Kelly?"

"From the Lambspun network, Burt," she said with a grin. "Our grapevine beats them all."

Eleven

"Fill 'er up, Pete," Kelly requested, leaning over the café counter with her outstretched mug.

Pete grinned. "You really know how to start the day, Kelly," he said, filling her stainless-steel mug with the dark brew.

Kelly's cell phone rang, and she struggled to grab her mug and knitting bag and answer her phone, all at the same time. "This is Kelly," she managed as she wound her way through the knitting shop.

"Kelly, I'm going up into the canyon in a little while to finish up the insurance claims," Debbie's voice came over the phone. "Will you be coming up today?"

"I'll be up this afternoon, Debbie," Kelly promised. "I have to get to a certain point with my office accounts, then I can head out. Probably after lunch." She dumped her knitting bag and mug on the library table, then waved hello to Jennifer and Megan, who were already knitting.

"Oh, good." Debbie sounded relieved. "I was hoping you would come. Tell me, have you made much progress with the financial reports?"

"I've reviewed all the income statements. Now I have to access the remaining records on the computer and update those. Once I finish that, then I can start to draw up the reports. Oh, that reminds me." Kelly dug into her bag and withdrew the completed blue and green scarf. "You'll need to call the investment bank and ask them to fax a statement showing all activity from the first of July. We've got last quarter's statement, but we need to see if Vickie made any withdrawals or deposits during those first few days. The statements are in a folder on the desk."

"I'll call as soon as I get to the ranch," Debbie promised. "Oops, got another call."

"See you this afternoon," Kelly said, then flipped off her phone. She picked up the peacock scarf and dangled it in front of her friends. "Ta-dah!" she announced.

"Whoa! Look at that," Megan said. "Good job, Kelly."

"See, we knew you could do it," Jennifer added, her needles busily working another long-fringed scarf. This one was tangerine and coral.

Kelly reached over and fingered the luscious summer colors. "I haven't seen these colors before. Did we get a new shipment?"

Jennifer nodded and pointed to the room behind her. "Check out the wooden crates in the corner. New yarns came in."

Kelly jumped up from her chair and headed for the yarns, nearly running into Steve, who had rounded the corner at the same moment.

"Whoa," he said, stepping out of the way. "You folks need traffic signals on this corner."

"How about truck mirrors?" Jennifer suggested. "They could stick way out so we'd see who's coming."

"Sorry," Kelly apologized. "You caught me in the midst of fiber fever. New yarns." She pointed to the corner.

"Do you have a minute?" Steve asked. "I'm on the way back to the site, but I wanted to check something with you." He pulled out a chair and straddled it backward, clearly not staying long.

"What's up, Steve?" Megan teased. "You trying to recruit Kelly for your team?"

Steve grinned. "I would if I thought I had a chance."

"Dream on," Kelly taunted as she settled back into her chair.

"No, I'm here to check out the itinerary

for tomorrow." He pulled a notepad from his pocket.

"Tomorrow?" Kelly stared blankly for a moment before she remembered. She slapped her hand to her forehead. "Oh, yeah, our Wyoming trip."

"Yeah, our Wyoming trip. Tomorrow. Early. So set your alarm. We're leaving at seven a.m."

Kelly's eyes popped wide. "Whoa. Guess I'll have to run at daybreak. Okay, who's driving? Do you need me?"

"Nah, we're covered. Curt's taking his truck, and I'm driving mine. We figured some of you might be up for a road trip."

"You know, Kelly, I could come along and take a look at your cousin's house," Jennifer offered. "Give you an estimate of market value. Let me check the Wyoming multilist this afternoon and see what the comparables are. Do you have a description of size, rooms, and all that?"

"No, but I'm sure the lawyer does. I could ask Chambers to fax me something," she replied. "Thanks for offering, Jen. That'll help a lot."

"Hey, I'd like to go, too," Megan piped up across the table. "I need a break after the project I finished yesterday. Brother. I'm exhausted."

"Sure," Steve invited. "We have plenty of room. Both trucks can take three up front."

"Chambers said he coordinated everything with Curt. Are we meeting with the ranch manager?"

Steve flipped open his notepad. "Yes. Chet Brewster. He'll be there to take us around and answer any questions. Then he'll take us on a tour around the entire ranch. We'll need to see which areas would work for a natural area and which areas wouldn't."

Suddenly the enormity of the endeavor settled in on Kelly again. "Wow, I don't know what I'd do without you guys," she said, nodding to Steve and Jennifer. "And Curt. I'd be clueless. Totally clueless."

"That's what friends are for, Kelly," Steve said, and gave her shoulder a squeeze.

Her cell phone jangled, and Kelly stepped away from the table to answer. Lawyer Chambers came on the phone. "Kelly, I thought I'd fax you a description of Martha's house and contents from my files. I figured you'd need it for your trip tomorrow."

"Mr. Chambers, you're a mind reader. I was just about to call you. Thanks so much."

"It's no bother, Kelly. One more thing. I've learned there are some alpacas on the ranch as well as sheep and cattle."

"Alpacas?" Kelly exclaimed, causing everyone at the table to turn and stare. "What am I going to do with alpacas?"

"The same thing you do with sheep and cattle, Kelly," Chambers said with a chuckle. "You count them, then decide to sell them or keep them. Take care and call me afterward. I'll look forward to hearing from you."

Once again, the wily old lawyer hung up before Kelly could register any more complaints. She swore she heard him laughing.

"You've got alpacas, too?" Megan asked. "Wow."

"Yummy," Jennifer decreed. "Think of all the wool."

"Oh, brother, now I've got alpacas," Kelly said to the heavens. "What next? Pigs and chickens?"

Megan giggled, but Steve patted Kelly on the shoulder as he turned to leave. "I think we've just filled that last seat in the truck. You're going to need someone to advise you on the alpacas."

"Can't you and Curt do that?" she asked.

He shook his head. "Nope. Curt and I

are cattle and sheep guys. You need someone who can check out the herd, then look at the alpaca registry papers and estimate what they're worth. I'm sure there's paperwork there." He grinned as he walked away. "See you bright and early tomorrow."

Kelly stared after him. Today had just started, and it was already jam-packed. There weren't enough hours to get everything done. Vickie's accounts would take quite a chunk of time. Kelly shoved her scarf back into the bag and grabbed her mug. "It looks like my day just exploded," she said with a good-bye wave. "I'll see you two tomorrow morning. Jen, I'll fax that house detail to your office as soon as I get it." Without waiting for a reply, Kelly was out the door.

The printer hummed, and Kelly reached both arms high over her head to stretch. Leaning back into Vickie's comfy desk chair, Kelly watched the pages of neat columns and figures drop into the printer tray.

It was dusk already, she noticed through the window, and she'd only finished half of what she'd planned to accomplish this afternoon. Of course, all the extra errands in town had slowed her down. Kelly rubbed her eyes. It had taken twice as long to enter all of the expenses since Vickie's death. Darnit. She'd hoped to get this part finished before she took off for Wyoming tomorrow. She checked her watch. Maybe if she worked a couple of hours more.

"What is this?" Debbie said from her cluttered table across the room. "This can't be right. Mom always paid her bills on time. She was scrupulous about that."

Kelly groaned inwardly. Every time she thought she had all the expenses, either she or Debbie found more. They really needed Jayleen's help, but when Kelly suggested it, Debbie shook her head no.

"Oh, great, there go the totals again," Kelly said, deliberately heaving a dramatic sigh. "How much is it?"

"Over five thousand dollars," Debbie exclaimed. "That can't be right."

"Boy, that's a lot of alpaca feed. Who's the vendor?"

"It's not a vendor. It's some organization of alpaca breeders, I think. All it says is 'Advance Registration Fees.' "

Kelly reached across the desk for the folder of assorted invoices and statements already paid. She thought she remembered one unpaid invoice in the pile. "Here's the bill," she announced, holding up the invoice. "And it's dated June first. Everything else is paid. Wonder why this one isn't."

"That is so unlike Mom. I can't understand it."

Kelly saw an opportunity and decided to reopen a closed subject. "I bet Jayleen knows what's up with this bill." She glanced out the window toward the empty pastures. "Darn. We missed her. She's already put the animals in and left. I wish we'd found it earlier. Why don't I call her?"

Debbie's mouth pinched in an expression Kelly was growing used to. "Yes, I suppose you'll have to."

"We could really use her help, Debbie," Kelly tried again. "It's taking us a lot longer to finish these accounts, because we're having to find everything first."

Debbie shook her head again. "No, we're doing fine. I'd rather pay you and make sure everything's done as it should be."

Kelly sighed out loud and debated asking the one question that kept playing through her mind. Then she decided, *what the hey,* and jumped in. "Debbie, why don't you like Jayleen? I mean, she's a cousin. Everyone said she and your mom were very close. What's up?"

Debbie fidgeted with the invoice for a moment. "I just don't like her. She's . . . she's so rough and crude." Debbie wrinkled up her face in displeasure.

"You mean the swearing and all that," Kelly said, remembering Jayleen's loud and liberal use of profanity when Lieutenant Peterson interviewed them.

Debbie rolled her eyes. "Yes, that, too, but she's just so loud and stomps around. Like a bull in a china shop."

"Well, she's certainly not a shrinking violet, that's for sure," Kelly joked.

"I also think she took advantage of my mother over the years. She was always borrowing money from Mom."

"Really? Did she borrow a lot?" Kelly's curiosity was piqued.

"Ohhhh, I don't know how much over the years, but my mom kept track of it." Her mouth pinched again. "Jayleen always had problems with money, and my mom always bailed her out. I used to tell her not to be so accommodating, but Mom would laugh and say Jayleen had had a rough life." She gave a disgusted snort.

"Did Jayleen pay Vickie back?"

"Yes, she always repaid the loans," Debbie admitted, begrudgingly, it seemed to Kelly. "And she hasn't borrowed any money for a couple of years, my mom said."

"Well, that's good. Probably a sign that Jayleen's business is doing better," Kelly ventured, compelled to say something in Jayleen's favor.

"Humph. My mom's the one who built Jayleen's business. She recommended her to every one of her friends. Jayleen wouldn't have anything without Mom's help."

Clearly there was more here, so Kelly gambled and probed deeper. "Debbie, I sense there's something else about Jayleen that bothers you. Not just the money. What is it?"

Debbie laid the invoice in her lap and stared out into the rapidly darkening sky. "She's a drunk. Or she used to be. And she was so awful. My mom always tried to help her out. Rescuing her, bringing her home, trying to sober her up." Debbie shivered. "I still remember seeing her one night, when I was in high school. Her husband left her and took the kids. And Jayleen went on a binge. She was staggering around the kitchen, screaming and crying, and threatening to kill herself. It was so awful . . . and so ugly." Debbie's voice dropped lower.

Kelly began to understand. Debbie's world was curtailed and circumscribed. Carefully controlled, antiseptic almost. No overexertion, no excess, no throwing caution to the wind. Debbie's life literally depended on restraint.

"That must have been scary to watch," she ventured.

Debbie nodded. "It was. I always ran upstairs to my room whenever she came."

"She's sober now, right?" Kelly pried. "I mean, I don't see how she could manage all she does and go out on binges."

Debbie stared into her lap. "Mom said she's been sober for ten years. Let's hope she stays that way."

"Okay, I'll give her a quick call tonight and see if she knows about that bill," Kelly said, changing the subject. "Meanwhile, I'll keep that invoice with the other."

"I should go now," Debbie said, gathering the papers on the table as she rose. She dropped the invoice on the desk. "I hate driving down the canyon when it's dark."

"I'd leave now, too, but I want to get a little further on these entries," Kelly said, noticing Debbie's pallor. "You know, maybe you shouldn't come up into the canyon tomorrow. You're looking really tired."

"I wish I didn't have to. But there's still so much I have to sort through. At least I finished with the insurance today," she said, hesitating at the door. "Thanks so much for all your hard work, Kelly. I can't tell you how much I appreciate it."

Kelly gave her a warm smile. Debbie looked as if she needed it. "You're welcome, Debbie. Now, you take care of yourself, okay? Drive carefully down the canyon."

Debbie nodded and gave a parting wave over her shoulder. Kelly found herself staring after her and not knowing why.

The jangle of her cell phone startled Kelly so much she jumped. The quiet of Vickie's office had settled over her like a blanket as she stared at the computer.

"This is Kelly."

"Hey, Kelly, Jayleen here. I got your message. Which bill are you asking about?"

Kelly reached for the file folder. "It's from some alpaca organization for registration fees. But it's a hefty sum. Over five thousand dollars." She sorted through the papers. "Here it is. Five thousand two hundred seventy."

There was a pause on the other end. "That's the bill for the local chapter's fees for next year's exhibition. You mean it's not paid yet?"

"Nope. This is stamped SECOND NOTICE, and it's unpaid. My concern is, do we have any more bills like this floating around? I'm really trying to get some totals so I can do the reports."

"No no, I get everything paid the very day Vickie asks me to. I don't understand. She told me she was paying that bill the first week of July. It was already a month overdue. I thought that was strange, because Vickie is almost fanatic about paying her bills on time. Are you sure there's no entry in the checking account?"

"Nothing. I checked the bank, too."

"That makes no sense. Listen, do you want me to come over and help you look? I'd be glad to. I've got some time tomorrow."

Kelly debated, then decided against. She didn't want to upset Debbie. "That's okay. Besides, I won't be here tomorrow. Say, that reminds me," she said, suddenly remembering. "I could really use your help another way, Jayleen. I'm afraid it would take most of tomorrow, though."

"I'd be glad to help you, Kelly. Any way I can. What do you need?" Jayleen replied, her voice revealing that Kelly's attempts at kindness had not gone unnoticed.

"Well, I have to go to Wyoming with some friends tomorrow and check out my cousin's ranch. She died and left a lot of cattle and sheep. And I learned today there's a bunch of alpacas there, too. Now, I've got cow and sheep people, but I need an alpaca expert."

Jayleen chuckled. "Well, I don't know if I'm an expert, but I think I can help you out, Kelly. Cow and sheep people, huh?" She laughed a husky, low laugh.

"Boy, Jayleen, you're a lifesaver," Kelly enthused over the phone, deliberately not revealing she'd asked Geri first. Geri had pleaded too much business in town. "Listen, here comes the bad part. We're leaving from my house near the Lambspun shop at seven a.m. We can swing by your place in Landport about seven thirty. How's that?"

"Why don't I meet you at Harvey's Restaurant at the crossroads? I like to have breakfast there. Besides, it's on the way out of town."

"That's great. Thanks again, Jayleen. See you tomorrow." Kelly snapped her phone off, relieved that the last lingering problem of the day had been solved.

Surveying the littered desk, Kelly decided, *enough*. It was nearly nine o'clock, and she was starving. Brewing some of Vickie's coffee had helped, but that had worn off long ago. She needed to go home. Besides, poor Carl was probably starving.

The image of Carl-in-Chains, starving no less, spurred her on. She closed out the computer accounts and straightened all the folders that lay open on the desk. Gathering what she needed into her brief-case, she snapped off the desk lamp and left the office.

Thank goodness she'd remembered to turn on the lights in the great room. The idea of being alone in a pitch-black house where her friend had been murdered wasn't a pleasant thought. Kelly felt a chill pass over her as she hurried toward the front door, deliberately not looking toward the spot where Vickie was slain.

She pulled open the front door and fum-bled for the keys as she stood on the door-step. "Darnit!" Kelly exclaimed in exasperation as she searched in her brief-case.

Just then she heard a loud slamming sound near the barn, and Kelly jumped around to peer through the night. The moon was shrouded, so she couldn't see distinctly, but she thought she saw the door to the alpaca barn open.

That's funny, she thought, as she stepped off the wide porch. Jayleen always closed the doors and dropped the metal hook through the lock every night. Kelly hesitated in the yard, debating whether to approach the darkened barn. She shouldn't leave it open. Predators lived in the canyon — mountain lions and coyotes. Alpacas were gentle prey, like sheep.

She swallowed down her uneasiness and walked to the open barn door, even though part of her wanted to run to her car as fast as she could. Kelly took a deep breath and entered, reaching around the corner for a light switch. The smell of hay and feed floated out to her in the darkened doorway, and she thought she heard the animals rustle.

Her fingers found the switch, and the barn flooded with light, causing her to squint. She stepped inside, quickly surveying the open stalls and holding pens. Several of the alpacas blinked back at her, then went back to sniffing the smoky gray alpaca in their midst. Kelly recognized Raja, surrounded by the others. Her stomach unclenched. Her imagination was running wild, that's all. Dark house. Murdered friend. She shook all the images away.

"Hey, guys. Have a good night," she said as she retreated through the doorway. Reaching for the door so she could close it, Kelly noticed the metal hook lying on the ground near her feet. She picked it up, flicked off the lights, and closed the door, shoving the hook through the slot. It must have blown off with the wind, she told herself as she walked toward her car.

But there was no wind tonight, not even a breeze, a little voice in the back of her mind said.

That thought caused a ripple to run up Kelly's spine. Had someone been sneaking around the property? She quickened her pace to her car. Whether her imagination was getting the best of her or whether someone had actually been poking around the property uninvited, it didn't matter. She was definitely not going to work alone at night in that house again.

Suddenly the deep rumble of a truck engine sounded in the distance. Kelly paused at her car door and peered down the driveway. The throaty rumble revved, rising then falling, like a truck was shifting gears and pulling away.

This time the ripple turned into real

fear. Had someone parked down the road and then crept around the ranch at night? And she was sitting all alone in an empty house, scene of a grisly murder.

Kelly yanked open the car door, swiftly checked the back seat, and jumped inside. Revving the engine loudly, she locked the doors and zoomed down the driveway, spitting gravel in her wake. Dark canyon roads be damned. She planned to beat all speed records back into Fort Connor.

Twelve

"Whoa, hold on, it's going to get rough," Steve said as he maneuvered his truck.

Kelly stared out the window at the deep ruts carved into the long road leading to Martha Schuster's ranch. "These aren't ruts, they're canyons," she observed as they bounced along, her head barely missing the truck ceiling.

"Is this the scenic part?" Jennifer asked, bracing herself against the dashboard and the door.

"You may want to put some gravel on this road before winter," Steve suggested, steering around a crevice.

"Is that expensive?" Kelly asked. She hadn't even seen the ranch yet, and she was already spending money.

"Well, it's a long road, so it won't be cheap. But I'll give you names of the contractors I use, so they'll give you a fair price."

"Are we there yet?" Jennifer asked in a plaintive voice as she braced herself against the ceiling. "I need three hands."

"Almost there," Steve announced. "See, there's the house and the barn coming into view now."

Kelly spotted the two-story, white frame house up ahead. It was bigger than she'd envisioned. The road curved, and she spied a huge red barn. Then a garage. Was that a triple car garage? A gray pickup, which she took to be the ranch manager's, was parked in front. Fences were everywhere. From the paved county road all the way up the dirt road leading to the ranch, Kelly saw fences. They seemed to stretch for a mile before they reached the ranch house.

"Whoa, that's a good-sized house, Kelly," Jennifer observed. "And a barn, a big barn, too."

"It's even bigger than it looks," Steve added. "Wait'll you get up close."

Oh, great, Kelly thought. The ranch kept getting bigger and bigger, and she felt smaller and smaller.

"Triple car garage, nice," Jennifer continued, pointing. "And look, there's another outbuilding. Looks like storage."

"Or an office," Steve said, as they drove into the barnyard area.

"All this and three hundred acres. Hmmmm . . ." Jennifer observed.

Kelly could almost see the calculator inside real estate agent Jennifer's head, tallying market values as she surveyed Martha's property.

Her property, soon, Kelly reminded herself and felt a flutter inside her gut. All of this belonged to her, or it would as soon as the lawyers finished passing paperwork back and forth. That old feeling of being overwhelmed settled over her again. "Wow, this is even bigger than I thought it would be," she said, her voice coming out softer than usual.

Steve pulled the truck to a stop beside the triple garage, then turned to Kelly with a smile. "C'mon, Kelly, let's go take a look at what you've got." He grabbed a cowboy hat from behind the seat, pushed open his door, and stepped to the ground. "Hold on Jennifer, I'll help you out," he said, then grinned up at Kelly. "I'd offer to help you, too, but you'd just scowl."

Kelly made a face and waved him away as she jumped to the ground. "Go help Jennifer."

"Oh, yes, Mistah Steve. I'd just love your help," Jennifer gushed in a perfect imitation of a magnolia-drenched drawl. "This big old door is so heavy."

Steve lifted Jennifer to the ground, then

tipped his hat. "Glad to be of service, Miss Jennifer, ma'am."

"Hey, I'm not old enough to be a ma'am," Jennifer teased, then pointed to Steve's Stetson. "Nice hat."

"I didn't know you owned one," Kelly said. Not every man could wear a Stetson. Some men wore the hat. Some, the hat wore them. Steve looked natural. "Colorado cowboy, huh?"

Steve laughed. "Part-time. The rest of the time, overworked builder."

Kelly walked over to the fence and stared down the road. She spotted Curt Stackhouse's black truck in the distance, spitting dirt and gravel as it drove. Letting her gaze roam over the pastures that surrounded the ranch compound, Kelly turned slowly in a circle, surveying her soon-to-be domain.

Ye Gods! Look at all that land. Those pastures stretched for miles — all the way to the mountains, surely. She visually outlined the low-lying, gentle ridges in the distance. Were those cows out there? Good grief. They looked like cows. Lots of cows. What was she going to do with cows? She'd never really felt comfortable around cows when she was a child. Whenever she'd visited a friend's farm outside town, she'd stayed clear of the big, clumsy creatures. Sheep were different. Aunt Helen and Uncle Jim had sheep when she was a child. She had a little bit of "sheep memory." But no memory for cows.

She scuffed her borrowed cowboy boots in the dirt, causing little clouds of dust as she rejoined Steve and Jennifer. "Cows. Lots of cows."

"Cattle," Steve teased. "Don't worry. That's what Curt and I are here for."

"Think of them as steak, barbecue, and roast beef," Jennifer suggested. "Can we cook one up for lunch?"

"I don't think it's that easy," Kelly said, laughing at last as she watched Curt pull his big black truck right beside Steve's big red truck. "Serious Trucks," her dad used to call these monsters of the road.

Curt Stackhouse stepped down to the ground. If ever there was a man who looked like he'd been born to wear a Stetson, Curt was it. A true cowboy, cattle and sheep rancher, and sometime land developer, Curt still reminded Kelly of that brash young cowboy in Aunt Helen's high school yearbook photo — the photo signed, "Yours, always. Curt." Kelly had to smile. She bet young cowboy Curt had been a heartbreaker back then.

Curt strode around the truck, clearly aiming to help Megan and Jayleen alight. No need, Kelly observed with a grin. Jayleen had already jumped down and was helping Megan make it to the ground. Jayleen, like Curt and Steve, wore her Stetson, and it fit her as naturally as her leather gloves. Colorado cowgirl, without a doubt.

Kelly glanced up at the sun. It was still early morning and not too hot. The wind hadn't kicked up yet, but it would. Wind was Wyoming's trademark. She adjusted her trusty USS *Kitty Hawk* baseball cap — her kind of hat.

Megan peered out at the landscape from under her floppy white sun hat, her face smeared with SPF 300+ sunscreen. "Wow, Kelly, look at all of this," she exclaimed.

Jayleen strolled over, hands shoved in her back pockets. "This is some spread you've got here, Kelly," she observed with a smile.

Curt walked up beside them, Steve and Jennifer close behind. He stared toward the mountains in the distance for a minute. "Kelly-girl, you've got yourself a nice piece of property," he said, then clapped her on the shoulder. "Congratulations, you're now a rancher."

Kelly visibly flinched in reply, which made everyone laugh out loud. “It’s so *big*. And it’s got cows. *Lots* of cows.”

“Cattle,” Curt echoed Steve.

“Cows, cattle, whatever,” Kelly said, rolling her eyes. “All I know is there’re a lot of them. Over there.” She pointed toward the mountains. “I swear, this place goes to the mountains.”

“It’s big, but it’s not that big, Kelly. Those mountains are farther away than you think,” Steve reminded.

“You’ve been out of the West too long, girl. Been working in those city canyons. Looking city pale, too. You’ve got that computer-green color around the edges,” Curt observed with a sage nod.

“Hey, I’m working on it,” Kelly protested with a laugh, holding up her arm. “I can’t help it if my job makes me sit in front of a computer all day.”

“I know what that’s like,” Jayleen chimed in, even though her ruddy complexion belied her fifty-some years. Even her sandy blond hair revealed only a few strands of gray. “But I don’t get on the computer till nighttime.”

“Well, Steve, you ready to check out some cattle?” Curt asked.

“Yes, sir,” Steve replied, squinting toward the mountains. "Wonder if that manager has some extra horses we could borrow. It'd be a lot easier on horseback."

"Sure would. Let's ask him," Curt said. "By the way, that's a fine-looking hat, son."

"Thank you. Had to replace my old one. It blew into the middle of a pigpen when I was helping some guy over in Greeley."

"Now that's a picture," Jayleen said, chuckling. "Sorry, couldn't help it."

"Please tell me we don't have pigs," Kelly begged.

Both Curt and Steve shook their heads. "You would have smelled them," Steve replied.

Kelly sniffed. "I smell something, and it's ripe."

Steve grinned. "That's the cattle."

"Oh, brother."

"Pigs are worse," Curt said.

"Much worse," Jayleen concurred, clearly enjoying Kelly's consternation.

A screen door slammed, and Kelly turned to the ranch house. A tall, lean young man bounded down the front steps.

"Whoa," Jennifer murmured beside her ear as the ranch manager drew nearer. "I pictured this manager guy being old and gray. Things are looking up."

"Hey, you're here to help me with the

house, remember?" Kelly teased.

"Morning, folks. I'm Chet Brewster," the young man announced as he strode into their midst. "Mr. Chambers said you'd be driving up today."

Tall, lean, and ruggedly handsome, Brewster looked like he stepped right out of the cowboy storybooks — or at least, Cheyenne Frontier Days.

Curt stepped up, hand outstretched. "Chet, I'm Curt Stackhouse." He gestured to Kelly. "We're all friends of Kelly's, and we're here to help her take a look at this spread."

Kelly took that as her cue and reached for Brewster's hand. "I'm Kelly Flynn, Mr. Brewster. Pleased to meet you," she said with her brightest meet-the-client smile.

Chet chuckled. "Call me Chet, ma'am. My father's Mr. Brewster. And I'll be glad to show you folks around."

Ma'am? Kelly thought in surprise. Did she look old enough to be a ma'am?

Steve stepped up and introduced himself as well as the others, then added, "Do you have any horses we could use, Chet? It would be much faster to check out this herd on horseback."

"Oh, yes, sir. We sure do," Chet replied. "I kinda figured you might want that, so

I've got three already saddled. Do you want to check out the sheep, too? They're over in the back pasture." He pointed behind him.

"We'll check those, too. How many have we got?" Curt asked.

"Over a hundred now, with the new lambs." He glanced to Kelly. "Are you riding with us, ma'am? I can saddle another."

"No, I don't think so, Chet," Kelly said. She hadn't ridden since she was a child and was sure she'd forgotten everything she ever knew. She'd probably fall off into a big, fresh cowpie. "That's why these guys are here."

Gesturing toward the house and barn, Chet said, "You and your friends are free to look at anything you want. House, barns, storage, pastures. I've got some coffee and doughnuts in the kitchen, too."

Kelly grinned. She liked this guy already. "Chet, you're a lifesaver."

Chet looked embarrassed. "It's nothing, ma'am. Make yourself at home. We won't be gone too long."

Jayleen stepped up. "I'm here to take a look at the alpacas, Chet. I can see where you've got the pastures separated, but I only see two animals. You got any more?"

"Yes, ma'am. We've got three more with

one on the way," he said proudly, then pointed toward the garage. "The garage was turned into an alpaca barn. They go between the corral and pastures and the barn."

Jayleen turned to Kelly. "Not bad. You've got the start of a nice little herd. I'll know more when I see the paperwork on them. Registry papers and all that."

"Do you know where the owner kept his records, Chet?" Kelly asked. "Is there an office in the house where we can look for documents?"

"Sure is, ma'am," Chet said with a respectful nod. "Right off the front hallway on the right."

Kelly didn't know how much longer she could take the "ma'am" moniker. "We'll be looking at more than animals today. My friend, Jennifer, is a real estate agent, and she's come to do a market analysis of the property while we're here."

"Charmed, Mr. Brewster. Absolutely charmed," Jennifer said in a sultry voice as she offered her hand.

This time, Jayleen wasn't the only one staring at her boots to keep from laughing, Kelly noticed. She watched Cowboy Chet fall beneath Jennifer's spell. "Ummmm, glad to meet you too, miss."

"Where're those horses, son?" Curt cut to the chase.

"Right this way, sir," Chet recovered quickly, pointing at the stable. "You ladies take care now," he added and tipped his hat as he followed after Curt and Steve.

"How come I'm a ma'am and you're a miss?" Kelly asked dramatically.

"You're his boss. You have to be a ma'am," Jennifer replied.

"That cowboy doesn't know what hit him," Megan predicted, then giggled.

Jayleen gave a loud laugh. "Damn, you girls are a hoot."

"Okay," Kelly said. "What do we tackle first?"

"We're closest to the alpaca barn, so why don't we start there?" Jayleen suggested as she headed toward the converted garage.

Kelly quickened her pace to keep up with Jayleen, who was already pushing the door open. A familiar smell of hay and feed greeted Kelly when she entered the barn. It was a little cooler, too, she noticed and wondered if the animals sought shelter from the brutal summer sun the same way humans did.

"There you are, little mom," Jayleen crooned to an ebony black alpaca in the large corner stall. Two alpacas stood beside her, one a creamy caramel color and another, milky white.

"Wow, they're pretty," Kelly remarked as she approached the stall. Jayleen was rubbing the pregnant female's nose, so Kelly extended her open hand, palm up, in case the alpaca wanted a sniff. The female took a tentative step forward and reached her long, graceful neck to sniff the tips of Kelly's fingers. It tickled, Kelly noticed.

"Good girl, make friends with your new owner. C'mon, you two," Jayleen continued in the same low, musical cadence as she beckoned the others over. "She's a beauty, Kelly. I can't wait to see who she's been bred to." Pointing to the others, she added, "And so are these two. Boy, I hope the owner has some pictures of them with their full coats before they were shorn."

"Do they bite?" Jennifer asked as she and Megan neared the stall.

Jayleen laughed. "They won't bite you. Go on, rub their noses." Both Megan and Jennifer extended their fingers to be sniffed.

"So, these alpacas look pretty good to you?" Kelly asked.

"Damn right, girl," Jayleen said. "But I want to see who they've been bred to and what the babies looked like." She bent down belly level with the animals. "Yep, I'm right. I thought these two are females. Good. They're worth a helluva lot more."

"Geri explained a little bit about how this business works," Kelly said, remembering. "You want female babies because they'll sell for more, and the better the sire, the better the colors of the babies' coats. Right?"

Jayleen grinned. "That's about it in a nutshell. That's why I'm hoping the owner kept pictures along with the records. Then, I can give you a much better idea of what this herd is worth."

Kelly glanced toward a second open door leading to a separate corral and watched the remaining two alpacas slowly approach. "Looks like we've got a gray and a dark brown."

"Smoky gray and chestnut. Good colors. Hey, I'm excited, almost like this is mine," Jayleen said, her tanned face creasing into a grin as she leaned over the other stall fence. "C'mon, you two, say hello. Bet you guys are the little boys, right?" she said as she bent to check. "Yep. You got yourself two young males, Kelly. Not old enough to breed yet, but they will be. They sure are pretty, too. Wonder what colors they'll throw."

Kelly rubbed the smoky gray nose of the closest male. To her surprise, he pushed his face toward hers. She jumped back.

"Don't be scared. He just wants a kiss, don't you, little boy." She shoved her face next to his, making kissing sounds. The smoky gray obliged. "Teenagers," Jayleen said with a laugh.

Kelly carefully leaned forward so the smoky gray could give her a half sniff, half kiss. "Tickles," she said.

"Boy, I really wish there were some fleeces left. I'm dying to know what these animals produce."

"Well, I think you've got your wish, Jayleen," Megan called from across the barn. She stood in the doorway of an adjoining room. "I see several bags of fleeces in here."

Jayleen let out a whoop and raced over, Kelly and Jennifer in her wake. "Doesn't take much to get her excited, does it?" Jennifer observed.

White plastic trash bags lined the floor, fleeces spilling over the sides. Caramel, charcoal, beige, and white, creamy white, and ebony. "Wow," Kelly said in admiration. "Look at that. Burt will be spinning into next year with all these bags."

Jayleen was already examining and fingering a charcoal gray fleece. She gently lifted it from the plastic bag. "Hey, help me with this one. I think it's the entire blanket. We can unroll it over here." She bent to one knee as the others did the same, and they slowly unrolled the thick coat.

"Whoa, this is even thicker than I imagined," Megan said. "And longer, too."

"That's why it's called a blanket," Jayleen explained. "It's shorn in one piece from the shoulder to the flank. That way it looks better for alpaca shows." She stroked the luscious wool. "This is a beauty. Someone must have planned to enter it."

Kelly let her fingers indulge themselves in the lusciously soft coat. The fibers were over six inches long and silky. "This really looks good enough to show?"

"Damn right. You've got some excellent quality, Kelly. In fact, you might think about entering next year's wool market." Jayleen glanced to the other bags. "Let's see what else we've got here." She started rolling up the charcoal blanket once more and slid it into the plastic bag.

Kelly noticed the other side of the storage room was filled with even more bags. Bags stacked on top of bags. Five alpacas couldn't have produced all this, she thought. "Has he been storing these fleeces for some reason? Why are there so many?"

"That's a good question," Jayleen said as she lifted two bags from the stack and checked inside. One fleece looked palomino gold. The other was long, white, and curly. "Well, of course," Jayleen said, chuckling as she fingered the fleeces in both bags. "These are sheep fleeces. We forgot about the sheep. Your luck is holding, Kelly. These look real good, too."

In the fascination with the five-alpaca herd, Kelly had completely forgotten over a hundred sheep. Yikes! Were there a hundred fleeces in here? Burt would be spinning the rest of his life. She'd have to put him on retainer.

Megan and Jennifer were already checking out the bags, exclaiming over the softness. Kelly chose a bag filled with creamy oatmeal-colored fleece and sank her hands down to her forearms in the soft wool. Surprisingly soft. She fingered the fibers, then chose another fleece, and another. Black, milky white, palomino gold. Each time enjoying the rich lanolin that coated her hands afterward.

Jayleen pulled out a notepad and pen from her pocket and began scribbling away, counting and checking bags, peering into containers. Kelly felt slightly guilty for playing in the fleeces while Jayleen was actually doing something useful. Then she reminded herself she hadn't found a way to be useful on this ranch yet. In time, Kelly hoped she could learn what she needed. Meanwhile, she was grateful she'd brought experts who knew what they were doing.

"Do you have any idea what all this is worth?" Kelly asked Jayleen.

"A general idea, but I need to see the paperwork. See what the bloodlines are, check some invoices, all that stuff." Jayleen shoved the pad and pen into her back pocket.

"I think it's time we checked out the house and found that office Chet mentioned," Kelly said, rubbing the lanolin into her skin.

"Good idea," Jennifer said. "I need to take a look at the house. I printed out the public records info from the state Web site, so I can start with that. Plus, I've got recent sales data for this area of Wyoming. Land sizes, property descriptions."

"Did you bring a camera?" Kelly asked, snapping off the light as they left the storage room.

"Digital, plus extra memory card. I'm ready."

"Bye-bye, guys," Jayleen called to the alpacas watching them from the stall. The teenagers had returned to frolicking with each other outside.

The sun's bright glare hit Kelly as soon as they emerged from the barn. She pulled her hat down and squinted into the distance. She wasn't sure, but she thought she saw three men on horseback in the far pasture.

Jayleen shaded her eyes. "We'll let the guys count the sheep and cattle. We'll take care of the tricky stuff, right?"

"I'd be glad to help," Megan offered as they walked toward the ranch house. "I may not know anything about alpacas or real estate, but I can certainly sort through papers."

Kelly paused for a minute at the front steps of the large, two-story, white frame ranch house. A weather-beaten front porch stretched the width of the house. Two rockers and a glider sat invitingly, beckoning her out of the sun. She could picture herself sitting there drinking a lemonade like she did years ago as a child on Aunt Helen's shady patio.

Brother, where did that memory come from, she wondered? She shook it away. This property was going to be sold. She could not afford to become attached to it.

"Okay, team, here we go," she joked. "Jennifer, real estate. Jayleen, registrations of all four-legged residents on this ranch. Megan, you can help me with everything else."

Suddenly, a horrifying thought struck. Kelly cast her face to the heavens. "Please let there be a file cabinet and not cardboard boxes." With that, she ran up the steps, her friends following behind.

Thirteen

"Found another one," Megan announced, paging through the stack of papers on the floor. "This one says Ryeland. Do we have that breed yet?"

Kelly ran down the list she'd made of the various breeds of sheep. "Yeah, we've got that one. Put it in the pile to be copied. I'm going to have to make a binder with all these certificates and pictures. Otherwise I won't be able to remember which one is which."

She took a drink of the last of Chet's coffee. Not bad. Not great, either, but right now she couldn't be choosy. It was nearly noon, and she was hungry. She hoped the guys didn't return from their cattle tour with big appetites, because the doughnuts and coffee were long gone. She and the others had convinced themselves that sorting through disorganized files had a much higher stress level than riding the range looking at cows. Therefore, they deserved the doughnuts. But she didn't look forward to explaining her line of reasoning to the guys.

Kelly leaned back in the cushioned armchair. Sunlight poured through the windows of the cozy ranch house office. She glanced around the cluttered desk, file folders stacked on top of each other and on the floor. Both Jayleen and Megan sat in opposite corners, each surrounded by piles of paper. It had taken three hours for them to get this far, and Kelly estimated they'd only checked a third of the files in the cabinet.

Then, there was the desk itself. Kelly didn't want to think about that. She'd opened all four drawers earlier and found stacks of developed photographs, all wrapped in rubber bands with sticky notes attached. All those memories shoved in a drawer, she thought sadly.

She reached her arms over her head and stretched. "I'm hungry. How about you two?"

Megan nodded over her pile. "Oh, yeah."

"Maybe Chet has sandwich stuff in the fridge?" Jayleen suggested.

"He doesn't. I saw some eggs and things, that's all," Jennifer said, appearing in the doorway. She collapsed in a nearby chair. "Wonder if they deliver pizza out here."

"Dream on," Kelly said.

Megan looked up. "Well, if he's got eggs,

I can take a break from sorting and make something for us. Let me take a look." She scrambled from the floor.

"Bless you," Kelly said. "We can't finish this office today anyway. There's simply too much. I'll have to spend a whole weekend here." She grimaced.

"Okay, let me see what I can find in the kitchen," Megan said as she left.

"At least we got all the alpaca certificates and most of the sheep and cattle info," Jayleen said as she set her stack of papers on a nearby table. "It's a good start, Kelly. Now we can come up with a rough idea of what these animals are worth."

"I can't tell you how much I appreciate your help, Jayleen. I'd be lost trying to figure out all this animal registry business." Glancing to Jennifer, Kelly asked, "How's your real estate survey going?"

"Except for a couple of shots of the pastures and views, I've got everything I need. I'll put it all together in the office and come up with a market analysis." She leaned forward. "Kelly, have you taken a good look at some of these furnishings? I think there're some antiques here. I'm not an expert, but I have a hunch. C'mon, let me show you."

"Go on, Kelly," Jayleen said, shooing her

from the office. "I'm going to get these registry papers in some kind of order."

Kelly followed Jennifer into the living room, which was darkened by heavy green drapes drawn across the windows. She stood for a moment, letting her gaze drift across everything — glass china closets, overstuffed sofas, portraits and paintings with ornate frames hanging on the walls, end tables, tea tables covered with lace cloths and crocheted doilies, curio cabinets filled with porcelain and glass figurines.

Memories were everywhere. Kelly could feel them all around her. Here were Martha's memories, she thought, remembering Martha's spare and empty house in Landport. All of her memories had been left here. It looked to Kelly as if Martha's husband had kept the room exactly the way it was when Martha ran away four years ago. Kelly could smell the dust.

"Boy, I don't think he ever cleaned in here," she said. "The dust must be inches thick."

"Hey, it protects the furniture," Jennifer joked. "Take a look at this end table." She pulled back the white lace cloth that draped across the top. "Looks like mahogany. And it looks old. Just like that one over there." She pointed to a round table at the end of the sofa.

"I don't have a clue about antiques," Kelly admitted. "We'd have to have an appraiser give us an idea."

"Don't worry. The auction people have appraisers they work with. Believe me, they know antiques when they see them. I bet this place is filled with them."

"Auction? I thought you said I'd list it with a real estate agency."

"You'll list the *empty* house. That means you'll need to sell off everything inside. And from what I've seen today, these furnishings will bring in a fair amount of money." Jennifer gave a firm nod. "Those antique dealers are all over estate auctions like fleas on a dog."

Kelly pictured strangers pawing through Martha's treasured belongings. That didn't feel right somehow. Martha wouldn't like that. "I don't think I want people poking around Martha's house."

"They won't. Everything's moved outside. No one goes into the house except you and the auction people. I've been to several over the years. Believe me, they're well organized."

"I don't know," Kelly hesitated, glancing around at the lifetime of Martha's family memories. Even though they weren't her memories, Kelly still felt protective. "I'm going to have to think about this whole idea. Something about selling all of Martha's memories at auction . . . well, it doesn't seem right."

"You could always put them in storage, I suppose," Jennifer suggested. "Until you get a bigger place."

Kelly shook her head. "This is getting way too complicated. Sheep and alpacas are easier than this stuff. I'll think about it later."

"There's no rush, Kelly. Take all the time you need," Jennifer said. "I'll be outside finishing the pictures."

As Kelly headed away from the world of antiques and back to the stacks of paper, she noticed an enticing aroma wafting from the kitchen. Was that bacon? Kelly homed in on the delectable scent.

There was Megan, mixing bowl in one arm, vigorously stirring something. "Wow, you really are fixing breakfast," Kelly said in admiration.

"Well, I found a lot more than eggs in the fridge. Then I saw all the flour and baking stuff in the cabinet and decided I might as well make a big meal. We'll be driving around the ranch this afternoon, and we're all hungry."

Kelly grinned. "You are something else, Megan. I didn't know you could cook."

Megan looked up, a smudge of flour on her nose. "Oh, this isn't really cooking, it's just breakfast."

"Whatever you call it, it smells delicious, and you're a lifesaver." Sniffing the air again, she detected a tantalizing scent beneath the bacon. "Do I smell coffee?" she asked, salivating already.

"I made a fresh pot. I've seen you without caffeine, and it's seriously scary."

"I am forever in your debt." Kelly made a deep bow, then poured herself a cup before she headed to the sunlit office.

Jayleen was rearranging piles on the floor. "I finished sorting the alpaca certificates by date, and I've updated your sheep list with what we've got so far." She set the clipboard on the desk, then pulled up a straight chair and straddled it backward.

Kelly glanced at the list as she settled into the armchair. "This is great, Jayleen. It'll make the rest of my search so much easier."

"I actually enjoyed seeing what you've got," Jayleen said. "There're some good bloodlines here. If you decide to keep those two males, I'd like to see what they can produce. If it's half as pretty as those fleeces in storage, I may use 'em as studs. You set your price."

"For you, Jayleen, no charge."

Jayleen closed her eyes and shook her head. "Absolutely not. This is a business. You never let friendship or relationships interfere in business. I learned that from Vickie."

"She was a tough businesswoman, huh?" Kelly asked, curious.

"The toughest," Jayleen said as she looked out the window. "I remember when I was building my herd and didn't have money for prizewinning studs. I asked Vickie if her stud, Raja, could mate with my best female. Just once. I was hoping I'd get some of those gorgeous colors and another female to sell." A crooked smile twisted her mouth. "Vickie didn't even take a minute to think about it. She refused flat out. She'd put too much time and energy into building Raja's reputation to give away his services free."

"That must have been hard to take, considering you two are family and you're very close." Kelly could almost feel the rejection coming across.

Jayleen shrugged. "I understood. Vickie worked damn hard to build that herd. Besides, she helped me in other ways. She helped me build my bookkeeping business by loaning me money to buy all the computer equipment I needed to start up. I always paid her back, though, with interest."

"She charged you interest?"

"Sure did. Market rate, too. That's okay. It's business." Jayleen gave a firm nod in emphasis.

"Boy, she didn't cut you any slack, did she?" Kelly said, trying to square this version of Vickie with Debbie's account.

"Hey, nobody else would lend me money," Jayleen said. "I'd just come out of a rough patch in my life. Real rough. My credit was shot to hell, my job history was spotty. I had a chance to turn it around, and Vickie helped me do it."

"Is that when you came to Fort Connor?"

She nodded. "Yep. I sold my house and took every dime I could to buy the place in Landport and start my herd. I bought two females from Vickie and saved up money for stud fees."

Fascinated by her story, Kelly probed, "Is that when you started the bookkeeping business."

"Yeah. I was working two jobs in town and barely getting any sleep. Vickie suggested I could replace the income from the second job with my own business. She loaned me the money to start. It was rough the first year, but it's getting better every year." Jayleen smiled. "I'm actually earning money now."

"I'll bet Vickie helped you build your client base," Kelly said, already knowing the answer but curious what Jayleen would say.

"Absolutely. I couldn't have built it without her. Thanks to her, I've got enough clients so I don't have to work in town anymore." Jayleen gave another one of her decisive nods. "It's been worth every penny of commission."

The accounting lobe of Kelly's brain perked up. "Commission? Who're you paying commission to?"

"To Vickie, of course. She gets a cut of every client's total business. Plus I do her books for free."

Kelly stared wide-eyed at Jayleen. Whoa. She hadn't expected to hear something like that.

"Vickie told her friends about her arrangement with you, right?" she probed, watching Jayleen's face.

Surprise registered. "I guess so. I mean, she told me it was done all the time and not to worry about it." Jayleen's blue eyes became huge. "I didn't do anything wrong, did I?"

"No, Jayleen, you didn't do anything wrong," Kelly said with a reassuring smile. "But Vickie may have. She encouraged all her friends to use your services. And if she didn't tell them about the commissions she received from you, then she was effectively getting money under the table off their business. Without their knowledge."

"I never thought about that," Jayleen said, staring out the window. "Well, I guess it doesn't matter now. Vickie's dead."

Kelly stared out at the Medicine Bow range as it sliced rough and barren across the landscape. Treeless ridges, not like Colorado. She also noticed three horsemen near the barn. The guys had returned from their mini–cattle drive.

"Hey, look who's back," she said, pointing out the window. "Shall we go out and greet them? I've about had it with this paperwork."

"Sounds good to me," Jayleen said, swinging herself out of the chair in one movement. "Say, do I smell bacon?"

"Megan's making a big breakfast, bless her. I wasn't looking forward to explaining why the doughnuts were gone," Kelly said as they headed for the front door.

Jennifer was standing at the foot of the steps, camera in one hand, shading her eyes with the other. “Well, ah declare, the menfolk have arrived at last,” she said, drawl dripping off her tongue.

Jayleen hooted. “Jennifer, you are something else.”

“Well, thank you kindly, Miz Jayleen. I’m just hopin’ that young handsome cowboy isn’t too tuckered out by the ride. I’d like to visit with him,” Jennifer drawled as she sashayed toward the barnyard.

Kelly and Jayleen followed after, not bothering to hide their laughter. “Which handsome young cowboy you talkin’ about, Miz Jennifer? I see two of ’em,” Jayleen teased.

“Why, that sweet little ol’ Chet, of course. He’s the only one not taken.”

Kelly jumped on that comment like a grounder to infield. “Hey, Steve’s not taken. He’s free as a bird,” she insisted. Jennifer ignored her, the menfolk clearly in her sights by now.

Kelly motioned to Jayleen. “Let’s stand here and watch. Jennifer in full flirt is an experience to behold.”

Jayleen chuckled. “Damn, that girl reminds me of me when I was younger. Lord, the trouble I used to get into.” She shook her head. “And the bad habits I picked up along the way. Along with the men. Picked up a lot of those along the way, too."

Surprised how forthcoming Jayleen was about her past, Kelly decided to ask the same question she'd asked Debbie. "Is that what I feel coming from Debbie? I sense she's uncomfortable around you, Jayleen. That surprised me, since you're all family."

Jayleen stared toward the mountains. "No surprise, Kelly. She remembers me from those bad times, when I was drinking." She let out a sigh. "I was an alcoholic back then. An ugly drunk. Vickie was the only one who cared enough to help me. She'd come get me and sober me up, let me stay with her. And, of course, Debbie saw all that. I guess she's never forgiven me." Her voice drifted off.

Kelly reached out and put her hand on Jayleen's arm. "Sounds like you've put all that behind you, Jayleen, and built a whole new life. You're to be congratulated — at least in my book."

Jayleen gave her a shy grin. "Thanks, Kelly. I've been sober ten years. You're right, it's a whole new life. Tough sometimes, but I wouldn't trade it for those highs and lows like before."

Jennifer and the "menfolk" approached, and Kelly noticed that Chet was already ensnared in Jennifer's spell. He strolled beside her, grinning boyishly, while Jennifer talked. Curt and Steve, however, looked like they were trying their best not to laugh out loud.

"Back from the range, huh?" Kelly greeted them. "Those cows stand still long enough for you to count them?"

"Nah, we brought 'em back here for you," Steve said. "They're your cattle. You can count 'em."

Sure enough, Kelly spotted black shapes coming across the pasture. Cow shapes, headed her way. "You did that on purpose, didn't you?"

Steve grinned slyly. "Curt and I thought you needed to spend some quality time with your cattle."

"Riiiight. Like I'm going to climb over the fence and start petting them. I'd just step in a fresh cowpie and mess up Ruth's boots."

"You got nothing to fear, ma'am," Chet offered earnestly. "Cattle are pretty docile unless you rile 'em up."

"Where's the bull?" Jayleen asked, surveying the pastures.

"Old Cujo is out there, ma'am. He'll be in when he wants to. Now, he has a pretty bad temper, but I don't reckon you'll be patting him." Chet grinned.

"Why didn't you bring in the sheep?" Kelly asked, peering into the far meadow. She could see the sheep grazing. "Sheep don't scare me. I'll pat them."

"We'll see all the sheep you want, Kelly, right after we've had something to eat," Curt said as he took Kelly by the elbow and led her toward the house. "Right now, we're going to find those pizzas Chet's got in the freezer. We've worked up quite an appetite out there."

"Any chance there's a doughnut left?" Steve asked.

"Nary a one, Mistah Steve," Jennifer said. "Kelly ate them all."

"Did not. Scarlett finished off her share."

"Lies, all lies." Jennifer fanned herself with the property description.

"Sorting through those files really wore you out, huh?" Steve said.

"Don't start," Kelly warned as they approached the front steps. "Nothing was in order. It was a big mess —"

"Hey, everybody," Megan called from the doorway. She'd found an apron from somewhere and looked positively adorable, standing there like she stepped right out of a magazine ad from yesteryear. "Breakfast is almost ready. Bacon's done and the biscuits are baking. But I could use some help setting the table while I scramble the eggs." Without waiting for a reply, Megan disappeared inside once again. The screen door slammed shut.

"Did she say biscuits?" Chet asked.

"She sure did, son."

"Oh, lord."

Kelly watched all three men race up the front steps, jostling each other as they crowded through the doorway, clearly eager to be the first one to offer his assistance to the cute cook. Imagine that, Kelly mused. Biscuits can beat out sex.

"Well, I nevah." Jennifer frowned, hand on hip. "I guess the way to a man's heart is truly through his stomach."

Jayleen laughed. "Gals, we'd better get in there now before the menfolk eat it all."

"You know, after that breakfast, we should be running around this ranch, rather than driving," Kelly said, as Steve's truck bounced over the pasture.

"I don't think I'd get very far," Steve said. "Not after all those biscuits."

Kelly laughed. "Yeah, I noticed you had your share plus half of mine."

"Hey, you finished the doughnuts, remember?" Steve countered.

Jayleen chuckled. "You two are something else."

Kelly heard a certain tone in Jayleen's voice but kept her mouth shut. What was it about people that made them want to pair others up? Like they were filling some modern-day Noah's ark. Kelly wasn't having any of it.

"Have to admit I never did quite get the hang of biscuits," Jayleen said. "I can grill up a steak and fix a mean chili, but biscuits? Never got the knack."

"You don't need a knack," Kelly teased. "You go to the refrigerator case in the store and buy them. They're in little cans that you whack against the counter. They practically jump right into the pan, ready to bake."

After she stopped laughing, Jayleen added, "Kelly, you'd be running all day to see this place. Three hundred acres stretches quite a ways. We've been driving for an hour, and we're still on your land."

Kelly stared out the window, amazed again at the amount of property that would soon be hers. She looked to the west. The Medicine Bow Mountains cut across the horizon, rough and rugged. The Sierra Madres and Continental Divide loomed behind, aching for winter's touch.

Martha was right. This land would make a beautiful natural area with its abundance of antelope and jackrabbits, coyotes and prairie dogs, songbirds and hawks, and all the myriad smaller wildlife that scurried and hunted in the day and in the dark. It would be perfect. But what would she do about the house? Would she section off the house and barns and sell them? Would she keep everything else as the natural area? Could she accomplish both? And what if they found oil and gas? What would she do then?

She couldn't think about all that now. She had her hands full wondering what to do with all the cattle, sheep, and alpacas. Should she sell some? If so, how many? Cattle, sheep, or both? Kelly had already started thinking about keeping the alpacas after Jayleen's enthusiastic description of their bloodlines. Plus, Kelly had to admit she loved those fleeces.

Oh, brother. She forgot the fleeces. She'd have to hire Ruth to clean and mill and spin some of them. She'd give Mimi first choice of which ones she'd like to buy. Then she'd give a bag to Lisa and Megan and Jennifer and two bags to Burt. Oh, and a bag each to Lizzie and Hilda.

Remembering the old nursery rhyme

from childhood, she almost laughed. *Baa, baa, black sheep, have you any wool? Yes sir, yes sir, three bags full.* Kelly had much more than three bags, for sure, and recalled Ruth's comment about selling them online.

"You know, Curt's wife, Ruth, said I could sell fleeces online to spinners. Do you think that's a good idea?"

"You bet you can," Jayleen replied. "You should save any you want for next spring's wool market, then offer the rest to spinners and weavers. Same goes for the alpaca fleeces. And I can help clean and spin some if you're in a bind."

Watching Chet's gray pickup turn to the right up ahead, Kelly figured they were coming up beside the sheep pasture again, which meant they'd circled the ranch as well as crisscrossed it twice. Spotting sheep in the distance, Kelly asked, "What do you think, Steve? How many of these cows and sheep do we sell?"

"Curt and I are still thinking about that," he said, steering around a low bush. "There's some good quality here, so you'd get a decent price. Curt's going to draw up a spreadsheet, then we'll have a better idea."

Kelly stared at him like he'd sprouted

horns. "*Spreadsheet?* You've got to be kidding. For cows and sheep?"

Steve grinned at her. "Modern-day ranching, Kelly. Get used to it."

She rolled her eyes. "Oh, great. More office work. That's all I need. I already spend most of my life on the computer."

"You can always hire it out," Jayleen suggested.

"Great idea," Kelly enthused. "I can pay you to do it."

Jayleen shook her head. "I don't do cattle operations, Kelly. I don't know enough about it."

"And I do?" Kelly exclaimed. "I don't even know enough to call them by their right names. Cows. Cattle. Whatever."

"Don't even worry about it, Kelly," Steve said. "You told me Lawrence Chambers already has an accounting firm doing the financial work now. You can keep using them until you've decided what you want to do with the ranch. Keep it, sell it, donate it, or a combination of all three."

That got her interest. "I could do all three?"

"Sure you can. But don't even start thinking about that yet, because everything could change if there's oil and gas on the property."

Kelly had momentarily forgotten about that scenario. She'd been focusing on what she could see on top of the land — the sheep and cattle — totally ignoring what might lie beneath.

"Whoa, oil and gas," Jayleen said, then whistled. "You're right. That would change everything."

"You mean I couldn't donate it?"

"Sure you could," Steve said. "You only lease the mineral rights below the ground. You still own the land. You could still designate land as a protected area if you want. Who knows? You might even want to keep some of those sheep and cattle. Jayleen said you've got some real good breeds. Curt's eyes lit up when she mentioned a couple." He laughed.

"He can have any sheep he wants," Kelly declared.

"He probably doesn't want to buy any, Kelly," Jayleen spoke up. "Most likely he wants to use your rams' services."

Kelly still hadn't integrated the concept of earning money when certain animals mated. Not only would she have to keep track of their food and shelter, but she'd also have to monitor what they did in their spare time.

"I notice you didn't mention selling off

the alpacas," Steve said with a smile. "Thinking about keeping them?"

She nodded. "I'm thinking about it. Those fleeces are beautiful."

"I told you," Jayleen teased. "It's contagious."

Kelly watched Chet holding the long metal gate open for them to exit the pasture and head back to the barnyard. Tour was over. She glanced at her watch. After three o'clock. If they left for Fort Connor now, she and Megan could still make ball practice tonight. Dinner would have to be a drive-through on the road. Unfortunately, she didn't remember seeing much in the way of food along the road.

Steve pulled his truck to a stop and opened his door. "Okay, quick stop before we head back to town. I've got practice tonight. How about you, Kelly?"

"Yep. Megan and I have to be at the ball field by six," she said, sliding out of the truck and into a gust of wind. She grabbed her *Kitty Hawk* cap before it blew into the nearby corral. The corral was now filled with cattle. Where there were cows, there were cowpies.

"You two are gonna play ball tonight?" Jayleen asked, stretching. "Boy, you make me feel my age. I've gotta go home and take care of my animals and Vickie's, then do my accounts. I plan to fall on the sofa after that."

Remembering an earlier comment, Kelly asked, "Is Raja acting okay? You said he was acting funny for a while."

Jayleen stared toward the back pasture where Curt's truck could be seen in the distance. "You know, he is, and he isn't. He's acting fine for a couple days, then I swear, he starts acting skittish again. I can't figure it out. And truth be told, I just haven't had the time to spend with the animals like I used to. Not right now. I've gotten a new bookkeeping client, and I'm staying up till two a.m. to set up his accounts."

"That sounds familiar," Kelley commiserated.

"Did you like what you saw, ma'am?" Chet asked as he joined them. "I've been trying real hard to take good care of it. It sure is a nice spread."

"I want to thank you again for the fine job you've done, Chet," she reassured, giving him her brightest smile. "I also appreciate your explaining things to me so I didn't feel stupid."

"Thank you kindly, ma'am," Chet said with a blush. "Do you, uh, have you decided yet what you're going to do? Are you going to sell it, you think?"

Kelly shook her head. "No, I haven't, and I probably won't decide for a while, Chet, so I hope you can continue on here as manager."

Chet beamed. "It would be a pleasure, ma'am."

Curt pulled his truck alongside them and jumped to the ground. Kelly noticed Chet was right at the door to assist Jennifer and Megan.

"The bull looks pretty good," Curt gestured to the corral as he approached. "Good bloodlines from what Jayleen told me."

Kelly stared toward the corral, peering at the cattle, trying to figure out which one was . . . whoa. That had to be him. Her gaze settled on a huge black steer with horns jutting out as thick as a man's arm. Almost as if he knew she was observing him, the bull turned toward Kelly and stared. Scowled would be more like it. He certainly didn't look friendly. The bull snorted and swiped his paw on the ground once, as if announcing who was the one in charge.

"Cujo, is that his name?" Kelly asked. "Surely he's got another name. Those alpacas and sheep have fancy names, and they're not even half his size."

"He's got a name almost as long as he is," Jayleen said. "Can't remember what it is, but I saw it on the certificate."

"That reminds me. I want to take a quick look at those registry records again," Curt said, settling his hat tighter on his head. "Is that okay with you folks? I know you and Megan have to get back into town for ball practice."

"Go ahead, Curt. Check all the papers you need. We'll wait for you here," Kelly said.

"Jayleen, I'm going to need your help. You still got that list?"

Jayleen slipped the notepad from her pocket. "Sure do."

Glancing over his shoulder at the threesome near the truck, Curt called out, "C'mon, son. I need to take another look at those sheep after I check the records." He headed toward the house with Jayleen right behind him, while Chet gave Megan a big smile before he followed after.

"Looks like I have time to make a few calls," Steve said, flipping a cell phone from his pocket. "Provided I find a signal." He walked toward the barn.

"Let me know if you find one," Jennifer called as she and Megan joined Kelly at the corral fence. "I've got to check in with my office. My cell's coming up blank."

Kelly wasn't sure, but she thought Megan looked a little flushed under her floppy sun hat. "Don't worry, Megan. We can make it back in time for practice," she said, hoping to distract an attack of Megan's super shyness. A gust of wind pulled at her hat, and she gave it another tug.

"Curt's really impressed with the ranch, Kelly," Megan said. "I mean, he was telling us all about different breeds of cattle and sheep. He knows all about them. Boy, he's a walking dictionary. It was fascinating, right, Jennifer?"

"He lost me after he explained how you cross one sheep with another."

"Actually, it was —" Megan cut her sentence short when another wind gust lifted her floppy sun hat and sent it sailing right into the corral. It landed right beside a large squishy cowpie.

"Oooops," Jennifer said, laughter escaping.

"Whoa! I just bought that yesterday!" Megan protested, clearly irate that her hat was about to become a cow doormat.

Kelly was about to say something reassuring when Megan spun about and climbed up and over the fence in seconds. Horrified, Kelly called out, "Megan, don't!"

It was too late. Megan had already jumped to the ground and raced across the corral to fetch her hat. Unfortunately, Cujo had also noticed the sun hat and the girl racing to get it. The huge bull snorted, pawing the ground.

Kelly didn't think twice. She scaled the fence and called out, "Megan, stop. Don't move," she ordered as she swung her leg over and dropped to the ground. Cujo lowered his big head and fixed Kelly with an angry glare.

Megan stood, seemingly immobilized at the sight of the bull across the corral, her face as white as the hat dangling from her hand.

Kelly slowly inched toward her, hoping to catch her attention as well as distract Cujo's. "Megan, back away and head for the fence," she warned. "Back away, now. . . ."

Suddenly another shape appeared at the corner of her eye. Steve dropped to the ground and let out a loud whoop, waving his hat in the air. Cujo spotted the moving Stetson and snorted in Steve's direction.

Megan snapped out of her trance just as

Kelly grabbed her arm, and they both took off for the fence. Megan scrambled over and threw herself onto the ground. Kelly grabbed the top of the fence just as Cujo let out a ferocious bellow. She swiveled around to check on Steve and nearly lost her grip. Steve let out one last whoop and tossed his hat right in front of the angry bull, then took off for the fence. Cujo charged the hat with a vengeance.

Kelly swung her leg over and climbed down. Steve was already helping a shaken Megan to her feet. The slam of a screen door brought Curt, Jayleen, and Chet running from the house.

"What in Sam Hill happened? I heard that bull roar," Curt demanded as he strode up, looking all the world like an irate father about to break up a rowdy teenage slumber party.

The three participants stood silent while Jennifer spoke up. "The wind blew off Megan's hat into the corral, and she climbed over the fence to get it —"

Chet's eyes nearly popped out. "Megan, you climbed in with that bull!"

"I didn't see him," she squeaked, clearly too scared to be embarrassed.

"And then Kelly climbed in to rescue Megan. Then Steve climbed in to rescue both of them. He distracted the bull long enough for Kelly and Megan to escape. But he sacrificed his new hat to do it."

Curt peered at both Kelly and Megan for a few seconds, and Kelly could tell he was dying to deliver a scolding lecture on using common sense. Instead, Curt took a deep breath and stared at the corral and Cujo and the flattened Stetson that lay at the bull's feet. Stomped flat. "That's a shame, son. It was a fine hat."

"Yes sir, it was," Steve agreed, staring into the corral.

Kelly saw Jayleen turn her head to keep from laughing. Chet, however, still looked appalled at what they'd done. "I'll get your hat, sir. Just let me move these steers along." He hurried over to the corral and started that same waving motion Steve had used.

Megan grabbed Steve's arm, the reality of what happened clearly settling in. "Oh, Steve, thank you, thank you, thank you! We would have been killed if you hadn't jumped in and caught that bull's attention."

"Thanks doesn't do it, Steve," Kelly said when she caught his eye. "Cujo would have stomped us instead of the hat. One of us for sure."

Megan shuddered. "Oh, my gosh. I can't believe I did something that stupid. We could have all been hurt!"

"Well, I, for one, think both of you owe Mistah Steve a new hat, don't you folks?" Jennifer said with a wicked smile. "Mercy, Mistah Steve, you managed to save two damsels in one fell swoop."

Steve laughed. "Actually, Kelly distracted Cujo long enough for Megan to escape. I jumped in to make sure Kelly didn't try to argue with him instead of running like hell."

This time, everyone laughed out loud, and Kelly didn't mind a bit being the subject. She felt the accumulated tension from the entire day release. "I was about to thank you again until you said that," she teased.

"I sure am sorry, sir," Chet said as he walked up, a crushed Stetson in his outstretched hand. "He stomped it pretty good."

Steve took the remains of his hat and popped the brim out. Casualty of the range. A bent and broken reflection of its former self. He exhaled a dramatic sigh. "It sure has been a bad month for hats."

Fourteen

Kelly stood in the middle of the asphalt parking lot and stared up at the pink stucco building's bright neon sign. "You sure this place has carryout? It looks like a casino." She reached her arms high overhead in a long stretch. It felt like she'd spent the whole day in a truck.

"It is a casino, but it also has a restaurant and hotel," Jayleen said. "I stopped here one night with a bunch of local breeders when a storm blew in. You know how this road gets in the winter."

"Well, at least it's more interesting than fast food," Kelly said, watching Curt and the others walk up. "Is it like Blackhawk and Central City?"

Jayleen shook her head. "No, not even close. It has slots and poker games, but that's all. Nothing fancy like those places."

"Casino, huh?" Jennifer said, as they approached. "Too bad I'm strapped for cash right now."

"You're always strapped for cash,"

Megan joked. "And you work two jobs. How do you manage that?"

"It takes concentration and consistent, steady spending," Jennifer replied.

"Hate to disappoint any of you who're gamblers, but we don't have time to play. We're gonna have to grab the food and go," Curt said, running a hand through his pewter gray hair.

"Accountants make lousy gamblers anyway," Kelly confessed as they headed for the casino entrance.

"I've gambled enough on my business," Jayleen said, grinning.

Steve slipped his cell phone back into his pocket as he stepped forward and opened the door for everyone. "Same here, Jayleen."

The sight of the phone jiggled Kelly's memory. She needed to call Debbie and check if those faxes had come in from the investment account. Debbie had called yesterday, so they should be there. With luck, she might be able to finish Vickie's accounts by this weekend. This double workload was beginning to pinch, and Kelly was feeling the pressure build. The sooner she could finish the work for Debbie, the better.

"I'll join you in a minute," she said and flipped open her phone. No signal. "Steve, can I use your cell phone, please? Mine's out of range."

"Sure thing," he said, handing it over. "Want us to order you something?"

"Thanks. Get me a cheeseburger, fries, and a diet soda, please. I'll be right in."

Kelly headed back into the casino parking lot, which was crowded already. The late afternoon sun was as brutal as midday in July, so Kelly searched for a bit of shade in the wide open. The casino had been planted right on the prairie land, only a stone's throw from the main highway into Fort Connor. Not a tree for miles. She found a sliver of shade beside Steve's truck and leaned against it while she dialed Debbie's number.

The phone rang several times, then finally switched to voice mail. She left a brief message, asking about the faxes and reminding Debbie that she'd meet her at the ranch tomorrow.

Kelly flipped the cell closed and was about to head back into the casino when she spotted Geri Norbert, exiting the casino from a side door. She started to call out a greeting until she spotted the expression on Geri's face as she strode to her truck.

Anger? Fear? A mixture of both? Whatever it was, it held Kelly in place. Instead of calling out, she stared as Geri slammed her truck door, gunned the engine, and roared out of the parking lot. Her truck turned south, Kelly noticed, back toward Fort Connor.

What on earth was wrong? Kelly wondered. Geri seemed to ooze calm and control, a cool self-assurance. Whatever had happened to upset her so?

Kelly entered the casino and glanced about for her friends. An expansive lobby opened in two directions — hotel, one way, casino and restaurant, the other. Kelly saw Jayleen hovering on the edge of the casino, while Megan and Jennifer strolled through the slot-filled aisles.

The brightly lit, mirrored room was nearly filled. Every machine had a person seated in front. Continuous, artificial machine-music filled the air, tinkling and jingling, punctuated by other game noises, honks, bongs, and bells. As Kelly drew beside Jayleen, she also detected the distinct sound that was so dear to every gambler's heart: *Ka-ching, ka-ching.*

"The guys are in the café." Jayleen gestured toward the casino room. "They always put the restaurant on the other side so you have to walk through to eat."

"Not much of a gambler, huh?" Kelly asked, noticing her hovering on the edge of the room. "Neither am I. I take a certain amount, use it, then leave. I'm not much fun."

"It's not the gambling that keeps me out," Jayleen said. "It's the liquor. The bar's in there, and of course, they bring drinks right to the machines for you. I can't be around that."

"Even after ten years?"

Jayleen nodded. "You never stop being an alcoholic, Kelly. That's why I still go to my meetings."

"You know, I just saw Geri Norbert outside when I was making my phone call," Kelly said, changing the subject. "She didn't see me, though. I was going to say hello, but she looked mad or something. She looked strange. Is she all right?"

Jayleen stared at Kelly solemnly for a moment, then glanced at her boots. "You sure it was her?"

"Positive. It was her truck, too."

"That is too damn bad, then," Jayleen said, shaking her head.

Something in the sound of Jayleen's voice set Kelly's instincts humming. "What's the matter? Is she a closet gambler or something?"

"Yeah, I guess you could call it that, although I don't think any addiction can be kept in the closet. Sooner or later, it's gonna come out and bite you in the butt."

"Brother, that's a surprise," Kelly said, sorting through all the images she had of Geri and trying to make these new pieces fit in the puzzle. "She always looked and acted so controlled and all."

Jayleen gave her a rueful smile. "The key word is 'acted,' Kelly. We learn to conceal what we're doing and what it's doing to us." She wagged her head sadly. "I thought she'd stopped. Vickie told me that Geri had sworn to her she stopped. And that was two years ago."

"Did Vickie try to help her like she helped you?" Kelly probed.

"She sure did. She loaned Geri money to make her mortgage payments when she was behind. Geri would have lost her house and land if Vickie hadn't done that."

"Same loan arrangements you had, right," Kelly continued, curious if Vickie showed favoritism between friends and family.

"Not quite. Geri didn't have another income like I did, so Vickie loaned her the money and had it secured by a lien against Geri's property. Kind of like a second mortgage. Geri made monthly payments, market rate, of course. I know because I deposit all the checks."

"Did she pay on time?"

Jayleen nodded. "Last year, she did. But she's been late several times this year. I remember Vickie being upset about that, too. She didn't like waiting for her money. That's why I always paid on time every month."

"Boy, if she'd nearly lost her property once, why would she risk gambling again? You'd think it would have scared her away," Kelly mused out loud, watching Jennifer walk toward them.

"Being scared doesn't even faze you, Kelly," Jayleen explained. "When you have an addiction, nothing else matters. It's a compulsion. And you've gotta admit you've got it before you can cure it. I offered to take Geri to the weekly meetings they have in town for gamblers. But she almost bit my head off for suggesting it. Boy, I wish I'd tried again."

"Hey, what are you two so serious about?" Jennifer asked as she strolled up.

"Nothing much," Jayleen said and walked toward the ladies room.

"Something I said?" Jennifer asked, pointing.

"No, I just saw a friend come out of the casino, and Jayleen told me she's a compulsive gambler who'd promised to stop. Now I'm worried about her," Kelly explained without saying too much.

Something in the back of her mind niggled at her. What was it? Something Geri had said when they were talking once. What was it? She'd remembered it for some reason. The day Geri came to the shop and introduced herself, wanting to hear all the details about Vickie's death. She recalled Geri saying, "My luck is about to change." When Kelly asked what luck had to do with the alpaca business, Geri had given her a sly grin and replied, "More than you think." There was something behind that grin that had bothered Kelly. Now, she wondered if Geri was talking about gambling and dreaming of "a big win."

"I've heard that's a hard habit to break," Jennifer said with a sympathetic nod. "I'm sorry for your friend."

Kelly stared out into the casino. She liked Geri a lot, and she didn't like the thoughts going through her mind right now. Maybe she was jumping to conclusions. Maybe there was another reason Geri was here this afternoon. Kelly wished there was some way she could know for sure. Perhaps she could ask someone here at the casino. Surely they would remember regular players.

She turned to Jennifer, an idea forming. "You know, I don't want to jump to conclusions about my friend. I want to find out. But I'm going to need your help."

"Sure. What do you want me to do?"

"They must have a bartender here, I bet. Why don't you go and chat him up and ask him about my friend. Tall older woman with dark hair in a braid down her back. She just left. She was wearing a red top with jeans. Find out if she comes here often. Say you were surprised she came here, blah, blah, maybe you two can share a ride next time, you know, whatever works."

"Don't worry. I know how to handle it, but I'm curious. Why don't you go ask him?"

Kelly grinned. "Because you're ever so much better at getting guys to talk to you than I am. You're a master."

"So let me get this straight. You're ordering me to flirt? On command?"

"If you would, please. Pretty please."

Jennifer gave a dramatic sigh. "Well, if you insist. See you later. Don't let anyone eat my chili burger." She headed for the far side of the room where Kelly glimpsed the bar.

"Where's she off to?" Jayleen asked when she returned.

"I sent her on a mission to pump the bartender. I figured he might know if Geri was a regular customer," Kelly explained. "I wanted to make sure we weren't making assumptions."

"That was smart," Jayleen said. "I remember lots of gamblers at the bar with me in the old days. They'd drink after they won, and they'd drink after they lost. Usually, they drank a lot after they lost."

"I like Geri a lot, Jayleen, and I don't want to jump to conclusions. Maybe she was here for some other reason."

"Boy, I hope we're wrong, but after your seeing her here today, I've got this bad feeling I can't shake."

"Me, too," Kelly confessed. "That's why I sent Jennifer in there to flirt and find out."

"Flirt and find out?" Jayleen said, smile winning out.

"Yes, I ordered her to go —"

"Hey, Kelly, go help Steve, will you?" Megan said as she approached them, hands filled with carryout bags. "He's got most of the orders. We're still waiting on a couple."

The unmistakable aroma of french fries permeated through the bags and straight to Kelly's nose. Her stomach growled on cue. "C'mon," she beckoned Jayleen. "We don't want the guys lifting all those heavy burger bags all by themselves."

"Curt gave me his key, so I'm putting these bags in the truck. Soon as we've got everything, we can leave," Megan called over her shoulder as she headed for the door.

"Why don't you help Megan. I'll help the guys," Kelly suggested to Jayleen as she turned toward the restaurant.

She found Steve and Curt leaning against the takeout counter, waiting for the last of the orders. Kelly wasn't the least upset at the delay. After all, even a consummate flirt like Jennifer needed a little time to extract information. Waiting patiently, however, was not one of Curt's strengths, so she tried to distract him with the continuing saga of Carl and the golf balls. Curt seemed mildly amused, but nothing really worked until the orders arrived. Then Curt was all smiles and heading for the door.

Kelly deliberately lagged behind her

hungry friends, hoping to spot Jennifer, when she scurried up from the side and fell into step.

"Here, let me help you carry these. That way I can steal some fries," Jennifer said as she reached for a bag. "Flirting for hire has its costs."

"Did you find out anything?" Kelly probed. "Did he remember her?"

Jennifer nodded, as she popped fries into her mouth. "Oh, yeah," she said when she could. "She comes regularly. Usually comes at night, though. He was surprised to see her this afternoon."

Kelly pushed through the entrance doors, her worries about Geri solidifying. "Darn, I was hoping it wasn't true," she said sadly as they crossed the hot asphalt. Heat shimmered off the surface at this hour.

"I know, Kelly. And I can tell you want to help her, but you can't. She has to do it."

Everything Jennifer said was true. Kelly knew it. But she didn't have to like it.

Kelly wiped sweat from her forehead and adjusted her *Kitty Hawk* cap. This was getting painful. The Greeley team's best batter was at the plate again. He'd probably hit another homer and bring in the runners on second and third, just like he did last time, she thought dismally.

She couldn't believe how badly her team was playing. Lisa couldn't throw a strike, the catcher dropped crucial throws, the infield bobbled balls, and the basemen dropped them. Everybody stunk tonight. Kelly couldn't understand it. When she and Megan starting dropping balls, she chalked it up to their road trip to Wyoming. Hours in a truck must have dulled their edge. But then everyone on the team started messing up, as if it were contagious or something.

Crack. The batter popped the ball high and took off for first. Kelly's foot instinctively touched the base as she watched the ball land foul. Maybe their luck would change. Maybe the other team's bats would go cold. Maybe she could get a hit this time rather than strike out. Maybe —

The batter connected on Lisa's next pitch, and Kelly squinted her eyes into the setting sun as she watched the ball sail up, up, up as if it were headed for the foothills. She exhaled an exhausted sigh. And then again, maybe not.

"I still can't believe how badly we played," Sherrie said, staring morosely at her beer.

"We stunk pretty bad," Kelly commiserated before she took a sip of her favorite ale, Fort Connor's pride and joy. The prizewinning ale slid down her throat, bringing its familiar and welcome tang. Even better, it was icy cold. "Whatever it was tonight, we were all off," she added.

Kelly leaned back in the outdoor café's metal chair and let the summer night settle over her. Glancing around the plaza of Fort Connor's quaint Old Town, she saw other groups like hers — friends out together on a summer night, sharing stories, celebrating victories and consoling defeats, enjoying each other. Enjoying the sweet summer languor that drifted by in the night breeze like the delicate white gauze from the cottonwood trees.

She liked it best like this, before the nightlife arrived in full force, ready to dance till dawn . . . or as long as the management would allow. Kelly didn't know how Jennifer did it. There was no way Kelly could keep numbers straight if she'd spent the whole night partying. She'd never been much of a partier, even in college. Wild binges and overdrinking never had appealed to Kelly. She liked being able to remember what she did the night before and not be embarrassed. That type of partying had never looked like fun to her.

Face it, maybe you're just boring, that insidious little voice in the back of her mind whispered. Kelly pondered that. Maybe she was. She'd always noticed the "wild and crazy" guys steered a wide path around her, even in college. Of course, that drop-dead-you-moron look she cast their way probably had something to do with it. It was fine with Kelly if they stayed away. Those guys seemed so childish. She always felt more grown-up than a lot of her peers. Maybe that was it. She was older. She was surely getting older. The Big 3-0 loomed this fall. Ye Gods!

Megan's voice caught her attention. "Personally, I think it was the bull's fault. My whole timing was off after that."

Kelly joined her teammates and their shared laughter around the table.

Steve came up to their table and leaned over Megan. "Well, I'm glad you guys have something to celebrate. We were whipped bad tonight," he complained.

"Us, too. We're just celebrating the bull," Megan joked. "Hey, let's toast Steve. He saved Kelly and me today."

Mugs and glasses were raised all around amid cheers and more laughter. "You're a good man, Steve," Kelly said, raising her glass before she drained it.

"Thanks, thanks, but I was just trying to get a workout after chowing down on Megan's biscuits. Those are lethal. Hey, maybe that's why we all lost tonight," he said with a wicked grin.

"Megan, don't you dare bake again," Kelly teased as she pushed back her chair and rose to leave. "See you guys later."

Waving good-bye to Megan and her teammates, Kelly started off through the plaza. Steve fell in beside her, she noticed.

"Hey, I've been thinking about old Carl's predicament, and I've got an idea that might get my buddy out of bondage," he said.

"Tell me, because Captive Carl is really laying on the guilt. I know he's running around when I'm not there, but whenever he sees me, he falls on the ground and lies there. Mister Morose."

Steve laughed. "What you need is something that will keep him from climbing over the fence, that's all. So you could either use a hot wire, you know, electrify the fence —"

"He'd get fried!" Kelly exclaimed as they walked through the adjoining streets lined with boutique shops of every description.

"All it takes is a couple of zaps, and dogs

get the message. After a month or so, you could probably turn it off."

Kelly pictured Carl getting zapped and didn't like it. Plus, the image of a month's worth of fried squirrels piling up on her lawn wasn't appealing. Even Carl would get tired of squirrel.

"Ooooh, I don't know about zapping." She shuddered.

"Then you could have angle arms installed and string fence wire around the top. That always works with climbing dogs. The arms angle in and keep the dog from reaching the top. They try, but they always fall off."

That idea sounded better. "They don't hurt themselves falling off?"

Steve shook his head. "Nah, they don't get that far up. It's the angled wire that keeps them in."

"That sounds promising," she said. "Is it expensive?"

"Not that bad, and cheaper than repeated court fines," he said with a grin. "I can give you the name of one of my contractors who does fencing. He'll give you an estimate. He's good, and he's fair."

"Boy, you have a contractor for everything," Kelly teased as they rounded a corner. “My car’s parked down here. Where are you parked?”

“One street over,” he said, pointing behind him, but staring at the building across the street from them.

“Something wrong?” she asked, watching him stare for a full minute.

“Nope, just dreaming,” he said. “I’ve always thought about what I’d like to do with this building.”

Kelly scrutinized the dilapidated old warehouse that occupied half of the small block. “Is it for sale?”

Steve shook his head. “No, a packing company is using it to assemble their shipments. But some of the other Old Town warehouses have already been renovated. Like that one over there, on the corner.” He pointed. “That used to be a dairy, and now it’s shops below and lofts above.”

Kelly surveyed the stylish lines of the building. The architect had captured some of the same design elements as the vintage buildings in Old Town. Yet, there was an updated, modern flair to the building as well.

“Retail and residences, huh?”

Steve grinned. “Yeah. Something like that. That’s why this warehouse appeals to me. It’s got potential. And that always fascinates me.”

"I'm glad you can see it. It looks pretty sad to me," Kelly observed.

"Hey, that's the challenge," Steve said. "That's what makes it interesting. You understand that, Kelly. You can't resist a challenge, either." Steve winked at her before he turned to walk away.

Fifteen

"Okay, Eduardo, fill 'er up," Kelly said, grinning at the café's grill cook as she set her mug on the counter.

"Hey, don't you mess with Eduardo. He's fixing my order," Jennifer intervened, grabbing Kelly's mug. "I'll get your coffee."

Kelly surveyed the café. Every table was filled. "Looks like you're pretty busy this morning."

"We're busy every morning, which sure helps my budget." Jennifer pointed to the outdoor deck. "See those guys with Pete? They're builders. He's thinking about adding on. Isn't that great?"

"Wow," Kelly said in admiration. "Pete has to be doing well to consider remodeling. That's a big investment."

Jennifer leaned against the counter. "Remember a few months ago, when we were all afraid Mimi would lose the shop and Pete would lose the restaurant? Boy, what a difference a few months can make."

"You're right," Kelly agreed, remembering the role she'd played in that situation. "I'm so glad Lawrence Chambers was able to convince the owners to keep the property."

"Gotta take care of my customers," Jennifer said, pushing away from the counter. "See you later. Your scarf looks great, by the way."

"Thanks," Kelly said, touching the peacock blue scarf for the fifth time since she'd draped it around her neck that morning.

It did look great, Kelly had to admit, catching sight of herself in a wall mirror as she headed into the shop. This scarf was different from everything else she had in her closet, but she didn't care. It was bold and bright, and it made her happy.

"Kelly, how are you?" Mimi greeted as Kelly turned a corner into the main room. "Isn't that your new scarf? See, I told you it would look fantastic. Now you should make another with a different kind of yarn."

"Let me bask in the pleasure of finishing this one first," Kelly said, admiring the new yarns Mimi was arranging for display. The round maple table was the focal point of the room, and it never failed to capture Kelly's attention, especially since Mimi and her staff kept the displays changing frequently. She fingered the ribbony yarns spilling from the top of a glass vase. Shiny rainbow colors, muted earth tones, an entire spectrum of light captured in each skein. "Wow, these are great. Would they work as a scarf?"

"Sure. Or, even better, an open lacy vest like the one Lisa made." Mimi pointed in the corner where a vest of ribbon yarns dangled. "It's simply the knit stitch with larger needles, of course."

Kelly stroked the ribbony yarn, now entwined in neat, open rows. Every time she saw a new yarn, her to-do knitting list got longer. The mention of to-do lists prodded her again.

"Oh, that reminds me, Mimi. We brought back some of the fleeces from the ranch. Mr. Chambers said it was all right. I want to give you first pick."

"Oh, Kelly, you're so sweet," Mimi said as she rearranged a bin of fringed yarns. "You don't have to do that."

Kelly waved away her objection. "Nope. Not a word. They're my fleeces, so I decide what to do with them. Besides, once this process is completed, I'll have so many I won't know what to do with them all. I'll have to put Burt on retainer to spin for me.

And I'll have to find another miller, because Ruth will be too busy to process all of these."

Mimi's smile disappeared. "I'm not sure Ruth will be able to take on any more, Kelly. She came in yesterday with some of my fleeces, and she didn't look good at all. She was so drawn and pale, I made her sit and drink a cup of tea with me before she left. I tell you, I'm worried about her. Maybe this work is too much for her. You know, lifting the bags, all that."

Bags of fleece don't weigh much, Kelly mused. Something else was wrong. "Does Ruth have any health problems you know of? She looked fine to me a couple of weeks ago when Steve and I went to their house for dinner. Then again, I'd never met her before, so I couldn't tell if she was always that pale or not."

"No problems that I know of," Mimi said, shaking her head. "And she's always so cheerful. Maybe I'm just worrying for nothing."

"You know, Mimi, when this ranch thing goes through, I'm going to really need your help," Kelly said, deliberately changing the subject. "Both Ruth and Jayleen suggested I sell all those extra fleeces that are in storage to spinners and weavers online. I'm sure you do that already, so I'd appreciate any guidance."

"Of course, Kelly. I'll walk you right through it." Mimi patted her arm.

The timer went off inside Kelly's head, and she turned toward the door. "I'll talk to you later, Mimi. I really should get more of my office work done this morning before I head into the canyon to help Debbie."

"How's that coming, Kelly?" Mimi asked. "I imagine Debbie is anxious to finish up so she can leave. She's been here much longer than usual. I'm starting to worry about her. The last thing she needs is a bad asthma attack."

"I'd hoped to finish today or tomorrow," Kelly said, pausing at the door. "But I had a voice message on my cell from Debbie yesterday. She said some investment statements came in by fax, and she has questions. So, it may take a little longer." Smiling at worrywart Mimi, she added, "Don't worry. I'll finish as fast as I can so Debbie can leave."

Kelly reached for the door, but it opened on its own. Megan and Lisa stepped inside.

"Hey, perfect timing," Lisa said, heading toward the main room. "I want to hear all about yesterday. Megan already told me the scary part."

"You'll have to fill her in on everything else, Kelly. After the bull, the rest is a blur," Megan said, dropping her knitting bag on the library table.

Kelly hesitated in the doorway, debating whether or not to stick to her regimented routine and go back to pore over client files, or . . . sit and knit with friends for a while. Friends won out. After all, she'd be spending the entire afternoon poring over Debbie's accounts.

"Go ahead, Kelly. I can tell you want to," Mimi said with a knowing smile. "Those files of yours aren't going anywhere."

"Don't start reading my mind, Mimi," Kelly warned with a grin. "My head can be a scary place sometimes. All those numbers and stuff."

She started toward the main room and her friends until she caught sight of a skein of the long-fringed fibers that had captivated her last week. Silky soft, wine-colored strands, rich purples from merlot to Beaujolais and rosé, spilling over into golds, the color of aged cognac and brash chardonnay. Kelly could almost taste the oak.

Mimi's soft laughter sounded behind

her. "I'm not reading your mind this time, Kelly. All I have to do is look. Go ahead and start a new scarf. I've seen you lusting after that yarn for over a week. Do it."

"But I don't have my needles with me," she said. "I can run back and get them. Size fifteen, right?"

"You take the yarn, and I'll get you some more needles," Mimi said, walking toward the front room. "If you go back home, you'll feel guilty and sit down at the computer and work instead of knitting with your friends like you want to."

Kelly watched Mimi speed toward the front room and the knitting supplies. Brother, she really hoped other people couldn't read her mind as easily as Mimi. How did she do that, anyway? Kelly selected a luscious skein and joined her friends.

"Megan says you've got fleeces to spare," Lisa said, her needles working another loose-weave vest. This fiber was different, not ribbons or fringe. It looked like feathery string.

"Yes, and you'll each get your own bag," Kelly said, setting her mug on the library table as she pulled out a chair.

"Wow, our own fleeces," Megan said. A soft gray mohair was forming into a shawl in her lap. "I may have to take Burt's spinning class again."

"Here you go, Kelly," Mimi said, bustling into the room. "Use these for now, then you can transfer it to yours later. Or keep these. You can never have too many needles, you know."

"If you say so. Besides, it sounds tricky transferring onto other needles." Kelly slipped the silky fibers from their wrapper.

"Nope. It's easy."

"I remember what happened the last time you said that," Kelly reminded, winding a length of the wine-colored fibers around her hand in casting-on fashion. "Ohhhh, it's *so* easy!" she taunted in a high-pitched voice.

"Cast on ten, like your other scarf," Mimi advised before she left the room.

"Megan said the ranch is huge. Cows, sheep, even alpacas. Sounds fantastic, Kelly. I can't wait to see it."

"Well, I'll be going back up there on a weekend to sort through files. Help me sort, and I'll buy dinner."

Lisa's reply was drowned out by a booming contralto voice in the doorway behind them. "Returned from the wilds of Wyoming, have you?" Hilda exclaimed as she strode to the head of the table and sat down. "Jennifer told us all about your adventures. Thank heavens you're safe and sound." Lizzie fluttered in behind her sister and perched on the chair beside Kelly. "Goodness, dear. You had quite an experience up there, didn't you? It was a very brave thing you did. But much too dangerous. Promise us you'll be more careful next time."

"Yes, indeed," Hilda said, peering over her glasses at Kelly. A frothy white shawl lay in her lap. "You're too brave for your own good, Kelly. You don't want to be foolhardy."

Kelly nodded dutifully as she cast on stitches. "I promise, ladies. I will never jump into a bull pen again. Megan will have to fend for herself next time."

"Megan, dear, you look in one piece. But I'm sure the experience was frightening," Lizzie said in a hushed voice, her eyes wide. Lizzie's nimble fingers were already working a salmon pink wool. Was that another baby sweater?

Megan nodded obediently. "Oh, yes. I definitely plan to stay out of Wyoming, in case that bull has a memory."

"I have a sun hat for you, Megan," Hilda added. "It ties under the chin. I suggest you use that when you're out and about in the countryside."

"Why, thank you, Hilda, but I plan to stay in the city for quite a while."

"If it has a floppy brim, we can give it to Scarlett," Kelly joked. "I'm sure she'll use it."

"I heard that," Jennifer said, pulling up a chair at the table. "And don't make fun of Scarlett. She has great taste in hats."

"Beg pardon," Hilda inquired. "Who is Scarlett?"

"She's one of the many personalities that Jennifer entertains us with periodically," Kelly said, pushing the needle beneath a soft strand. The big needles and the silky-soft fiber made for slower going, she noticed. Like the boa eyelash yarns, it would be easy for extra stitches to "accidentally" creep onto the needle. Kelly vowed vigilance and counted the row.

"There was a dear Southern lady in our altar guild several years ago," Lizzie mused aloud. "Charlotte Something-or-another. Such a lovely, melodious accent, too. I loved listening to her speak."

"Why don't you channel Scarlett for a couple of minutes?" Megan teased. "Lizzie would enjoy it."

Jennifer gave an airy wave of her hand.

"I'm afraid Scarlett is busy right now and does not want to be disturbed. She's sharing a julep with a handsome riverboat gambler. I'm sure you understand."

Lizzie giggled. "Oh, my, that does remind me. All the gentlemen used to flock around Charlotte, like flies to honey. Southern charm, I suppose."

"Nonsense, Lizzie. Her first husband left her a sizable estate, if I remember correctly," Hilda remarked. "Money sets them buzzing."

"Well, there's something else that sets men buzzing," Jennifer said, a new sweater taking shape on her needles. "I learned that much in Wyoming."

Lizzie's bright blue eyes lit up. "Really, dear. Do tell."

"Honestly, Lizzie. You're incorrigible," Hilda said, wagging her head in older sister fashion.

"It's biscuits," Jennifer said solemnly.

"Biscuits?" Lisa laughed. "What do you know about biscuits? You don't cook."

"That's precisely my point." Jennifer heaved an exaggerated sigh. "I learned there's a definite limit to sex appeal. Biscuits win out in the end."

Kelly noticed a flush creep up Megan's

pretty face as she concentrated on her knitting.

"Okay, what's with the biscuits?" Lisa demanded. "Megan didn't say a thing."

"Megan made this fantastic breakfast for everybody at the ranch," Kelly explained.

"It wasn't fantastic," Megan demurred.

"Was, too."

"The guys were all out roaming the range," Kelly explained. "Jennifer, Jayleen, and I were working on ranch records, and we were all starving. So Megan goes into the kitchen and whips up this feast with bacon and eggs and homemade biscuits. She saved us all from starvation."

"Wow, homemade biscuits," Lisa said. "I'm impressed."

"It was nothing," Megan replied, cheeks tinged pink.

"It was wonderful," Kelly continued. "You should have seen her standing in the doorway calling us in to eat. She looked absolutely adorable in this cute apron —"

"Oh, stop."

"Definitely adorable."

"— with flour on her nose," Kelly continued with a grin.

"Did not!"

"Did, too."

"That's all very charming, dear, but

what does that have to do with sex?"

"Lizzie! I don't know what I'm going to do with you."

"I'll tell you, Lizzie." Jennifer turned to her with a wicked smile. "Scarlett was making progress with this handsome young cowboy named Chet. He's the ranch manager. Anyway, things were coming along marvelously until Betty Crocker steps out on the porch and announces breakfast. With homemade biscuits, yet. Chet ran up those steps and into the house faster than you can say 'Tara.' He was gone with the wind."

"Enough," Megan begged with a laugh.

"Scarlett's not exaggerating," Kelly added. "Those three guys nearly killed each other trying to be the first one in the door. It was all we could do to find a seat at the table."

"I declare, it was so demoralizing," Jennifer said, hand to breast. "I may be forced to take cooking lessons."

"That'll be the day," Lisa retorted.

"Well, it all goes to prove what my mother said many a year ago," Hilda intoned, fingers nimbly working the milky white froth foaming into a shawl in her lap.

"Which saying was that, dear?"

Hilda stared off into the yarn bins. "You

can catch a man with cookies and cake, but you'll hold him with good biscuits."

"Amen," Jennifer said with a righteous nod.

Kelly snickered. "Well, it's a good thing I'm not trying to hold on to anybody, because the biscuits I make come from a can."

"I didn't want to hold on to Chet, just play with him for a little while."

"Jennifer!" Megan fussed, flushing brighter, as everyone else laughed.

"I predict little ol' Chet will be heading down to Fort Connor some weekend. Mind my words," Jennifer said.

"Well, he's coming to see you, then," Megan declared, picking up the knitting that had fallen in her lap.

"Not on a bet," Jennifer continued with a devilish smile. "He'll be coming to see you. I may have nice buns, but he's much more interested in your biscuits."

Kelly joined the laughter that rocked the table while Jennifer dodged every ball of yarn that Megan threw at her.

Sixteen

The curving road wound through the rugged, craggy ravine. Kelly steered easily around the curves as the road climbed up, up, up into Bellvue Canyon. Thick pines clustered on both sides of the road, separated by boulders that looked like the slightest nudge would send them crashing down.

She never minded this drive. Even though consulting for Debbie had doubled her workload, Kelly still looked forward to driving to the ranch. It was peaceful and relaxing. Of course, she'd never had to drive this road in the winter with snow and ice. Remembering some people's stories, Kelly decided she definitely wouldn't want to slide all the way to the bottom of this canyon.

The road opened to patches of pine forests dotted with homes and fences. Modest bungalows perched beside a creek that cut through the canyon. Log homes, sturdy, two-story framed houses, and more elaborate construction appeared one after another along the road. Some sat side by side, others were separated by acres of pastures.

Now that she'd climbed higher, Kelly could glimpse the vistas through the opening in the pines. It would be nice to have a mountain home here, a stray thought teased. Kelly pondered the idea for several minutes as she guided her car around the familiar bends and twists.

That could only happen if she quit her Washington, D.C., job and stayed here permanently. But she couldn't afford to quit. She'd been over this again and again in her mind and always came back to the same place. Still, the question danced through her mind like a feather on the wind, darting about when she least expected it.

Another thought teased. What would happen if the Wyoming ranch turned out to be an income producer? Would she be able to quit the D.C. job and stay here? She'd already been away from the corporate accounting atmosphere for so long, Kelly wondered if she'd ever be able to "suit up" again and live in such a regimented fashion as before. These few months here in Fort Connor had given her a taste of something she'd forgotten, something she didn't even know she lacked: freedom. Kelly had never thought of her former life as lacking freedom, until she came here. Until she came back home.

What *would* she do, Kelly mused, if she had the choice? That thought played in her mind while she drove through the alpine scenery of the upper canyon. The images her imagination created were intriguing enough to hold her attention until she turned a bend in the road and approached Vickie's ranch. Then, the unwelcome sight of police cars in the driveway scared every pleasant thought away.

Kelly drove down the driveway, her heart pounding. What happened? Had a burglar broken in at night? Where was Debbie? She screeched her car to a halt and jumped out, slamming the door. Debbie was nowhere in sight. Kelly surveyed the pastures. Vickie's alpacas were grazing normally. They didn't look perturbed at all, Kelly noticed. Maybe Debbie had heard a prowler.

She spotted a uniformed officer heading her way, and Kelly sped toward him. "Officer, what's happened here?"

"Ma'am, we're going to have to ask you to leave," the young man said. "When we have more information, we'll answer questions, but not right now."

Kelly's breath caught in her throat. "Officer, I work with the owner of this property. My name is Kelly Flynn, and I've been working with the ranch owner, Debbie Hurst." Kelly caught sight of Lieutenant Peterson standing on the front porch. "There's Lieutenant Peterson," she said, pointing. "He knows me. Could I speak with him a moment, please?"

"Lieutenant Peterson is very busy right now," the officer replied in a perfunctory tone. "When we have —"

"Officer, I was the one who found Vickie Claymore's body two weeks ago," Kelly interrupted. "I believe Lieutenant Peterson will give me a couple of minutes. Please."

The young man's expression changed instantly. "I'll be right back, ma'am," he said and scurried off.

Kelly watched him speak with Peterson and saw the detective turn her way. To her relief, Peterson walked toward her. "Lieutenant Peterson, you remember me, don't you?" she asked as he drew near.

"Yes, I do, Ms. Flynn. What brings you out to this ranch today? You've got incredible timing," he said.

"I've been helping Debbie Hurst sort through her mother's business records and create financial statements so the estate can be settled. Usually, I meet Debbie here in the office in the back." Kelly pointed toward the other side of the house, even though she had a sinking feeling Lieutenant Peterson already knew where it was.

"Ms. Flynn, when was the last time you spoke with Debbie Hurst?" he asked, slipping a familiar notepad from his pocket.

The cold feeling that had been creeping into her gut claimed Kelly now. "Where's Debbie, Lieutenant? Is she all right?"

Peterson caught Kelly's frightened gaze and held it. She could feel his probing. "No, Ms. Flynn, she's not. I'm afraid she's dead."

Kelly froze for a second. She was sure her breath was frosted. "How . . . what . . . what happened?"

"That's what we're trying to discover, Ms. Flynn. Ms. Hurst was found on the floor of the office last night. She was not breathing. Apparently, she suffered a severe respiratory attack, so we're trying to determine the exact cause of death. Now, back to my question. When did you speak with her last?"

The ice in her brain started melting. "Yesterday, I had a message from her on my cell phone. I was in Wyoming with some friends all day yesterday, then I was playing softball last night, so I didn't speak with her personally. It was the day before when I spoke with her. We were here working in the office together."

"Did she seem upset? Or did she look as if she were having trouble breathing?"

"Well, she always has difficulty breathing up here at the ranch, because of the grasses and all. That's why she uses an inhaler. But she was acting normally. I mean, she's been very anxious to get these records finished so she could leave for her home in Arizona. This whole trip has been stressful for her, and all of her friends have been worried."

"Was she disturbed about anything? Anything recent?" Peterson asked, scribbling in his notepad.

"No," Kelly answered, surprised at the question. Then she remembered Debbie's voice message. "The only thing I recall was the voice message she left yesterday. She said the faxed bank statements had some discrepancies, and she wanted to go over them with me. That's why I'm here," Kelly added in a plaintive voice.

"What time was that call? Can you check your phone?"

Kelly obediently flipped open her cell even though she knew she wouldn't have a signal. "I'm afraid I don't have a signal, Lieutenant. I can call you when I get back into range. My call log will have a record of the time."

"Thank you, Ms. Flynn, I'd appreciate that." He reached into his pocket and handed her a card. "Here's another, Ms. Flynn. I'm assuming you no longer have the first one I gave you." A small smile appeared for a second.

"Thanks, Lieutenant. I'll call as soon as I leave the canyon," Kelly said. "Can I ask a question, sir?"

"You can ask, Ms. Flynn, but I make no promises to answer." This time Peterson gave her a real smile.

"Who found Debbie? Was it Jayleen Swinson? She takes care of the alpacas. As soon as we got back into town last night, she headed up here."

Peterson started scribbling again, which wasn't a good sign. "No, Ms. Flynn, it wasn't Ms. Swinson who discovered the body, and I'm not at liberty to say who it was. We'll make it a point to speak with Ms. Swinson, though. You take care now, and drive safely out of the canyon."

With that, Peterson turned around and headed back to a small group of investigators assembled on the porch. Kelly watched a uniformed officer start to wind yellow tape around the sprawling log home. Again. She stared almost in disbelief that death could strike twice in this peaceful mountain setting. Part of her still couldn't believe it.

Kelly headed for her car. Jumping in, she sped away from the ranch as fast as she could. This time, she didn't even pay attention to the beautiful mountain scenery as she tore out of the canyon. The awful memories from Vickie's death were tugging at her, and this time they'd brought a new friend. Guilt.

This would never have happened if she'd been there yesterday. If she hadn't gone to Wyoming, then she would have been there to help Debbie when she had her attack. Surely that's what it was. A sudden asthma attack. Hadn't Mimi told her how worried she was about Debbie? This very morning Mimi was worried about an asthma attack. And it happened. And Kelly wasn't there to stop it.

The sporty car shot forward, picking up speed, responding to the increased pressure of Kelly's foot. It was all her fault. She knew Debbie was getting tired. She'd seen how pale Debbie looked these last few days. Why had she gone to count cows when Debbie needed her? Debbie probably spent the whole day up here working while Kelly was gone.

She wheeled around a curve, feeling the centripetal force tug at the car, pulling it over the line. It was all her fault. If she'd been there, Debbie wouldn't have over-worked. She wouldn't have died.

Kelly rounded another curve just as a red SUV swerved into view. Thanks to razor-sharp reflexes, Kelly was able to hug the inside of the curve just in time. She braked immediately, slowing to a safer speed.

Idiot! What are you doing? You know better than that. Slow down and stop this drivel about your being responsible for Debbie's death. Kelly recognized the voice of her guardian angel. Nary a fluffy feather on this angel. Kelly's angel specialized in kicking butt.

Kelly realized the truth. She was not responsible for Debbie's death. Debbie could have died just as easily in the motel room all alone.

Checking the scenery, Kelly noticed she was almost out of the canyon. She flipped open her cell phone and tossed it on the seat, waiting for it to wake up with a beep. Meanwhile, Kelly tried to figure out who had found Debbie and called the police.

She'd been sure it was Jayleen until

Peterson said it wasn't. After all, Jayleen headed over here last night about six o'clock. That means Debbie hadn't been discovered yet, or there would have been police cars all over. Jayleen would have called. So, it had to be later in the evening. Who would come that late? Who would even know Debbie was here?

Geri. It had to be Geri. She's the only one who kept in regular contact with Debbie like Kelly did. Jayleen said she tried to stay out of Debbie's way, because she didn't want to upset her.

Kelly glanced accusingly at the little phone, willing it to resurrect. It lay silent on the seat as she wound toward the mouth of the canyon. Finally, as she reached the edge of Landport, the phone beeped into life. Pulling over to the shoulder, Kelly punched in Peterson's number and left a voice message. Time of Debbie's call was eleven twenty yesterday morning. She searched the directory as she headed back into traffic, then dialed Geri's number. Geri answered on the third ring.

"Geri, it's me," Kelly exclaimed, breathless. "I went up to the ranch to finish the accounts, and the police were there. They told me Debbie died yesterday! An asthma attack. It's horrible. I cannot believe this happened."

Geri's voice sounded strained and raspy, as if she'd been crying. "I know, I know. The police told me this morning. I drove by and saw the cars. . . ." Her voice faded away.

"You didn't find her?" Kelly asked in surprise. "But, but I thought it surely was you who called them."

"No no, it wasn't me," Geri said. "I saw her yesterday afternoon, but then I ran some errands and went back to the ranch."

Kelly remembered Geri's late-afternoon trip to the casino. Lots of errands, indeed. "Who in the world found her, then?" she wondered out loud.

"Wasn't it Jayleen? I assumed it was her. I haven't called or anything."

"No, I asked the detective in charge if it was Jayleen, and he said it wasn't," Kelly replied.

"Who could it have been? Oh, God . . . I can't believe this," Geri's voice quavered. "Poor Debbie, dying all alone like that."

That image bothered Kelly too. "I know, that haunts me as well."

"I . . . I've got to hang up, Kelly. I'll talk to you tomorrow." Her phone clicked off.

Kelly flipped off the phone, puzzling

over who would come to the ranch in the evening. As she passed by a stretch of properties, Kelly recognized Jayleen's truck pulling into a driveway. Without hesitation, Kelly wheeled in behind her, following Jayleen all the way to the barn area. A modest house and barn occupied the edge of what Kelly guessed to be about five acres. Not much, but enough to raise a small herd, she thought as she exited her car.

"Thought that was you behind me," Jayleen said as she strolled up, hands in hip pockets in her trademark fashion. "What's up? You look like hell."

"Debbie's dead," Kelly blurted. "I went up there to meet her in the office, and police are crawling all over the ranch again. Just like when Vickie died."

Jayleen's mouth dropped open, and her eyes popped wide. "What! That can't be! Wh-what happened?"

"They said it looked like an asthma attack."

Tears sprang to Jayleen's eyes, and she ran her hand through her tousled hair. "Not Debbie, too. No! This can't be happening." She turned from Kelly and walked several paces away, her head hanging.

Kelly stayed silent, watching a hawk sail

from the pasture into the foothills, hunting. After a minute, Jayleen rejoined her, wiping the back of her hand across her face.

"I'm so sorry, Jayleen. It hurts to lose family. I know."

"When did it happen? Yesterday, when we were gone?"

Kelly nodded, somber. "Yeah, and you can imagine how I feel because I was up in Wyoming and not here with Debbie." Guilt twisted its knife once more.

"There's plenty of room in that guilty tree, Kelly," Jayleen said. "I went out there last night and raced through the chores. Got those animals in the barn in two shakes flat. I saw Debbie's car in the driveway, but did I go in and check on her? Noooo. And this morning, too. I was in such a hurry to get back to my own business."

Kelly watched the emotions play across Jayleen's face and offered the same advice to her she'd given to herself. "Jayleen, don't do that to yourself," she said softly, her hand reaching out. "I blamed myself all the way out of the canyon and nearly ran into some guy on the curve. I'm not to blame for Debbie's death and neither are you. You didn't check in on Debbie because you knew it would bother her. You told me so before. And she could just as easily have had the attack at night in her hotel."

Jayleen snuffled and swiped at her eyes. "I guess you're right, but I feel so bad! Her dying alone and all, right after her mother. Who . . . who found her? Geri?"

Kelly shook her head. "No. I talked with Geri on the way here. She said she last saw Debbie in the afternoon, but not after that. She also mentioned she ran some errands yesterday. I guess those errands included a trip to the casino."

Jayleen stared off. "Well, who in hell found her then? Nobody else knew she was working at the ranch except us."

"That's what I've been trying to figure out," Kelly said, catching sight of a police cruiser coming down the county road.

It slowed as it approached Jayleen's driveway and turned. Uh-oh, Kelly thought. Time for her to leave. She didn't want to test Lieutenant Peterson's patience.

"Sorry, Jayleen," Kelly apologized. "I should have mentioned this earlier. Lieutenant Peterson told me he was coming to interview you."

Jayleen gave Kelly a wan smile. "That's okay, Kelly. I'll try to behave myself better this time. I think he got upset with me last time we met."

Kelly smiled and waved good-bye as she headed for her car while the police cruiser pulled up in the graveled driveway.

"This is horrible, just horrible," Mimi said, a tear trickling down her cheek.

Kelly reached across the secluded café table and squeezed Mimi's arm. "I know, Mimi. It's tragic to lose both of them."

Mimi leaned her face in her hands and wept quietly. Kelly gently patted her arm, not knowing what else to do. It was impossible to console another's grief. Not really. It was best to let them mourn. Tears had helped her, Kelly recalled.

"I'm losing too many friends, Kelly," Mimi said. "This is heartbreaking."

"I understand, Mimi, I truly do," Kelly soothed as best she could. Pete peered around the corner then and looked at Kelly with concern. She lifted Mimi's cup so he would bring some more tea. "Mimi, why don't you go home and take some private time to yourself. Everybody understands. We're all concerned about you. You've known Vickie and Debbie the longest, so this hurts you the most."

Mimi sniffled into a tissue. "I don't know. . . ."

"This has been a terrible shock. You

need to go home and rest. Take care of yourself, otherwise we'll be hovering around you."

Mimi stared at the new cup of tea that miraculously appeared. "Thanks, Pete," she whispered. "Maybe I will go home. Tell Rosa to —"

"I'm right here, Mimi," Rosa said, slipping into the chair beside her. She patted Mimi's other arm. "Don't you worry about a thing. Jennifer will take you home. You drink your tea. Everything will be fine here."

"And don't come in tomorrow morning, either, or we'll send you back home. Right, Rosa?" Kelly warned as she rose to leave.

"You got it," Rosa said, nodding her head.

"I'll call you tomorrow, and you'd better be at home," Kelly said as she headed to the shop entryway. Mimi was in Rosa's capable hands now.

Kelly stopped by the library table long enough to grab her things. She needed to return to her own office now, where she imagined client files were stacking up in her computer mail in-box. Thankfully, there was no practice tonight, so she could catch up on her office workload. Another night spent in front of the computer.

All of the work she'd done for Debbie was in limbo. The ranch office and all its files were off-limits for now. Kelly had no idea when she'd be able to finish. And who would be in charge when she did finish? The lawyer handling the estate? Maybe she should call the lawyer. Debbie had been in regular contact with him over the will and its provisions. Kelly needed to introduce herself and tell him the financial reports were nearly finished. After all, the estate couldn't be processed without them.

As Kelly approached the foyer, Burt entered the shop. "Kelly, I just heard," he said. "Jennifer is outside waiting to take Mimi home, and she told me. How's Mimi doing?" His gaze was warm and compassionate.

"Heartbroken, as you can imagine," Kelly answered truthfully. "We told her to go home and stay there for a couple of days. She needs to take care of herself."

Burt nodded, staring off toward Mimi's office. "You're right. Is there anything I can do? I'm teaching a spinning class tomorrow, but I'll be glad to do whatever you folks need."

Thoughts began pulling at Kelly, demanding her attention. She'd been chewing on some of them all the way from

Landport. "Actually, Burt, there is something you can do." She gestured toward the main room once again and chose a spot at the end of the library table for them both. "There are several things about Debbie's death that are puzzling me, and I was hoping you could find the answer," she said as she sat down.

Burt smiled as he settled his large frame in the small chair. "Tell me what's puzzling you, Kelly, and I'll try to find the answers, if I can."

Kelly pondered for a moment. "First, I'd like to know who found Debbie. I asked Geri Norbert, but she said it wasn't her. Lieutenant Peterson told me Jayleen didn't find her, either. Then he added he 'wasn't at liberty to say' who it was. But Geri, Jayleen, Mimi, and I were the only ones who knew Debbie was working up at the ranch."

"More people than that knew Debbie was there," Burt countered. "Think about it, Kelly. She'd been here for over two weeks and had been contacting lawyers and banks and all sorts of people, including police."

"Okay, you're right," Kelly conceded. "But I want to know who found her and why Peterson is being so secretive about it."

This time Burt grinned. "Secretive? Sure you're not exaggerating, Kelly?"

"Not at all, Burt." Kelly leaned forward over the table even though they were the only ones in the room. "When I drove up to the ranch yesterday to meet Debbie, Peterson and his guys were crawling around there just like they did when Vickie died. They were putting police tape over the place like before. Something told me they wouldn't do that if it was a natural death."

"Well, she didn't die a natural death," he said. "Apparently it was an attack of this asthma or whatever. Peterson was just following procedures, Kelly."

"I don't think so, Burt. My instinct tells me something else is going on. Peterson came out and started asking me questions just like he did when Vickie died. Writing down everything in his little notepad."

"What kind of questions?"

"When did I last speak with Debbie? Did she seem upset or disturbed about anything? Anything recent?"

The expression on Burt's face changed. Imperceptible, but Kelly saw it. "Anything else?"

"No, he said he'd talk to Jayleen after I reminded him she was there the night before with the animals."

"Did she talk to Debbie while she was there?"

Kelly shook her head. "Debbie doesn't like Jayleen because she . . . well, she had an alcohol problem years ago, and Debbie still has a lot of bad memories of her mom trying to help Jayleen. I could feel it when Debbie talked to me about it in the office one night. So Jayleen tries to keep her distance."

"So, Jayleen was there last night to care for the animals, and Debbie's body was found later, right?" Burt asked.

The change in Burt's tone was slight, but Kelly detected that as well. He was suspicious. "What are you thinking, Burt? That Jayleen might have done this? That's crazy."

"Nothing's too crazy to be ruled out in murder," he said. "Tell me, does Jayleen go to the farm in the morning to care for the animals?"

"Yes, and she told me she'd been in a terrible hurry, that's why she didn't check on Debbie. She feels terrible that she didn't, just like I felt awful for being away in Wyoming."

"Did Jayleen mention there were police cars at the ranch?"

Kelly shook her head. "No, there

couldn't have been, or she would have called me. In fact, she would have gone to talk to them herself. I know Jayleen."

"Do you? How long have you known her?"

"Well, not very long, actually," she admitted. Now, Burt's suspicions had magically transferred to her mind. How well did she really know Jayleen? Sure, she liked Jayleen as a person. Really liked her. But maybe there was a side of Jayleen she hadn't seen. A side she kept hidden.

"What time did you folks return to town?"

"About six o'clock. Megan and I rushed to ball practice, and Jayleen took off for the canyon. She was way behind with her chores and all her work. She has a bookkeeping business on the side, too, you see." Kelly added the last part in an effort to explain Jayleen's hurried state. Surely Burt couldn't be serious. Jayleen couldn't kill Debbie. Could she?

"Sounds pretty busy to me. Is money a problem for Jayleen?" he asked.

"Yeah, like it is for all of us, I guess," she answered lamely. Burt's interrogation was making her very uncomfortable. Kelly didn't like the thoughts that roamed around her head now. In one last effort to deflect Burt's attention from her friend, Kelly offered, "Hey, maybe Peterson was asking all those questions because they saw signs of a prowler. You know, a break-in, or something."

"Maybe," was all Burt said, but it was the way he said it that convinced Kelly her questions had brought more suspicions than answers. And in the process, had put her friend, Jayleen, right in the middle of the police radar screen.

Seventeen

"Okay, Carl, that's enough," Kelly called out. "The guy will be finished in a moment. Don't scare the man to death, or he'll never come back."

Carl looked over his shoulder at her, as if he was considering what she said, then launched into another ferocious series of barks at the Intruder Who Dared.

Kelly watched the fencing contractor measure and scribble, scribble and measure around the fence and yard. She hoped the estimate wouldn't be too high, but she'd already convinced herself that angled fencing was the only remedy she could live with. Something had to be done to release Captive Carl.

She clicked the mouse, and her printer hummed, client account pages obediently drifting into the tray. Kelly leaned back in her desk chair and drained the last of Eduardo's coffee — early morning version. It was now mid-morning, and she needed a refill.

Her cell phone jangled, and Kelly

flipped it open. Maybe it was the estate lawyer returning her call.

"Kelly Flynn."

"Ms. Flynn, Gerald Huff here. I got your message. Yes, please finish up the financial statements as soon as you can. We're adrift in the water without them, you know."

"Yes, I know, Mr. Huff, and I promise I will get to them the moment police allow me onto the property," she said.

He paused. "This is all so unfortunate. I must confess I've never had an estate quite like this one."

"It's more than unfortunate. Several of us were friends with both women." Kelly couldn't resist adding, "I suppose this makes it much easier for Mr. Claymore, right?"

"Yes, it does. He's the sole heir now." Huff's sympathetic tone changed back to business. "Please drop the statements by my office when you're finished, Ms. Flynn. And be sure to include a bill for your services. When the estate is finally settled, you'll receive payment. I wish I could pay you now, but alas, the only ones with access to Vickie Claymore's bank accounts are now dead."

"That's all right, Mr. Huff. I don't mind waiting." Finishing the call, Kelly tried to shove the phone in her pocket and realized she was still wearing her spandex running shorts from this morning's workout.

Rounding the corner into her sunny bedroom, Kelly quickly changed clothes. Carl was barking at the fence guy again.

Brother, what would she do when the fence was being built? Carl would have to be inside all day, giving him even more reason to be morose. Kelly didn't think she could stand those guilty stares much longer.

"Okay, let's go outside for a pit stop," she called out to Carl, who was still standing sentry at the patio door. Kelly scooped up her phone and Carl's leash, hanging beside the kitchen cabinet. At the sound of the magic jingle, Carl raced over to the front door, jumping in place. It took three tries to snap the leash.

"Calm down, Carl. We're not going out to bark at the fence guy. He's scared of you enough as it is," Kelly explained as she tried to hold back her enthusiastic dog. She knew she should have taken him to obedience classes when he was a puppy. "C'mon, let's go find a bush or something."

Unfortunately, the bushes Carl was attracted to were across the driveway in the knitting shop's gardens. Kelly jerked Carl away and searched the driveway area for a less offensive place. Spying a telephone pole hiding inside some scraggly pine trees, Kelly made a beeline for it. Carl needed no prodding.

Her cell phone jangled again, and Kelly flipped it open while Carl proceeded to sniff every neighboring bush. "Kelly Flynn here."

"Kelly, this is Jayleen."

Kelly felt the uncomfortable thoughts from last evening return. She'd managed to push them away with account files and workload this morning. Now, they were back. "Hey, Jayleen, how're you doing?"

"Okay, runnin' ragged, as usual. I just wanted to let you know that I survived the police questions yesterday."

"Oh, good, good. What'd he ask, anyway?"

"Just what time I came to check on the animals that evening. Then he asked me why I didn't go in to see Debbie. I didn't really want to get into all that stuff from the past, so I just told him that I was runnin' behind. Same thing yesterday morning."

"Did he have a problem with that, you think?" Kelly probed.

Jayleen paused. "He did look at me kinda funny after that."

"Well, he probably looks at everybody

that way," Kelly said. "After all, he's a detective."

"Yeah, I guess," Jayleen replied. "You know, he did say something that made me think."

"What was that?"

"He asked me if I saw the police notice on the front door yesterday morning. I told him I didn't because I was in such a hurry, I didn't even look. Now, I'm wondering. Why didn't they put that yellow tape around the place right away, rather than waiting until yesterday afternoon?"

Good question, Kelly thought. She'd been wondering the same thing. Did the police assume it was an accidental death at first, then find something to change their minds?

"I don't know, Jayleen. Maybe because they had a bunch of investigators with them yesterday afternoon. Maybe they're the ones with the yellow tape," she joked in a really feeble attempt at humor.

Jayleen chuckled anyway. "Maybe so. Listen, girl, I've gotta run and take care of business. Talk to you later." She clicked off.

Kelly stared out at the golfers wandering the greens while she let all of Burt's suspicions about Jayleen dart about in her head. Burt was a skilled investigator. If he was suspicious about Jayleen, she should be too. Why, then, was it so hard to picture Jayleen as a killer? Was it because she'd gotten to know her and liked her? That had to be it. Even so, wouldn't Jayleen have said something that tipped her off? Kelly prided herself on her good instincts. Surely she would have picked up some signal, some feeling about Jayleen. If Jayleen was guilty, then she was one heckuva good actress.

A memory triggered. Something Jayleen had said to her in the casino. Kelly had mentioned that Geri always "acted" in control. Jayleen pointed out the key word was "acted."

"We learn to conceal what we're doing . . . ," she'd said.

That made Kelly feel even worse as she pictured Jayleen playacting for everyone's benefit, pretending to be a helpful friend. If that was true, Kelly had never been so wrong about someone in her entire life.

She guided Carl back to her cottage doorstep and ushered him into the house before she closed the door. "Stay here for a minute, boy. I've got to talk to the fence guy."

At the mention of the Intruder Who

Dared, Carl's ears perked up, and he raced to the patio door, on patrol. Kelly rounded the corner to the yard as the fence man approached. She saw him anxiously peer around her, clearly worried that Carl was hiding, ready to jump out.

"Don't worry, he's inside," she reassured.

"Good, good," the man said, visibly relaxing. "Sorry, but big dogs scare me. I've been bitten one time too many."

"Ohhh, Carl would never bite anyone," she declared with a wave of her hand. "He's really a big sweetie."

The man stared at her like she was totally crazy, but he was too polite to point it out.

"He is a good watchdog, though. He keeps prowlers away," she went on. "He probably thought you were a prowler."

"Whatever you say, ma'am," he replied, scribbling on a clipboard. "I've come up with an estimate. We can use the fence you have already and add the extra height we need. And the angle arms, of course." He handed her a sheet of paper.

Kelly read the notations. It wasn't cheap, but she could live with it. "That sounds good. When can you start?"

"I can have a crew here tomorrow morning. It'll take no more than one day, if we get an early start." The man jerked his thumb toward the house. "Can he stay in the house again? My guys can work a lot faster if they're not looking over their shoulders." He gave Kelly a small smile.

"Absolutely. I'll keep Carl inside with me while I work. No problem."

"Okay, ma'am, we'll be here at seven in the morning," he said as he strode to his truck. "See you then."

Kelly waved good-bye and felt one of the burdens on her shoulders slide off. Now, if she could return to Vickie's ranch and finish those reports, she'd really feel better.

Time for a mid-morning coffee fix, she decided, then headed toward Pete's café. As she walked through the garden patio, she heard a familiar voice call her name.

"Kelly, I was looking for you inside," Geri called from the parking lot.

"Hey, Geri, how're you doing?" Kelly asked. "I was about to have some coffee. Join me."

Geri tossed her long, dark braid over her shoulder as she approached. "Sure. Why don't we stay outside?" She pulled out a chair at a nearby umbrella table.

Kelly signaled the waitress as she sat down, then waited for her to scurry away with their orders before she spoke. "How are you doing, Geri? You sounded pretty upset on the phone."

Geri stared at her jeans. "Better. It was just too much at one time. Vickie, then Debbie, and then all the extra work with my business. I mean, I've had two different females arrive for breeding this week. On top of all this horrible . . ." Her voice drifted off.

"Your business sounds like it's doing well," Kelly said, making room for the huge pottery cup filled with black nectar. She took a deep drink and savored it.

"It's getting better," Geri said, staring off into the backyard of the café as she sipped her coffee. "I mean, there's always risk in this business. You don't know if the breeding will take and then what type of babies come out. That's the crucial part. Reputation can make you or break you as a breeder."

Kelly watched Geri worry as she stared, lines creasing her face. She even looked older than she did the last time Kelly saw her. Worrying over a business can do that to a person, Kelly mused. Then another thought intruded. Maybe the worry was caused by something else entirely. Maybe it was the gambling. Maybe Geri has lost more money than she could afford. Kelly remembered Geri's stormy expression from the day at the casino.

"Is everything all right, Geri?" she probed gently. "You look really worried."

Geri turned to her with a startled expression. "Me? Oh, no, I'm okay. Just super busy, that's all." Then, she abruptly drained her cup, pushed back her chair, and stood. "Listen, Kelly, I've got to run now. I have a whole list of errands today. But promise me you'll call if there's anything you need for Debbie. Do you have someone to handle the funeral arrangements like I did for Vickie?"

"Mimi's handling it. She wants to, and it's helping her, you know, deal with the deaths."

"I understand," Geri said as she turned away. "Let me know if there's anything else, okay?"

"I promise," Kelly said with a good-bye wave and watched Geri climb into her truck and drive off, wondering if those errands included a run to the border casino.

Kelly finished her coffee alone, then returned to her cottage. Securing Carl on his backyard chain, she ignored the resentful pout as she settled back at her computer. If she worked straight through without stopping for lunch, she could catch up with her clients. Then, maybe, she could escape to the shop for a late-afternoon knitting break. Maybe.

"Everybody left?" Rosa asked as she hurried through the knitting shop's main room.

"Yeah. I'm leaving in a few minutes, too. Practice tonight after dinner," Kelly said, slipping the needle beneath a silky strand.

"That scarf's looking good," Rosa said.

Kelly stroked the lusciously soft fiber. "Thanks. I think so, too. It'll be great for fall."

"Well, don't wait till then to wear it," Rosa teased as she turned a corner.

Not a chance, Kelly thought, as she admired the scarf. Halfway done, she couldn't wait to show it off.

"All alone, Kelly?" Burt's voice sounded behind her.

All warm and fuzzy thoughts fled. She watched him pull up a chair beside her, which was a sure sign he planned to talk. The last time they spoke, she'd asked a lot of questions. Maybe Burt had some answers.

"Hey, Burt, how are you? Did you have a chance to talk with your contact?"

Burt leaned one arm on the table and

hunched forward. "Yes, I did, and I learned a lot."

Kelly couldn't resist looking up with a grin. "Good."

Burt smiled. "I figured you'd like that."

"Okay, tell me, was I off base thinking Peterson was sniffing around for more?"

Burt nodded. "You were right. They first treated Debbie's death as 'illness-related' because of her asthma history — until the medical examiner had a chance to check her. He found bruising on her neck. Not really obvious, unless you looked closely."

Kelly stared, wide-eyed. "Was she choked to death?"

"I'd say it sounds more like someone 'helped' an asthma attack kill her. And with someone as frail as Debbie appeared to be, it wouldn't take much to do that. A steady grip on her throat would keep her from drawing a breath. Then maybe the asthma kicked in and did the rest. Who knows exactly how it happened."

The awful suspicion that had lurked in the shadows of Kelly's mind slid through her now, cold as a snake. "Murder," she whispered.

"That's how they're handling it and have been since yesterday. You happened to go up to the ranch at the same time Peterson and his boys were searching for evidence."

"I knew he was up to something," Kelly said, nodding. "And that explains the tape."

"What do you mean?"

"Oh, Jayleen brought up something this morning that I found odd, too. We had wondered why the police didn't put any tape around the house until yesterday."

Burt nodded. "That's because it was considered death due to illness until the ME gave his report. Tell me, what else did Jayleen say?"

"Peterson asked her why she didn't check on Vickie, and she told me she pleaded too busy, rather than go through all that old baggage."

"Old baggage can hide some interesting things."

Kelly decided to veer the subject away from Jayleen if she could. "Who found Debbie?"

Burt glanced over his shoulder, even though they were alone in the room. "Bob Claymore," he whispered.

That surprised Kelly. "What? Why would he go up there? Debbie hated the very sight of him."

"Well, they were jointly inheriting the property. Maybe he went to the ranch to discuss it with her."

Kelly shook her head vehemently. "That wouldn't happen, Burt. Every time Claymore suggested talking with her, she refused. I know, because I asked her to meet with him, too. He begged me at the funeral to intercede for him. He looked so wretched that I agreed and asked her. Debbie flat out refused. She was convinced he killed Vickie. She didn't want Claymore near her. You can understand that."

"Claymore approached you at the funeral?" Burt asked, peering at her.

She nodded. "He looked awful. I tell you, Burt, if he was acting then, he should go pro. He was drawn and haggard and kept talking about these accusations Debbie was making to the police and all. And how ashamed he was when the police came to his office at the university." Kelly stared at the scarf lying quietly in her lap. "I confess, that got to me."

Burt took out a small notepad and pen and started making notes. "Why'd he ask you?"

"He said he'd asked everyone else, and she'd refused to see him. He'd heard I was working with her up at the ranch. I guess he thought he'd give it another try."

"So, he knew she was up at the ranch regularly, right?"

Kelly nodded. She could see those wheels spinning in Burt's head. "When did Debbie die, Burt?"

He flipped through his notepad. "Time of death was approximately twelve noon to two o'clock."

The same time she and her friends were sitting down to a rowdy and hearty breakfast in Wyoming, courtesy of Megan. Back in the canyon, Debbie was dying.

"When did he go up there? When did he find her?"

Burt paged through his pad again. "Not until that evening. The call came in to 911 about seven thirty. Ambulance and cruiser were dispatched. Apparently, the dispatcher said he sounded distraught."

"That's understandable. I can attest to what it feels like to walk in on a dead body," Kelly said, then grimaced. She watched Burt continue to jot down notes. "Once an investigator, always an investigator, right, Burt?"

"Yeah, I guess so," he agreed, then slipped the pad into his shirt pocket.

"This makes Bob Claymore look even worse, doesn't it?"

"It sure doesn't help. He was pretty high up the list of potential suspects in Vickie's death, and now he's the one who finds

Debbie dead." Burt shrugged. "Either he's incredibly stupid, or incredibly smart."

"Smart? How do you figure that?"

"If he's really devious, he could be purposely acting the distraught, disorganized professor, stumbling onto a murder scene. After all, there's no proof to link him to either murder."

"Did they find any fingerprints on her neck? Or something like that?" Kelly asked.

Burt shook his head. "Nope. No prints."

Kelly pondered. "I guess the main thing against him is motive. Without a divorce, he inherited half the estate. Now that Debbie's gone, Bob gets it all." That thought brought a taste of indignation with it. "Son of a . . . sailor."

Burt chuckled. "That's a new one."

"One of my dad's sanitized navy curses. Burt, do you think Claymore is really that conniving?"

"Kelly, I've seen a lot of criminals over the years, and anything is possible. The human heart is capable of harboring all sorts of emotions, good and bad, no matter what the situation. Mix money into the stew, and it gets more complicated." He glanced at his watch. "I've got to go. I promised Mimi I'd take her spinning class tonight."

Kelly carefully folded her silky scarf and placed it in her knitting bag. She'd learned to be more careful with these delicate fibers. Pushing back her chair, she joined Burt as he walked to the door. "You know, Burt, part of me suspected Debbie was murdered, but I didn't want to see it. I mean, losing Vickie that way was bad enough. Now, this killer has taken both of them." She shook her head.

"Well, it might not be the same person, Kelly. We don't know that," he said as he pushed the door open. "I'll talk to my friend tomorrow. Meanwhile, take care of yourself." He gave a wave as he walked to his car.

Kelly pondered the possibility of two separate killers as she headed toward her cottage. She did not like the thoughts that invaded her mind. One killer was bad enough, but two?

Her cell phone jangled, and she slipped it from her pocket as she opened the cottage door.

"Kelly, this is Jayleen again. I was just up at the ranch putting the animals in, and the cops are removing the tape. Thought you'd like to know."

"Really? That's great," Kelly said as she dumped her bag on the sofa. "Maybe I'll be able to go back to the ranch tomorrow. Thanks for telling me, Jayleen."

"It's nothing. I knew you'd be pretty anxious to finish. Gotta go. Bye now."

Kelly scooped dog food into Carl's supper dish while she checked her cell phone directory. Punching in Lieutenant Peterson's number, she left a brief message asking permission to return to finish her murdered friend's accounts. She was hoping the sympathetic look she'd spotted in Peterson's eyes was genuine. Kelly needed to bring closure to this business. Peterson was doing it his way, and she was doing it hers.

Eighteen

Kelly stared at the papers and folders littering Vickie's desk. She'd looked through every folder, sorted through every stack of papers, even searched the desk drawers, and still there was no sign of those faxed statements. Kelly knew she hadn't imagined Debbie's message on the phone to her. It was Debbie's last message, so it radiated in Kelly's mind.

Debbie had received the faxes from the investment bank and noticed several "discrepancies," as she put it. She had questions. Kelly was determined to examine those statements thoroughly as soon as she arrived at the ranch this morning. She owed both Debbie and Vickie her very best effort, nothing less.

There was only one problem. The statements were nowhere to be found. Kelly had been looking for over an hour and getting more aggravated by the minute. "Darnit! Where are they?" she exclaimed to the empty office.

A long black nose pushed against the

window screen. Carl. He'd heard her voice. "Hey, boy. How're you doing?"

Carl replied with a whine.

"Sorry, Carl. I can't let you run free. You'd spook the alpacas," she said as she sank into the desk chair.

Carl barked this time, then looked over his shoulder at the alpacas that were placidly grazing in the pasture. Kelly did notice they'd moved farther from the house than usual.

"I know, it's boring, but it's still better than being locked in the house all morning."

She leaned back and took a deep drink of coffee as she surveyed the office for the third time. This made no sense. Why weren't those statements here? Debbie wouldn't have thrown them away, and neither would the police. Debbie wouldn't have hidden them, either. She kept all Vickie's documents in three folders, which were stacked neatly on the desk. Kelly had gone through each folder twice.

She released a frustrated sigh. All her plans for finishing up this assignment were "blown out of the water," as her dad used to say. She couldn't finish the accounts without them. And she was so close, too. Kelly swished the remaining coffee in her mug. Thank goodness she'd brought a refill.

There was nothing left to do but call the investment bank and ask them to refax the statements. Maybe she'd get lucky, and they'd fax them today. If not, she'd simply have to return tomorrow. Meanwhile, she'd finish everything else this morning.

"Okay, then," Kelly said out loud, causing Carl to poke his face in the window once more. "Let's find that phone number and get this moving."

Kelly shuffled through the folders until she found the one labeled "Banks." Paging through, she located the investment bank's quarterly statement ending June 30. Punching in the phone number, she worked her way through two menus until she found a real person who could facilitate her request.

"Account and PIN number, please," the young woman demanded.

Kelly rattled off the account number on the statement, then searched for the requested PIN code. "Hold for a moment while I get it," she said and reached into the stack of folders. She'd remembered seeing a list that had account numbers on the inside of one of the folders. Finding the folder, Kelly ran her finger down the long list of numbers and repeated the necessary PIN number.

"Thank you. You should receive the faxes by tomorrow," the woman said.

Kelly hung up the phone and stared at the open folder in her lap. Vickie had written bank account numbers, PIN numbers, credit card numbers, even e-mail IDs and passwords all inside the front of the folder. Not a good idea under most circumstances, Kelly knew, but she figured it made sense in Vickie's business. After all, Jayleen did the bookkeeping. She had to have access to all the account information.

"Okay, back to work," Kelly muttered as she sorted through the folders on the cluttered desk.

At least one big job would be finished today, even though it wasn't hers. Carl would have a safe and secure backyard playground. No more Mister Morose. Look out, squirrels. Carl would be on patrol once again. Good thing, too. Those squirrels were getting too brazen for words. Kelly was sure she'd spotted a fluffy-tailed chorus line dancing across the patio this morning.

"I told you to lie down, Carl," Kelly called to her dog as she turned another corner of the curving canyon road. "All we've got is curves and more curves. Give up and lie down."

Carl ignored her, continuing to stick his head out the window, ears flapping in the wind, as Kelly sped up the canyon road.

She wound around another curve, and Carl hit the seat once again. Doggie wipeout. Clearly undaunted, he scrambled to his feet and shoved his head out the window. Flying, no doubt, Kelly thought.

"Not much farther, Carl," Kelly said. Since she was leaving earlier than planned, she'd decided to stop by and check on Geri. She'd remembered how worried Geri looked yesterday. Maybe there was some way Kelly could help.

She rounded the last curve leading to Geri's place. Geri's herd of alpacas was grazing in the pasture, but Kelly barely glanced at them as she turned into the driveway. Her attention was completely drawn to the man standing beside the fence with surveying equipment. Measuring instruments and clipboard in hand, he was obviously surveying Geri's property.

Was Geri refinancing or something? Kelly wondered. Another thought intruded. Geri had gambled with her house once before, according to Jayleen. Had she been foolish enough to jeopardize her property again?

Her curiosity really pushing now, Kelly

pulled her car onto the side of the driveway and got out. She deliberately parked away from the surveyor so Carl would not go into a frenzy of barking.

"Hi, there," she called to the man as she approached. "You're surveying, right?"

The older man glanced up at Kelly. "That's right. Are you Ms. Geraldine Norbert?" He glanced at his clipboard.

"No no, I'm a friend of hers," Kelly said. "I was wondering why the property was being surveyed, that's all." She gave the man her brightest smile.

"I just work for the county, ma'am. I survey what they tell me to," he replied, bending over his instrument once more.

Kelly was about to pry again when a truck engine sounded down the driveway, coming closer. Geri roared up and jerked the truck to a screeching halt, kicking up dust clouds.

Geri leaned out the window. "Listen, don't do another thing. This is all a mistake," she said to the surveyor, her face ashen. "I've paid the mortgage, I swear!"

"Ma'am, I'm sorry, I just survey the properties the county tells me to," he explained.

"Look, I'm going to the courthouse. I'll get a receipt! Whatever it takes. Just take my name off that list, please!" Geri begged.

"Ma'am, I don't make the list, I just follow my instructions."

Kelly stepped forward. "Geri, is there anything I can do?" she offered. The fear on Geri's face was heart-wrenching.

Geri stared at Kelly, as if seeing her for the first time. "No, no . . . I just need to get to the courthouse . . . This is all a mistake . . . a mistake. . . ." She jerked the wheel and gunned the engine. The battered green truck lurched out of idle and roared down the dirt driveway to the canyon road.

Kelly watched the truck disappear around the curve. The surveyor continued to measure and jot information on his clipboard. "Look, mister, I know it's none of my business, but I'm really worried about my friend," she said. "What list is she talking about? Is the county taking her land for taxes or something?"

The man looked up from his clipboard. "No, ma'am. The list I work from shows properties coming up on foreclosure." He shook his head. "This is the part of the job I hate," he said, returning to his instruments.

Kelly walked back to her car, a sinking feeling in her gut. Geri had looked so scared — and with good reason. She was about to lose her house and land. That meant she'd lose her business, too. If only there was a way to help. Should Kelly even try? Vickie had tried helping Geri before. Why had she slipped back into those old habits? Why?

Carl woofed as she approached. Kelly leaned against her car and patted Carl's smooth black head while she gazed out at the mountains. Geri had a beautiful view — rolling ridges with high peaks behind. In September, those high peaks would be snowcapped. Glancing around, Kelly noted the small farmhouse, barn, and a couple of outbuildings. It wasn't as big as Vickie's, but the setting more than made up for that.

A creamy white alpaca wandered into her line of vision as it grazed in the adjacent pasture. Ample pastures, too, Kelly noticed. Another alpaca caught her eye then — a smoke gray, almost bluish color. Kelly blinked. That looked like Raja. Or his twin. That had to be Geri's young herd sire, Raleigh. She'd said he was sired by Vickie's prizewinning male.

Carl whined. "Okay, we're going," Kelly said, settling into her car. "You've got a big surprise waiting for you when we get home." Waving at the surveyor as she drove past, Kelly flipped on her phone and was surprised when she had a signal. She called Jayleen, who answered on the second ring.

"Jayleen, this is Kelly. I've just been to Geri's, and there's a surveyor there measuring her property. He said it was on the foreclosure list."

"Oh no!" Jayleen cried. "I can't believe Geri'd do that again."

"Well, there's a chance it's a mistake," Kelly went on as she rounded a curve. "She came tearing down the driveway and told him she'd be back with a receipt. She claims she made the payments, so maybe there's a mix-up. I sure hope so."

Jayleen sighed. "I hope so, too, Kelly. Dammit! How could she do that to herself all over again? And Vickie's not here to bail her out this time."

"Part of me feels sorry for her, and part of me doesn't," Kelly admitted.

"I know what you mean, Kelly," she said with a sigh. "I'd like to kick her butt around the block. Damn fool! Risking her business she'd worked on for years. Every year her herd's been growing, and now she's risked it all."

"You know, I saw some of her herd a few minutes ago, and that male of hers is

Raja's twin for sure. She ought to get some beautiful babies out of any breeding with that bloodline."

"Well, sometimes it doesn't work that way, Kelly. You can have a great sire and expect the offspring to be the same, and they can turn out to be a bust. I'm afraid that's what happened with Geri's male, Raleigh."

"What do you mean? Doesn't he produce the same colors as Raja?"

"Not yet, he hasn't. But on top of that, he seems to be a dud at breeding. He'll mate, but it doesn't seem to take. When the females are checked in a month, the ultrasound shows no baby. Not good."

Brother, this breeding business was definitely trickier than she thought. "Wow, maybe that's why Geri got into trouble with the gambling," Kelly speculated. "Maybe she was trying to make up for losses in the breeding business. Maybe —"

"Kelly, don't get ahead of yourself. We don't know what happened to put Geri back on that path."

"You're right. I just wish there was some way to help," Kelly said, hugging the curve as she slid around it.

"So do I, Kelly. But this is something Geri's going to have to take care of herself this time. Gotta go now. Bye."

Kelly closed her little phone and tossed it on the seat while she tried to stop worrying and enjoy the luscious alpine scenery surrounding her.

"Go get 'em, Carl," Kelly said as she opened the gate to the newly finished backyard. Carl took off, racing around the perimeter, nose to the ground, sniffing every footprint. He'd be occupied for hours. Kelly fingered the sturdy addition of extra chain link topped off with twelve inches of metal and strung wire angling inside. There was no way Carl would be able to climb out of there. It was like a penitentiary. Thank goodness, she thought with relief. No more shouts of angry golfers on a Saturday morning or threatening notices posted to her front door.

"Hey, the fence looks great," Steve called out as he crossed the parking lot. "I was passing by and thought I'd cheer up Captive Carl. Looks like he's got his freedom back."

"Yeah, he's no longer Captive Carl. I guess he's Convict Carl, now," she joked. "This is a penitentiary. He'll never get out."

Steve chuckled. "Yeah, it does look formidable. But that's the only way you'll keep him inside." He pointed. "Look, there he goes now, checking it out."

Kelly watched Carl stand on his hind legs, front paws on the chain link, staring at the metal above his head. "Golf ball party is over, big guy," she said with a laugh.

Carl turned, took one look at Steve, and forgot about the penitentiary. He bounded over to the gate, barking a friendly greeting.

"Hey, how's my golf ball buddy," Steve said, laughing as he let himself in the gate. He grabbed Carl about the neck and they both fell on the ground in a rottweiler version of Wrestlemania. Kelly wagged her head, watching the two of them do the slobber-and-roll. It's gotta be a guy thing, she decided. Rolling in a yard with dog poop. Not her idea of fun.

"Thanks again for suggesting that guy Manny," she said when Steve had extricated himself from Carl's embrace. "He certainly does good work."

"Yeah, Manny always does a first-class job. That's why I use him." Steve escaped through the gate with a final pat.

"He was afraid of Carl, though, so I took the big guy with me up to the ranch today to work."

"How's that going, by the way?" Steve asked as he strolled toward his truck. He'd obviously come straight from the building site, dirt on his jeans and denim shirt, mud on his boots. You could mistake him for one of his workmen. Kelly had the feeling Steve liked it that way.

Kelly exhaled an exasperated breath. "Brother, it's the job that doesn't end. Every time I think I can finish and close up the accounts, something new appears."

"Think of it as your first consulting job, so you're working out the kinks," he suggested with a smile.

"I guess," she said, peering toward the sun angling over the mountains. "Well, I'd better go in and do some of my work before I run off to practice."

"Me, too. I think we play you guys next week." Steve stopped beside his truck and leaned against it. "By the way, pick a night when you're free next week. I want to take you out to dinner. There's this great little bistro in Old Town. Good food. Good jazz."

Kelly didn't see that coming, so she didn't have a quick response ready. Instead, she just stared back at him.

Steve grinned slyly. "Caught you by surprise, didn't I? Come on. You have to eat dinner, don't you? So do I. What about it?"

"Uhhhh, ummmm," she hesitated while she thought of a viable excuse. Steve's suggestion was unsettling, and she didn't know why exactly. She had an idea, but she didn't want to go there. Not yet.

"C'mon. I think you'll really love this place."

"Yeah, well . . . why don't we just go somewhere after practice next week?"

"Because you'll invite the whole team. I want to go to this place with you."

He was teasing her, and Kelly knew it, but she wasn't ready to give in. Not yet. "Alone, huh?" she said archly.

Steve laughed. "Not exactly. There'll be a bunch of people in the restaurant with us."

"Well . . . ," she hedged.

"C'mon, Kelly. We've already gone to dinner together at Curt and Ruth's house. This is exactly the same, just without Curt and Ruth." His grin turned wicked.

Rats. He was outflanking her. Kelly didn't like being outflanked. But she also didn't want to act like an idiot, either. Steve was right. They had already been to dinner together.

"Okaaaay," she agreed in a bargaining

tone. "Only if we meet at the restaurant after work."

"Separate cars again, huh?" Steve chuckled. "You really are afraid someone at the shop will see us going out."

"No, I'm just afraid you'll roll around with slobbery Carl before we go, that's all," Kelly teased as she headed for her front door.

Steve laughed. "Okay. Friday night, next week. Six o'clock."

Kelly gave him a thumbs-up sign and waved good-bye as she escaped into the cottage. As long as they were joking and teasing, it was fine. Anything other than that was . . . well, was something else. And she just wasn't ready for something else. At least, not yet.

Nineteen

Kelly rounded the corner from the café into the knitting shop and nearly ran right into Mimi. "Whoa, I'm sorry, Mimi. I've gotta slow down on those corners," Kelly apologized, stepping back.

"That's okay, Kelly. I was lost in thought and not paying attention," Mimi said.

Mimi still looked pale, instead of her usual radiant self. "How're you doing, Mimi?" she asked gently, unable to conceal her worry. "You still look tired. Maybe you should go back home."

"No no," Mimi refused, shaking her head. "I'm rattling about like a bean in a can back at home. This is where I want to be. The shop is home to me, Kelly. You know that. Besides, I'm much happier when I'm busy."

Kelly understood. Nothing drove her crazier than being idle. Her engine didn't idle well. It choked and stalled. "You know best, Mimi," she said with a smile. "It's great having you back."

Mimi beamed her warm smile as she

turned toward her office. “Thanks, Kelly. You just missed Lisa. She had to leave for a morning appointment,” she said as she left the room.

Kelly set her mug and knitting bag on the library table as she pulled out a chair. She didn’t mind knitting alone for a few minutes. Her scarf was nearly finished anyway. A few more rows and she could bind off the silky creation before she headed into the canyon to Vickie’s ranch.

She slid the needle beneath a colorful strand and started another row, letting the quiet of the sunny morning settle over her. That relaxed feeling settled in as well, Kelly noticed. Almost meditative. She knitted several rows, savoring the tranquility until a familiar voice sounded beside her.

“I’m glad I found you here, Kelly,” Burt said, drawing up a chair beside her.

Meditation over. Kelly let the scarf and needles drop to her lap. The expression on Burt’s face commanded her attention. “You’ve heard something, haven’t you?” she said.

Burt nodded. “I spoke to my friend yesterday and asked how the investigation was going. He told me Bob Claymore was called into the department for questioning again. This time, he brought his attorney with him."

Kelly's eyes widened. "That means Bob Claymore really is the chief suspect, right?"

Burt shrugged in the way he did when he didn't want to say yes, she noticed. "Let's just say he's aroused considerable suspicion. My friend also said that Claymore swore Debbie called him at his office asking him to come to the ranch that night."

"Riiiight," Kelly said skeptically.

"Well, Claymore maintains she called and left him a message. Apparently, she talked with his secretary at the university."

"There's no way. Debbie hated his guts, remember?"

Burt nodded. "I know what you said, but my friend says they checked it out. The secretary confirms she received a call from a woman named Debbie that afternoon."

That took Kelly completely by surprise. "What!"

"I was surprised to hear that, too, considering what you'd told me about Debbie's feelings toward Claymore. But he's telling the truth, and the secretary backs him up."

Kelly pondered the surprising bit of information. "What in the world was so important that Debbie would ask him up to the ranch?"

"Maybe she'd decided to drop her grudge and settle the estate reasonably," Burt suggested. "People do change their minds, Kelly."

"Well, whatever it was, it got her killed," Kelly said in a bitter tone. "What do you think happened? Did they start to argue? Did Debbie accuse him of killing her mother to his face? Whatever it was, it drove him to murder!"

Burt held up both hands. "Whoa, Kelly. You're jumping to conclusions here. There is absolutely no proof that Bob Claymore killed Debbie. He may have had incredibly bad luck to show up there and find her dead, that's all."

Kelly gave a disdainful snort. "But there's no one else who could have done it, Burt. Debbie didn't have any enemies. Neither did Vickie."

"Each one of us has done or said things in our past that have hurt others," Burt said sagely. "Sometimes those things come back to haunt us. Maybe there's someone else out there who harbored ill will toward these women."

That thought wormed its way into Kelly's mind, wiggling stray thoughts loose. Disturbing thoughts about other people. Burt was right. Bob Claymore was the obvious choice of killer. But what if he wasn't? That meant the real killer had cleverly concealed his or her identity.

"You're right, Burt," she admitted with a sigh. "I guess Bob Claymore is the easy choice."

"That's why investigation is tricky, Kelly," Burt said as he rose from the chair. "We have to look at the obvious as well as the hidden." He pointed toward the front. "You take care now. I promised Mimi I'd help with the spinning. See you later."

Kelly waved as he walked away, then checked her watch. Once again, her scarf would have to wait. Time for her to head back to the ranch. With luck, those faxes would be waiting for her, and she could finally finish the job that refused to end.

Leaning back into Vickie's desk chair, Kelly flipped through the folder in her lap until she found last month's bank statement. She sipped her coffee as she ran her finger down the entries at the end of the month. Then, she picked up the two faxed pages from the investment bank. Sure enough, there were several entries during the first week of July. It was a good thing she'd waited. The financial reports would be totally skewed without this information.

She flipped on the computer, relieved to be in the homestretch at last. All she had to do was enter these transactions into the accounts and run new balances. Then she could create the necessary reports and be finished. Finally.

Kelly would have cheered out loud, but it might have startled the alpacas. Without Carl's presence, Vickie's large herd was grazing closer to the house today.

The computer screen beeped into life, and icons popped into view. Kelly was about to click on the accounting software program when she noticed a flashing symbol at the bottom of the screen. The tiny envelope flashed brightly, indicating e-mail. Probably the last of Debbie's correspondence, Kelly thought. Since she couldn't finish the accounts yesterday, Kelly never turned the computer on.

She clicked the flashing mail icon, feeling uncomfortable reading Debbie's mail. There might be a business letter here as well, she told herself, as the in-box appeared on the screen.

The name highlighted on the message caused Kelly to catch her breath. Bob Claymore. Her mouse hovered over the message while Kelly debated whether or not to continue. Curiosity overcame privacy, and she clicked.

"I can't thank you enough for calling, Debbie. I'll be there at seven. Bob," the message read. It was simple, yet that wasn't what riveted Kelly's attention. It was the second message printed below Claymore's. A message from Debbie.

"If you want to speak with me, then come to the ranch after dinner. I'll be in the office. Don't call. My cell isn't working."

An alarm went off inside Kelly's head. That message wasn't from Debbie. It didn't even sound like her. And Debbie's cell phone was working fine that day. She'd called Kelly earlier that morning. Who sent this e-mail?

Kelly stared at the computer screen, her mind buzzing. Maybe Bob Claymore really wasn't the killer. This message surely came from the ranch office computer. Here was the proof. The message was sent — Kelly stared at the date and time — at one fifteen in the afternoon. Burt said Debbie was killed between noon and two p.m. that day.

A chilling thought snaked its way through the others. The killer sent this message. Whoever murdered Debbie deliberately invited Claymore to the ranch to discover the body, knowing that Claymore would be the primary suspect.

Kelly leaned back into the chair and tried to order her thoughts. She needed to let the police know. Grabbing the phone, Kelly searched her briefcase for Lt. Peterson's card and dialed the number. Once she'd worked through two different levels of police department personnel, she finally reached the detective.

"Ms. Flynn, the desk officer says you have something of importance." Kelly could picture the middle-aged detective peering at her.

"Yes, sir. I'm at the Claymore ranch right now finishing the financial reports, and I've discovered an interesting e-mail that was addressed to Debbie Hurst. I can forward it to you right now, if you'd like."

Peterson paused. "Who is the e-mail from?"

"The e-mail itself is from Bob Claymore, but I think you'll see the message preceding that one is of the most interest. It's supposedly sent from Debbie, but I noticed the time on the message was one fifteen p.m. of the day she was killed."

Another pause, then Peterson replied

with his e-mail address and a curt "thank you."

Kelly dutifully entered the detective's address and forwarded the suspicious messages. Unfortunately, the unsettled feeling didn't leave.

Closing the e-mail program, Kelly clicked open the accounting records. Only one thing would distract her from the disturbing thoughts racing through her head. Numbers. Lots of numbers. She reached for the faxed statements and clicked into the expenses screen.

Kelly methodically entered the cash withdrawals into the records. She understood why Debbie had questions. The transactions were larger amounts than usual. Two thousand dollars. Three thousand dollars. Five thousand. Forty-five hundred. Thirty-five hundred.

Picking up the quarterly statement again, Kelly scanned for withdrawals. Much smaller amounts. She looked at the faxes. Brother, Vickie must have had some hefty expenses come due at the first of the month to be taking out several thousand dollars.

A remembered conversation flashed into Kelly's mind. She recalled Jayleen saying that an alpaca exhibition bill still wasn't paid. That must have been it. Vickie withdrew the money to pay for that. Kelly sorted through the bank statement folder for the checking account and scanned that statement. No deposits matched those amounts, either.

That didn't make sense, Kelly thought, as she sipped her coffee. Vickie wouldn't pay a bill that large in cash, would she? Surely Jayleen would know. Kelly reached for her phone again, then something stopped her. Something about those withdrawals, what was it? She studied the statement again, the amounts, the dates . . . the dates.

The last entry jumped out at her. She'd been so focused on the actual numbers, she'd scanned right past the last entry. "Withdrawal Transaction Denied." Then the date was listed. The day Debbie was killed.

Kelly carefully set her mug on the desk before she dropped it. She studied the list of withdrawals again, paying careful attention to the dates of each of the transactions that had gone through successfully. Her heart started beating faster. Two thousand dollars were withdrawn the day Vickie died. Three thousand dollars, the following day. Five thousand dollars, one week later. And so on.

Debbie didn't make these withdrawals. Kelly knew it. Debbie was scrupulously coordinating every check she wrote and every bill she paid with Kelly. Plus, Debbie was using her mother's business account exclusively. Never the investment accounts. And Vickie certainly couldn't have withdrawn the money. The transactions didn't start until the day Vickie died.

Kelly's heart skipped a beat this time as the implication of these transactions crystallized. The killer had gained access to Vickie's accounts and was stealing money. Had Debbie discovered something that led to her death? She must have. Kelly recalled Debbie's last message. She found "discrepancies" in the statements. Indeed, there were. Had Debbie noticed the suspicious dates first? Something caused the killer to strike again.

This time the disturbing thoughts weren't content to race through Kelly's mind. They went into hyperdrive. Surely Vickie wasn't killed for a few thousand dollars, was she? Who needed money so badly they'd kill for it?

Kelly flipped open another folder on the desk, the folder with all of Vickie's account numbers and PIN codes written on the inside cover. Anyone who had access to this office could have found the folder, copied the numbers and withdrawn the money.

Jayleen's face popped to mind first. Kelly wanted to kick herself, but she had to consider it. Jayleen kept Vickie's books. It would be easy for her to steal. Had she? Did Vickie find out and threaten to turn her in to the police? Kelly tried picturing that, but it wouldn't come into focus. Besides, Jayleen had been in Wyoming when Debbie was killed, so she couldn't be guilty. Could she? Were there two killers?

That question was too confusing to even think about.

Another face appeared. Geri Norbert. Geri seemed to have fallen into serious money problems. Kelly hated herself for considering it. Geri's panicked, fear-pinched face still radiated in her mind from yesterday when the surveyor appeared on her property. Had Geri needed money so badly she'd killed for it?

Enough, Kelly thought to herself as she sprang from the desk chair and headed for the kitchen and her coffee refill. She couldn't think about this anymore. Her head was spinning. Right now, she needed to concentrate on finishing the financial reports so she could deliver them to the estate attorney.

Then, she'd pay a visit to the bank and see if she could pry some information loose. Kelly wanted to see the time of those withdrawals. Who knows? Maybe the ATM had a camera.

Kelly tapped her pen against the files in her lap while she waited for the bank account manager to return. It had taken over half an hour plus a call to the estate attorney's office to convince the bank personnel that they could answer one simple question: What time of day was each withdrawal transaction processed?

Recrossing her legs again, Kelly shifted in her chair. She'd given up trying to relax. It was impossible to relax. She was sitting next to the window and was roasting in the July sun. The bank's air-conditioning seemed to be nonexistent, and the music was starting to get on her nerves.

Mercifully, the manager's assistant scurried in Kelly's direction, a sheet of paper in her hand. At last.

"Sorry to keep you waiting, Ms. Flynn, but it took me awhile to find all the transactions," the woman explained as she sat down. Spreading the computer printout on her desk, she pointed to several lines of text that were highlighted. "Here's each one, with date and exact time of day and the amount."

Kelly quickly scanned the lines. The first transaction occurred on the afternoon of Vickie's death, approximately the same time Kelly had brought the visiting knitters to the ranch. Then she read the last entry for the denied withdrawal. Five thirty-eight in the afternoon on the day Debbie was killed.

Recalling that day, Kelly remembered checking her watch when they drove into the casino parking lot. It was almost four thirty in the afternoon. Minutes later, she watched Geri drive off toward Fort Connor, which was less than an hour away. Geri would have had enough time to return to town and drive to the bank. If she had lost more than she bargained for at the casino, Geri may very well have risked another withdrawal.

"May I keep this copy, please?" Kelly asked, reaching for the sheet.

"Of course, ma'am, I printed it for you," the woman replied. "I hope we've been able to help."

"You definitely have. Thank you again," Kelly said as she dropped the paper in her portfolio and rose to leave. As she started to walk away, Kelly remembered something. "By the way, do your ATM machines have cameras?" she asked the assistant.

"No, ma'am, they don't. We hope to install them next year."

"Several of the other banks in town have them, don't they?" Kelly probed.

"Yes, I believe so. Our branch has been a little slower to adopt, but we're catching up." She gave Kelly a beginner-salesman's smile.

Darnit, Kelly thought, as she headed for the parking lot. A picture would solve this entire puzzle. They'd see who withdrew the money. Her cell phone jangled, and she flipped it open as she slid into her car.

"Kelly, Jayleen here. I've just found out why Raja has been acting funny lately. Last night, I finally had some breathing room, and I took some time with Vickie's herd like I used to. Raja was acting skittish again, so I checked him out, and, well, I started getting suspicious."

"Suspicious?" Kelly asked, merging into Fort Connor's version of rush hour traffic.

"I began to notice little things, like his teeth and other stuff. Enough to make me check his ID tag."

"I don't remember seeing tags on the animals. Are they in their ears, like cows?"

"No no, we don't do that with alpacas.

We insert a tiny metal ID under the skin behind their left ear. The number is recorded on their registration certificate. That way, we can ship these guys and gals all over the country and make sure we get them back. The right ones, I mean," Jayleen explained.

"Hey, that's slick," Kelly said. "But if it's inserted under the skin, how do you check it?"

"With a handheld scanner unit. It reads the code on the metal ID, and the number flashes on the screen. Anyway, I scanned him, and it's another number entirely. It's not Raja."

"Ohhhh, brother," Kelly said. She didn't have to think very long for someone's face to come to mind. "Are you thinking what I'm thinking?"

"I'm afraid I am," Jayleen said with an aggravated sigh. "Geri Norbert's Raleigh is a mirror image of Raja. I'm thinking she switched them so she could use Raja to breed those two females that arrived last week. Damnation! Why would she do something like that? It's gotta be the gambling."

Jayleen bit off a few choice expletives while Kelly pondered the new information. Had Geri stolen Vickie's prize male as well as Vickie's money? Kelly had no proof of the withdrawals, but maybe they could prove Geri had switched the alpacas. First, they needed to scan the male in Geri's pasture.

"Jayleen, are you at your ranch? I need to talk to you right now," Kelly said, switching into a westbound turn lane.

"I'm here. What're you thinking? I can hear something in your voice, girl."

"I'll tell you when I'm there. It's all speculation right now. But first, we need to check out Geri's male. See if it's really Raja. Could you use your scanner for that?"

"Sure, but I'd have to sneak into Geri's barn at night to do it."

"Is there any way you can track the number on the look-alike in Vickie's pasture?"

Jayleen paused. "Yeah, I can check with the vet. Geri uses the same one that Vickie and I do. The vet will be able to check the records. I'll call her first thing in the morning."

"Are you okay with all this, Jayleen? I don't want you to do anything that makes you uncomfortable," Kelly added.

"I'm fine, Kelly. In fact, I'm startin' to get mad now. If Geri took Raja to breed those females, that's the same as stealing in my book. And she's got to answer for it. I'll be glad to help any way I can."

"I've got an idea, Jayleen. But I'm going to need your help. See you in a few minutes." Kelly tossed her phone to the seat. If she was right, then Geri Norbert had even more to answer for than switching alpacas in a pasture.

Jayleen leaned forward in the ladder-back chair, her hands clasped between her knees. She stared at Kelly, her blue eyes wide. Even Jayleen's normally ruddy complexion had paled as Kelly repeated her suspicions about Geri. "Good Lord A-mighty," Jayleen said softly. "That's more than I want to think about. I mean, stealing Raja and Vickie's money is bad enough, but . . . but killing . . ."

Kelly swirled the coffee in her cup before she drank. Thank goodness Jayleen had a pot on the stove when Kelly arrived. She didn't think she could tell this story without sustenance of some kind. Lacking food, she'd take caffeine. Kelly shifted position and sank deeper into the upholstered chair. Most of the furniture in Jayleen's small, but cozy, living room showed years of wear. Comfortable and broken in, Kelly's dad would call it.

"I know, Jayleen. I don't like to think Geri could do it, either. But those withdrawals are simply too damning to ignore," Kelly said. "Only someone who was close to Vickie would have access to her office so they could see the folder with account numbers. And unless you know of someone else, that leaves Geri, you, and me."

Jayleen screwed up her face. "What about Bob Claymore? That bastard had the most to gain from all of this. Maybe he took the money."

"Why would he?" Kelly countered. "He was about to inherit half the estate."

"You've let him off the hook, haven't you?"

Kelly shrugged. "Well, it's pretty clear he's telling the truth about Debbie. That e-mail message came from the ranch office, no question. Plus, he didn't show up until evening. Debbie was killed earlier in the afternoon, the police say."

Jayleen shook her head. "I just hate letting that bastard off. He's . . . he's . . ."

"So easy to suspect," Kelly finished the sentence. "I know. I felt the same way. But that e-mail shows the killer was trying to frame Claymore by luring him up to the ranch."

"You think Geri schemed all of this?"

"I don't know, Jayleen, but all these circumstances keep adding up. Geri needed money badly. Whether her business was going bad or whether she gambled too much, her house was going up for foreclosure. The surveyor said so. I called Jennifer on the way over here and asked her how foreclosure works, and Jennifer said there's all sorts of time built into the process so the home owner can save their property. I mean, they just don't sweep in and grab your house if you miss a couple of payments. It has to be more than that, and the person is given every chance to pay up before the county steps in. So that means that Geri had been missing payments for several months before it got to this point."

Jayleen leaned back in her chair and crossed her ankle over her knee. "Well, she'd been making her loan payments to Vickie every month. Maybe she was skipping her mortgage to do it, hoping she could catch up later."

"Maybe she was hoping she'd win big and be able to pay everything off," Kelly suggested. "Who knows what the final straw was. Maybe the county contacted her about the looming foreclosure. Something happened to drive her to desperation."

Jayleen stared off into the room for a full minute before speaking. "Or maybe she had a blowup with Vickie."

The tone in Jayleen's voice captured Kelly's attention. "What do you mean? Was there a problem between the two?"

Jayleen exhaled a long sigh. "Whenever Geri was late with her loan payments, Vickie would lay into her. She could be pretty harsh at times. I was there when it happened a couple of months ago, and, well, there was this look that flashed on Geri's face . . . just for a moment." Jayleen stared at her boots. "Well, it was ugly, that's the best I can describe it."

"Had they argued about the loan before?"

"Not in front of me, but I could tell Geri chafed about the lien Vickie put on her house. But she was careful to keep that below the surface."

Below the surface, simmering, Kelly thought. "If Geri was skipping her mortgage payments to pay Vickie and then lost more money at the casino, that could drive her to do something desperate. Or at least ask Vickie for an extension on her loan or maybe forgiving a payment."

Jayleen shook her head vehemently. "Vickie would never agree to that. Friends, family, it didn't matter. She was hard-nosed about money and never budged an inch. Plus, she'd be suspicious if Geri even asked. Vickie would know right away that

Geri'd been gambling. She'd smell it out. Then, she'd hit the ceiling." She flicked some caked mud off her boot. "Damn, now I wish I'd lied when she asked about those commissions."

"You mean that percentage you gave to Vickie for every client?"

Jayleen nodded. "Last month, Geri was in the office when I was doing the books, and she overheard a message on Vickie's answering machine when I talked about the commission on my new client. Geri asked me straight out if I'd paid money to Vickie for everyone's business, including hers." Jayleen shut her eyes, as if the memory bothered her. "She caught me off guard, and I couldn't lie. Not with her staring daggers at me like that."

"Was Geri mad?"

"Furious. That ugly look flashed over her face for a second."

Kelly thought about that for a moment. "Maybe that's what happened. Maybe Vickie refused to help her, and Geri got mad and accused Vickie of using her friends for her own financial gain."

"Oh, no. I could have stopped it. Why didn't I lie?"

"Jayleen, none of us can stop what's going on inside someone else's head. You know that," Kelly countered. "Geri may have killed Vickie in rage. We don't know what happened between those two."

"But why kill Debbie?" Jayleen asked. "What threat was she?"

"I think Debbie discovered those suspicious withdrawals first. She left me a message on my cell when we were in Wyoming. Maybe she spoke to Geri, and Geri got scared. Who knows?"

Jayleen stared at Kelly. "You know, all we've got is a bunch of suspicions, Kelly. No proof at all. How're we gonna go to the police with that?"

Kelly swished her coffee again. It was cold, but she drained it anyway. "I've been thinking about that. And the only thing we can do is confront Geri and try to make her confess."

Jayleen's eyes nearly popped out. "What! Confess to two murders? Are you kidding? She'd never do that. Why would she? She probably thinks she's in the clear. Everybody thinks Bob Claymore killed both of them."

"That's why you and I will have to put pressure on her. Tell her we know about the gambling and the alpaca switch. Make her think we know even more. Push her hard and see if she cracks."

Jayleen whistled between her teeth. "Boy, that's a big gamble, Kelly-girl."

"It's the only thing I can think of, Jayleen." Kelly glanced out the window. Nearly dark. They'd talked for over two hours. She pulled herself from the comfy chair. "Listen, call me as soon as you find out if that's Raja in Geri's barn, okay? Do you recognize his ID?"

"Sure do, but it'll be after midnight, probably. I figure the wee hours would be better for sneaking around," she said with a wry smile as she rose from her chair.

"I'm willing to bet next month's salary that Geri has switched alpacas. She's got Raja, and Raleigh's in Vickie's barn. And if you confirm it, then I'll call Geri early in the morning and ask her to meet me at the ranch office. I'll tell her that I've found something in the records concerning her loan, and I need her help to explain it. I'll make it sound urgent."

"Boy, Kelly, I hope you have a backup plan if this doesn't work," Jayleen said as she walked Kelly to the door.

"One crazy plan at a time, Jayleen," Kelly said as she left, the sound of Jayleen's laughter drifting after her.

Twenty

"You're up to something, Kelly, I can tell," Jennifer said, as she refilled Kelly's mug in the corner of the café. "All these questions about foreclosure. And you're more antsy than usual, even for you." She held the mug out of reach. "Go on, spill it, or no Eduardo coffee." She sniffed the steamy brew. "Aaaah, smell that."

"You are cruel, you know that?" Kelly said, then laughed as she glanced over her shoulders at the filled tables. "I can only give you a hint right now, but I promise I'll come over late this afternoon and explain the whole thing. Right now, I don't know if I'm being overly suspicious or if I'm on to something."

"My money's on overly suspicious. You're an accountant. It's what you do."

Kelly grinned as she headed toward the knitting shop. "Well, there is that. I promise I'll tell you later. Until then, I'm just trying to do my civic duty as a good citizen."

Jennifer eyed her skeptically. "Somehow,

I don't think you mean picking up trash along the highway."

Kelly waved and scooted out of voice range. She was hoping to find Burt before he started his early morning spinning class. She needed a favor.

It was after one a.m. when Jayleen had called to tell Kelly the alpaca in Geri's barn was indeed Raja. Not only did he nuzzle her like usual, the ID tag number matched when she scanned him. That was all Kelly needed to hear. She called Geri first thing in the morning.

Geri had hesitated a moment when Kelly asked for her help, but when Kelly prodded once more, Geri agreed. She'd meet Kelly at the ranch office after one o'clock. Kelly and Jayleen planned to be there waiting for her.

Kelly's cell phone rang, and she slipped it from her pocket as she huddled beside several bins of yarn. "Jayleen?" she said, recognizing the number.

"It's me. We were right. The vet confirmed the alpaca in Vickie's pasture is Geri's herd sire, Raleigh."

Kelly felt another piece of the puzzle fall into place in her mind. "Okay. My salary's safe then. I'll see you around ten thirty." She flipped off the phone as voices came around the corner. One of the voices was Burt's.

"I can move that wheel for you, if you'd like," Burt said, as he and Mimi walked into the room.

"Oh, would you? That would be wonderful," Mimi said, then glanced up. "Hi, Kelly. You missed Megan and Lisa, but they'll be back this afternoon."

"That's okay. I'm only here to ask Burt a question."

"Well, drop by later, why don't you?" Mimi suggested as she headed toward the front of the shop. "I've missed talking with you."

"What's up, Kelly?" Burt asked, peering at her almost the same way Peterson did. "You've got that look."

Brother, she couldn't hide anything. Jennifer could read her, and so could Burt. Kelly gestured Burt toward the empty library table and pulled out her phone. "Burt, what's your cell number?"

Burt recited the number, then added, "There's something else on your mind, Kelly. What is it?"

Kelly grinned. "Everybody's reading my mind today. Boy, I'm going to have to work on that. What an invasion of privacy."

Burt didn't reply. He folded his arms across his chest and waited.

"Burt, I need a favor."

"What kind of favor?"

"If I called you this afternoon, would you be able to get in touch with your friend in Peterson's office quickly?"

Burt's eyes narrowed. "What're you up to, Kelly?"

"I'm going up to Vickie's ranch to meet with Geri Norbert. Ask her some questions. And if the answers are what I think they'll be, I'll need you to send Peterson's boys up there."

Burt reached out and took Kelly by the shoulders. "Kelly, don't you go getting into something you shouldn't. You could get into trouble. What do you know about this Geri?"

"I've uncovered enough to suspect her of Vickie's murder, and Debbie's, too."

Burt drew back in shock. "Exactly what have you uncovered, may I ask?"

"Jayleen and I have proof that Geri stole Vickie's prizewinning alpaca stud. He's in her pasture right now. And we think she's been stealing money, too. These withdrawals were made after Vickie's death." Kelly reached into her bag and handed Burt a copy of the bank printout. "The last entry was made while we were coming back from Wyoming, right after we spotted

Geri driving away from a gambling casino. Geri was also about to lose her house in foreclosure. You may want to give this bank statement to your friend in the department."

Burt took the printout and scanned it. "Kelly, this is all just —"

"Circumstantial, I know," Kelly agreed, feeling Burt's wave of skepticism wash over her. "That's why Jayleen and I are going to confront Geri and see if she'll confess." Somehow, saying it out loud to Burt made the plan sound even crazier than it did last night at Jayleen's.

Burt stared at her in disbelief, then rolled his eyes. "Kelly, Kelly, don't be naïve. You have absolutely nothing on this woman."

"I know. But Bob Claymore has been interviewed twice based on circumstantial evidence," Kelly countered. "Admit it. There's no proof he killed either woman."

Burt frowned at her. "What if this Geri gets violent? Have you thought about that?"

Kelly shrugged good-naturedly. "Hey, there's two of us. Jayleen looks pretty sturdy. We can take her." Deciding retreat would be a good idea, Kelly backed away.

"Keep your phone turned on, okay?" she said, giving him a bright smile.

"Depend on it. You be careful, and don't press your luck."

Kelly gave another wave and escaped out the door. Burt didn't understand. Luck was all she had to press.

Kelly rearranged the folders on Vickie's desk, carefully concealing the small tape recorder she'd brought along.

"Hey, don't cover that, or it won't pick up anything," Jayleen warned from her spot beside the window, which looked out toward the driveway. Alpacas were scattered about the pastures, grazing peacefully.

"Maybe beside the in-box," Kelly said, moving the recorder. "There it's partially hidden by the clock, now."

"Whoa, here she comes. Better make that call, Kelly."

Kelly flipped on the recorder as she grabbed her phone. Burt picked up on the first ring. "It's me, Burt. Could you make that call, please? She's driving up now."

Burt sighed loudly. "Okay, Kelly. But if you're wrong, you're gonna do more than piss off a friend. You're going to piss off the county police, and that's never a good idea." He hung up before Kelly could reply.

"Okay, let's get to work over these papers and look busy," Kelly suggested, waiting for Geri. A moment later, she heard the sound of boots walking across Vickie's hardwood floors. Kelly took a deep breath and bent over the folder on the desk.

"Hey there, Kelly," Geri said as she entered. Glancing over at Jayleen, she added, "Hi, Jayleen. Are you helping Kelly?"

"Yeah, we're both trying to get these records done so that damn lawyer will get off our backs," Jayleen said as she looked up from the stack of bills she'd strewn across the desk. Debbie would have been appalled at the mess.

"Thanks for coming, Geri," Kelly said, leaning back in the chair. "Why don't you sit down. I've got a few questions that I'm hoping you can help me with."

Geri tossed her dark braid over her shoulder and pulled up a chair on the other side of the desk. "Sure. Be glad to. You said you saw something with my loan. What exactly did you find?"

"First of all, I was surprised to see that the loan was secured by a lien on your property. Was that your idea or Vickie's?"

"It was Vickie's. She, uh, she was kind of

a fanatic about money, you know," Geri said with a shrug. "She wanted to have extra security, I guess."

"But why your loan? Vickie had loaned money to Jayleen before and never asked for a lien. Why you?" Kelly probed.

Geri glanced back at Kelly, then Jayleen, then examined her jeans. "I don't know. Vickie could be funny sometimes."

Kelly let the warm tone disappear from her voice. "Was it because of your gambling? Vickie had loaned you money once before when you were about to lose your house, right?"

A flush crept up Geri's neck, spreading to her cheeks. "That's past history," she retorted. "I stopped all that. I'm paying back every damn dime!"

"But history has a way of repeating itself, doesn't it, Geri?" Kelly continued. "You broke your promise to Vickie. You're gambling again. I saw you leaving the casino last week when we were driving back from Wyoming. The bartender says you're a regular. How much have you lost? Is that where your mortgage payments went? Into the slots?"

Geri's cheeks flamed. "Are you spying on me?"

"You gambled away the mortgage money,

didn't you, Geri?" Kelly pressed. "You paid Vickie's loan so she wouldn't get suspicious. Were you planning to make a big score and pay everything back? Instead, you lost even more, didn't you? That's why your house is on the foreclosure list, isn't it?"

"Not anymore it isn't!" she declared hotly. "I paid up everything I owed. And I've got the receipt to prove it."

"Where did you find the money to make all those back payments?"

Geri glared at her. "My business is growing. I . . . I've had two new breeding females arrive. I've got the breeding fees and . . ."

"And you've got Vickie's Raja as the stud, right? What better way to build your reputation than to use a prizewinning stud, rather than your own. Clever, Geri. Except Jayleen and I found out."

"Wh-what are you talking about?" Geri's face started losing color.

"I heard you sneaking into the barn last week. You left the barn door open, and I heard your truck drive off," Kelly said. "Plus, Raja was acting different. That's because you were sneaking him over to your place every time you had a new female to breed, weren't you? You switched Raja for Raleigh, hoping we wouldn't notice."

"You — you're crazy, I never —"

"We scanned them, Geri," Jayleen spoke up, walking across the room to the file cabinet beside the door — blocking any sudden escape, Kelly thought. "I found Raja in your barn last night. And Raleigh's in our pasture right now. If you don't believe me, we can go out and scan him again. I verified the ID number with the vet. It's Raleigh." She leaned against the file cabinet and fixed a hard gaze on Geri.

"Is that how it started? Stealing Raja?" Kelly went on. "But you needed more, didn't you? That's when you went to Vickie, right? Did you ask her for more money, and she turned you down? Did she find out what you were doing with Raja? Did she threaten to turn you in to the police?"

Geri leaped out of her chair, her fury evident. "I am not going to sit and listen while you two trash me! To hell with both of you!"

Jayleen stepped forward. "Sit down, Geri. You're not going anywhere until you answer our questions," she said in a low voice.

Geri pulled herself up, clearly indignant. "Who are you to ask me questions?"

"You and Vickie had a fight, didn't you?"

Kelly continued, as if Geri hadn't said a thing. "When she refused to give you money, you accused her of stealing from her friends by taking commissions from Jayleen. Am I right?"

Geri glared at Kelly, then Jayleen, then sank back into the chair. "You bet I was mad about those commissions. That's illegal, and she knew it. Dammit! She knew how hard it was for me to make everything work, and she was stealing from me all that time. And she had the nerve to refuse me when I asked for an extension on my loan payment. That's all. Just one extension, so I could catch up. She went on and on about bills to pay and exhibition fees and how she was depending on that money and how I was causing her trouble. Hell, she had plenty of money in the bank. I knew it."

Geri stared toward the window for a moment. Kelly deliberately didn't interrupt, watching different emotions flash across Geri's face instead.

"That's when she started her sermon," Geri continued with a sneer in her voice. "On and on. I couldn't listen to that crap again. So I snapped back at her. That's when she really went off on me. Accused me of gambling. I don't know how she guessed, but she ranted and raved. How could I do that after she'd bailed me out years ago? Didn't I learn my lesson? Over and over, like she was some kind of preacher. Finally, I just had it, and I yelled at her to shut up."

Geri's face darkened. "Well, that did it. She told me she was finished with me. Told me to get out of her sight. Never wanted to see me again. She was through helping me, because I didn't appreciate it. Told me to get out." Geri gave a derisive snort. "She was supposed to be my best friend, and she treated me like dirt. I couldn't believe it. And then, she had the nerve to warn me that I'd better never be late with my loan payment again. 'Remember, I've got a lien on your ranch,' she said."

Kelly watched the storm clouds rage across Geri's face, and gambled. "Is that when you picked up the bust and hit her?"

Geri gave Kelly a look that chilled her all the way to her toes. "I don't know what you're talking about. Bob Claymore killed Vickie so he could get her money."

"No, he didn't, Geri." Kelly dropped her voice to the floor. "You killed Vickie in a rage. Then you stole her money. You found the account numbers in this folder, didn't you?"

Geri's gaze darted to the desk, then back to Kelly. "You're crazy if you think you can pin this on me," she said, then sprang out of the chair again. "I'm getting out of here right now!"

This time, Jayleen stepped right in front of Geri, hands on hips, as if she dared Geri to get around her. "Geri, you're makin' me mad. You'd better start tellin' the truth about what happened that night, or I swear I'm gonna break your arm."

"Back off, Jayleen. You don't scare me," Geri said scornfully as she pushed against her. Jayleen grabbed Geri's arm in one smooth movement and twisted it behind her back. "Stop, you're hurting me!" Geri cried out.

Jayleen let go and shoved Geri back into the chair. "Start tellin' the truth, Geri, or I'll really get mad," she warned.

"I *am* telling the truth," Geri whined, rubbing her shoulder. She shot a belligerent look at Jayleen.

Kelly had only one thing left to gamble with, and it was a bluff. She took a deep breath and deliberately changed her harsh tone to one of sympathy. "You and Vickie had an argument that got out of hand, didn't you? You killed Vickie in a rage. Then you stole thousands of dollars from her investment account. That's how you paid up your mortgage, isn't it, Geri?"

"I told you! I got that money from breeders."

"We went to the bank, Geri. They have pictures of you at the ATM. And we know you lost money gambling. We've been to the casino to ask about you."

Geri paled in an instant. Kelly watched fear dart across her face briefly, then it was gone, replaced by a hate-filled glare. Her eyes narrowed. "You have no right to pry into my private life. You don't know what I've been through."

"We know you were struggling. You were about to lose your house and ranch and everything you'd worked for. That's why you went to Vickie for help. You were desperate. And when she refused you and threw the gambling in your face, you snapped. That's what happened, isn't it?"

Geri's mouth flattened into a thin, angry line as she stared out the window for a long minute. Even from the side, Kelly could see different emotions raging across her face.

"She told me I didn't belong in the business since I was so careless with money. She said I deserved to lose my ranch," Geri continued in another voice — a voice Kelly hadn't heard before. This voice seethed with animosity. "Vickie had everything, everything. And she still wanted more. Stealing from her friends. From *me*. And I was the one she called on whenever she needed help. *Always.* Never once did she pay me. *Never.* She didn't even give me a break on stud fees, either. Even when she knew I was scraping by, trying to build my herd. *Selfish bitch.* She had it all and wanted to take mine, too. I knew what she was thinking. She was planning to grab my herd. *Steal them.* That's why she didn't lend me the money. She wanted my animals. Well, I wasn't going to let her steal everything I'd worked for. Took years to build. No way. I stopped her. She'll never get her hands on my ranch. *Never.*"

Kelly sat mesmerized. A bone-deep resentment oozed out of Geri, pooling at her feet in a rancid puddle. Kelly could almost smell the stench.

Geri turned another face to Kelly, and Kelly caught her breath. There was someone or something looking out from Geri's eyes. "Yes, I hit her," Geri continued in that strange, calm voice. "I only wanted to hurt her, but once I saw her lying on the floor, then I knew I needed to finish it. That's when I pulled out my knife and slit her throat. Then I watched her bleed to death on that new rug of hers." Geri's mouth twisted into a chilling smile. "Served her right. She was too arrogant. It was time to settle accounts."

Kelly watched the strange light dance in Geri's eyes as she recalled killing her best friend. "Did you leave that bracelet there?"

"Yes. Eva dropped it in Denver, practically under my nose. I was going to sell it to a guy at the casino. Then I had a better idea. I knew the cops would trace it to Eva, and she would point right back to Bob." She sneered. "Those two deserve each other."

After a moment, Kelly asked softly, "And, Debbie? Why kill her? She was harmless."

"No she wasn't. She had a mean streak like her mother. When she saw those statements, she started asking questions. Too many questions. So . . . I shut her up." Geri smirked. "It didn't take much. She started to have one of those attacks, and I just helped it along. Then I destroyed those statements so you wouldn't find them."

Chilled by what she'd just heard, Kelly stared back at Geri, or whatever Geri had become. A slight movement from Jayleen caught Kelly's attention. Jayleen gestured out the window and nodded. The police.

In an attempt to appeal to what was left of Geri's sanity, Kelly spoke up. "You're going to want to get this off your chest, Geri. You can't live with something like this."

Geri snickered. "Don't be ridiculous. There's no proof that I had anything to do with Vickie's death. Or Debbie's. You have nothing."

"We have those photos at the bank," Jayleen spoke up, picking up Kelly's ruse where it left off.

"That proves nothing. I'll simply say Vickie gave me permission to withdraw the money to pay my mortgage. You can't prove otherwise." Geri rose from the chair and shoved her hands in her jeans pocket. She smirked at both Kelly and Jayleen. "Now, if you'll excuse me, I've got a ranch to attend to."

Kelly rose from her chair and leaned across the desk. "I think you'll be staying a while longer, Geri. The police will want to talk to you."

"Give it up, Kelly," Geri said disdainfully. "You've got nothing on me. It's just your word against mine."

"Look outside. They're here now," Kelly said.

Geri stared at her, incredulous for a split second, then went to the window. "Son of a . . ." Geri let loose a stream of expletives that made even Jayleen stand up straighter.

"You better start practicing those lies, Geri. It's easy for the police to trip you up. You may forget and slip and make a mistake," Jayleen warned.

Geri flashed both of them an incendiary glare. "You two are desperate, aren't you? Well, it won't work. I told you, you've got nothing on me. Nothing! It's just your word against mine."

Kelly reached over the desk and picked up the small tape recorder, tape still running. She held it up for Geri to see. "I think we've got all the words we need."

Geri's jaw dropped as she stared at the recorder. Her look of shock changed to rage in an instant. "Damn you!" she swore and lunged forward.

Jayleen stepped in front of the desk, as if to block her, until voices called out from the living room.

"Ms. Flynn? Lieutenant Peterson, here. Where are you?"

Jayleen stepped away and drew back. "I think I'll let the police handle it from here," she said.

"I'm in the back, Lieutenant," Kelly called out. "In the office."

Geri stared from one woman to the next, panic darting across her features as she backed into the corner. There, another transformation occurred. Kelly watched the malevolent Geri disappear like smoke and leave a terrified Geri crumbled in a heap, collapsed in the chair.

"Don't let them touch me, don't let them touch me," she whimpered. "Please! Please, I didn't mean to do it, please."

Lieutenant Peterson appeared in the doorway, and the sight of him elicited a wail from the corner. Peterson peered at Kelly. "Ms. Flynn, exactly what is going on here?"

"I think you'll want to hear this, Lieutenant Peterson," she said, holding out the recorder as she approached. "Then you may have some questions for Ms. Norbert."

"Ms. Norbert is going to need a lawyer, Lieutenant Peterson. She's not in real good shape right now," Jayleen said, gesturing to Geri, who was hunched over and weeping softly in the corner.

Peterson accepted the recorder, then glanced from Kelly to Jayleen to Geri, then Kelly again. "Ms. Flynn, why don't you and I go into the living room and have a little talk? We'll start from there."

★ ★ ★

The silky fibers caressed her skin as Kelly wrapped the finished scarf around her neck. "How's it look?" she asked her friends seated at the knitting shop's library table.

"Fabulous," Lisa commented, glancing up from the fringed string she was turning into a vest.

"Told you it was easy," Jennifer teased, relaxing with a mug of coffee. "It looks great."

"See, you are getting better. Lots better. I can't wait to see your sweater when you're finished," Megan said, another bright boa eyelash yarn in her lap.

"Where is that sweater, Kelly?" Mimi asked, holding a china cup and saucer — her afternoon appointment with Earl Grey.

"Well, it's back at home, spread out on the table, waiting for my love affair with the scarves to stop, I guess." She fingered the luxuriously soft yarn. The love affair may never end, she thought.

"That'll never happen," Jennifer joked. "There are too many luscious yarns that keep coming into the shop."

"It's all Mimi's fault," Kelly said with a laugh. "She keeps buying yummy yarns. I could spend my whole salary here, if I let myself go."

She turned to Burt, who was sitting in

his favorite spinning spot at the end of the table. "Burt, stop spinning. No more mohair and silk or other gorgeous yarns. Mimi's going on a yarn diet."

"Never!" Mimi protested with a laugh as the others joined her.

"I think we should start Kelly spinning. Then maybe she'd get hooked on that rather than running around solving crimes and getting into trouble and worrying all the rest of us in the process," Burt said, hands methodically working the roving as it fed onto the wheel. He glanced up at Kelly and gave her a wink.

"Knitting's complicated enough for me, Burt," Kelly said, stroking the silky fibers again.

"That's one incredible story," Jennifer said, staring out into the room. "Who would have thought that nice Geri Norbert had all that hate inside her."

Lisa and Megan nodded silently as they bent over their busy needles. Mimi set her teacup on the table and leaned back into her rocker as she continued a light blue sweater, the color of Colorado skies.

Her soft voice spoke up. "Well, I'm glad it's over and justice has been done. Thanks to our Kelly."

Kelly smiled. "I was just trying to help,

that's all. So was Jayleen. I couldn't have done it without her. Or, her muscle."

Jennifer chuckled. "That Jayleen is something else, isn't she? We'll have to see more of her."

"Maybe she'd like to teach a class," Mimi said. "I could ask her."

Kelly was about to encourage that suggestion when Rosa appeared around the corner, her face white with concern. "Mimi, someone just called and said Ruth Stackhouse is in the hospital. She's had a heart attack. A real bad one."

Mimi's needles dropped to her lap. All color drained from her face. "Ohhhh no!" she whispered. "I knew something was wrong. I just knew it! When did it happen? Who was it that called?"

"I don't know who it was, Mimi. She said she was calling all Ruth's friends. Apparently it happened yesterday. She's in Front Range Hospital Cardiac Unit."

Mimi gathered up the yarn in her lap. "I'm going there right now," she announced.

Burt appeared by her side. "I'll drive you over there, Mimi. I don't want you on the road worrying like you are now. You could have an accident."

Kelly unwrapped her scarf and shoved it

gently into her bag as she stood up. "I'm going, too. We can all go together."

"Don't worry, Mimi, I'll close up like usual. Everything will be fine," Rosa promised. "You go see Ruth. I'll say a prayer for her."

"I'm so sorry, Mimi," Megan spoke up. "I didn't know Ruth, but I heard wonderful things about her."

Jennifer looked up at Kelly. "I'll say a prayer, too. I remember a few from all those years ago."

Kelly glanced around the table at the concerned faces of her friends. She was lucky to have such good friends. And she kept making more friends. Expanding the circle. Friends who cared about her, and she cared about them. The longer Kelly stayed here, the harder it was to leave. She didn't want to leave these friends.

She gave Jennifer a pat on the shoulder. "That's sweet, Jen. Prayers are good."

Burt and Mimi hurried to the door, Kelly following behind. She paused in the doorway and glanced back to her friends. "I'll be there tonight for practice."

"Promise?" Lisa called after her.

"Promise," she yelled over her shoulder before she stepped outside into the late-July sunshine. Kelly always kept her promises.

Tropical Shell in 4 sts/in

This sleeveless shell is great for summer or to wear as a vest or under a jacket or cardigan in colder weather. It's made in the round up to the armholes and the shoulders are knitted together.

FINISHED MEASUREMENTS IN INCHES:

Sizes:	XS	S	M	L	XL
Bust (at underarm)	31	33	37	39	45
Armhole Depth	6	7	8	9	11
Length*	16	17	18	19	21

**Length is easily adjusted between the bottom edge of the sweater and the armhole.*

MATERIALS: Heavy worsted weight yarn or any combination of yarns to obtain gauge.

Sizes:	XS	S	M	L	XL
Yardage	400	425	450	500	600

NEEDLES: U.S. Size 7 — 24- or 32-inch